Matteo

The 4 Seats
Book 1

Cassandra Doon

Author's Note

Dear Reader,

Before you step into this world with Matteo and Eleanor, I want to take a moment to speak with you honestly about the story you are about to read. This book is dark, intense, and unapologetically gritty. It is a world built on blood, loyalty, and power — and it does not flinch from showing you the cost of both.

On the Subject of the Mafia

This story immerses you in the brutal reality of organised crime. Matteo's world is one of violence, control, and ruthless ambition, where power is taken and held by force, and where mercy is often a luxury no one can afford. The mafia life I have written here is not glamorised — it is dangerous, morally complex, and deeply human in all the worst and most compelling ways. Drug running, kidnapping, and the machinery of criminal empire are woven into the fabric of this story, and I have tried to portray them with honesty rather than romance.

On the Subject of Human Trafficking

As with the later books in this series, we continue to confront the devastating reality of human sex trafficking. This is one of the gravest injustices in our world, and I refuse to treat it as anything less than that. Where it appears in these pages, it is presented as the horrific violation it is. The darkness belongs to the crime. The tenderness belongs to the healing.

On the Subject of Violence and Sexual Assault

This book contains graphic, on-page murder and depictions of violence. It also references rape, which occurs off the page. I have not included these elements for shock value — they are part of the truth of this world and of these characters' journeys. If these are subjects that may be harmful for you to encounter, please take care of yourself first and foremost.

On the Subject of Intimacy

Matteo and Eleanor's story is also one of heat, hunger, and connection. There are steamy, explicit chapters and the exploration of kinks within their relationship. The intimacy between them is a counterpoint to the darkness — raw, consuming, and real.

My Commitment to You

I write difficult stories because I believe they matter. I believe in the power of fiction to hold space for the darkest parts of human experience while still finding the light on the other side. No matter how dark the road, I promise you this: Matteo and Eleanor will find their way to a Happily Ever After. Every couple in this series does.

Thank you for trusting me with your time and your heart. Thank you for walking into the dark with me, knowing I will always bring you home.

With gratitude and respect,

Cassandra XXX

To Heathcliff,

I know, I know — I keep being told I'm not allowed to dedicate all my books to you.

But honestly?

Meh.

I'm doing it anyway.

Because deep down, I don't just want a man who loves me. I want a man who goes full-blown feral after I'm dead — the kind of love that digs up my rotting corpse just to sleep beside my bones because he misses me that much.

Sorry not sorry.

Welcome Back, Dark Mafia Romance Readers.

Before you dive into the world of Matteo and Eleanor, here is a list of what is inside this book. Please don't read if anything here bothers you. Your mental health and comfort are paramount.

- Extreme Violence & Gore
- On-Page Murder
- Kidnapping & Captivity
- Drug Running & Organised Crime
- Human Trafficking & Sexual Exploitation
- Non-Consensual Acts (off-page)
- Torture & Interrogation
- Strong Language
- Explicit Sexual Content & Kink
- Possessive/Controlling Behaviour

**To everyone who reads this, like a shipping list:
Welcome back.**

Chapter 1

Matteo Ricci

It's been 10 years.

A full fucking decade since I've buried myself inside a woman. The rage I carry inside has become a constant fire, licking at the base of my skull. A low burn that never quite goes out.

Don't get it twisted, it would be a goddamn lie to say I've been living as a monk. I just haven't put my dick inside a cunt. Not once. Because they're all treacherous. Every last one of them is a snake waiting to strike. None of them can ever be trusted.

You see, that's the curse of it all. Once you've gotten a taste of your forever, of that one soul that was forged in the same fire as yours, everything else turns to ash in your mouth. Every other woman after is a pale, pathetic imitation that makes the hunger for what you lost even worse.

And mine. Yeah, mine ran from me 10 years ago. Vanished into thin air like a ghost, and I've torn this city and half of the world apart looking for her. A relentless, bloody search that cost me more than 10 million dollars and left a trail of bodies. But she's just gone. Erased from the face of the earth, as if she never existed at all.

So, no. I haven't buried my cock in anyone. Not since her; I'm no saint. I'm a man with needs and a girl on call. A nameless, faceless whore who knows the rules, knowing she's only there for her mouth. A quick empty release giving me a temporary fix for a problem with no solution and does nothing to quiet the storm inside me; But it's better than nothing.

But no bitch, not a single one, has ever come close to her, to the fire, the fight and the way she looked at me like I was the only man in the world.

Eleanor Motherfucking Wang.

The name is a curse on my lips, a brand on my soul, the bane of my very existence and the missing half of me, all at once. She's the ghost that haunts my every waking moment. The star I still search for in the endless, black night.

The last time I saw her is burnt into my memory. A perfectly torturous loop playing over and over in my mind. She was walking into her apartment. The scent of her perfume, a sweet, intoxicating mix of vanilla and something wild that is just her, Clung to the air around me. Her last words a soft, breathless promise; "I love you, Matteo."

Then, Poof; She was gone. Swallowed by the silence of her empty apartment. She just vanished. Never to be seen or heard from again, leaving everything behind as if she was just raptured.

Her apartment is a museum of our life; untouched and frozen in time. Her handbag and wallet sits on the hall table right where she always left them. A half-empty glass of water on the counter. While her car collects dust in the underground car park. Everything exactly as it should be, except for her.

Not a trace. Not a clue. Not a single goddamn thing.

10 years. 10 motherfucking years of this emptiness. This cold, gnawing void she's left in my chest. The mere thought of her, of her smile, her touch and the way she used to say my name, still has the power to bring me to my goddamn knees.

Chapter 2

Matteo Ricci

Present Day

"Fuck!" The word tears from my throat as I push her face further down onto my dick. My fingers tangling in her hair as I take control of the rhythm; controlling everything, because that's what I do. I control everything and everyone around me.

"Swallow it." I command, my voice low, brooking no argument. She complies without hesitation because she knows the rules, she knows exactly what she's here for and nothing more.

Candy, or whatever the hell she calls herself, hums lightly around my shaft, letting me fuck her face with the kind of desperation that comes from a decade of emptiness. Her mascara running in dark rivulets down her cheeks. Her gag reflex is as trained and reliable as a well-oiled machine.

"That's it, I'm gonna cum," I growl, feeling the pressure building at the base of my spine, my balls draw up tight and my legs go rigid as the orgasm tears through me.

"Fuck!" is all I can manage as I empty myself; it's a hollow release that does nothing to fill the void within and nothing to quiet the constant, gnawing hunger that only one woman has ever satisfied.

Candy pulls off my dick, rocking back onto her heels as she looks up at me with those practiced eyes. Yeah sure, she's hot; she's the kind of hot that makes men do stupid things. The kind of hot that has other men mortgaging their houses just for the privilege of getting their dick sucked by this chick. But she means nothing to me; just a temporary fix for a temporary problem.

She's a regular of mine, one quick call or text and she arrives thirty minutes later. Ready and willing to do exactly what I need her to do. No questions asked. No complications. No expectations; she knows the drill, knows it better than anyone. Suck it and then fuck off. Disappearing like she was never here and I wire the cash into her bank account later; it's like clockwork.

She doesn't talk and doesn't look at me after either. Maintaining a beautiful, blessed silence that makes the whole transaction feel less like a betrayal of the promise I made to a ghost. She's a good little slut and I pay her well to be exactly that; to ask for nothing and to give nothing but her mouth.

I roll the condom off my shaft with deliberate care, walking into the bathroom and tipping it down the sink. I rinse it out methodically before I tie a knot in it and throw it out; because I'm not stupid. I've seen what women can do with a man's cum, the traps they can set and the leverage they can gain. I own a billion-dollar company; I'm not about to get trapped with some random slut and a bastard kid that isn't mine.

No fucking way.

But there's also more than that, more than the business, the money and the empire I've built. A long time ago, I made a promise to one girl, who was everything to me. That promise still holds, even though she's been gone for a decade. Even though I don't know if she's alive, dead or somewhere in between.

I promised her that my cum, would only ever belong to her, Eleanor. And because I'm a Ricci and I don't make promises unless I intend to keep them, it doesn't matter if Eleanor is missing. doesn't matter if she ran from me or if someone took her and she's dead in a ditch somewhere. I'll find her. I'll always find her. It doesn't matter if it's been ten years or ten decades. She is it for me, and no one else will ever compare or ever be enough.

"Boss," Spike says, as I walk back into my office, his voice cuts through the silence like a knife pulling me out of the dark spiral my thoughts had become.

"What?" I ask. Already knowing it's business and feeling the weight of it settling on my shoulders.

"Mr. Morelli is here."

"Let him in," I command.

Spike turns, heading out to collect Mr. Morelli. Looking at Spike, you wouldn't think he is my right-hand man. His real name isn't even Spike; it's Domino. The guy is tall, well over 6 foot, with long blonde hair that he ties up in one of those man-bun things, most men would look ridiculous with it but somehow he makes it work. He's all lean muscle, sharp edges and as slender as a bean pole.

And the man has a liking for knives that borders on obsession, he loves to slice up our enemies with a precision and artistry that's almost beautiful in its brutality. My other second in command is a man who actually looks a lot like David Boreanaz, all dark, brooding and dangerous. So, I mean it seriously would have been a travesty if I didn't nickname the guys after the Buffy characters.

Though I admit, I didn't technically nickname them, Eleanor did. Back when she was still here. And still mine. The first time she met the two they were her protection detail, she had them pegged immediately. Saw through their exteriors to exactly who they were. Since that day, I haven't ever called Spike by his real name; because my girl had been a Buffy fan and her instincts were always spot on.

"Matteo, it's a pleasure," Enzo's slimy voice infiltrates my office like an infection.

Suppressing the urge to reach for the gun in my desk drawer.

"Pleasure as always Enzo," I reply. The words like ash in my mouth. Because fuck I hate this prick; hate him with a burning intensity that surprises even me. Just the sound of his voice has the hair on my neck standing up and my instincts are screaming at me that something is off; something is wrong.

"What can I do for you today?" I ask, taking my seat behind my desk. Settling into my position of power because that's what I do. I control the narrative, I control the room, I control everything.

"I wanted to bring it to your attention that Eleanor has been sighted."

Well, that's a bomb I wasn't expecting. My entire body tenses, my heart rate spikes into the stratosphere. But it's also not the first time Enzo has said this, it's not the first time he's dangled this particular carrot in front of me. The last three times had been complete bullshit. False leads that sent me on wild goose chases across the globe, only to come up empty.

"And what makes you think it's her this time?" I ask in a carefully controlled tone, laced with a razor's edge of danger running through it.

"My sources say they saw her on the tube in London, heading into the city centre," Enzo .

I can fell the blood roaring in my ears as my heart rate thumps a mile a minute.. I know that if this is just another false lead, if this cocksucker is wasting my time again, I'm going to gut him in his sleep and make it look like an accident, then I'm going to make him disappear, so thoroughly, even his own mother won't be able to find his body.

"I can prove it," Enzo says and throws a pile of printed photos on my desk.

I scoop them up, flipping through them one by one with trembling hands. They look like her; they really do. Tall, slender, with long black hair and Asian features that match her perfectly. But none are taken close enough to be one hundred percent certain; until I get to the last one.

My breath catching instantly in my throat.

It's a close-up of her standing on the platform. It's her; It has to be her. There's the beauty mark just above her lip on the left side, that I've kissed a thousand times. Her eyes, light amber eyes that I've stared into while buried deep inside her. Eyes that I've searched for in every crowd for the past ten years. She's wearing a tight, black business dress, with long-sleeves so none of her tattoos are on display. The very ones I've traced with my fingers, lips and tongue.

But I need to see her to be absolutely sure. I need to be face-to-face with her to confirm that this isn't just another cruel trick of fate.

"When were these taken?" I ask. My voice barely above a whisper.

"Yesterday," Enzo smirks. His smirk only makes my trigger finger itch more.

"WHAT DO YOU WANT FOR THE INFORMATION ENZO?" I ask.

Because this cunt always wants something. He always has a price, but he's as rich as I am, so I know money is off the table. Enzo likes to trade in information, to play games with other people's lives. The Morelli family make up one of the four seats that run the countries underworld. I occupy one, as well as the Gallos and the Rossi's.

Together we run Australia's largest crime ring. The Ricci's and Morelli's rule over Sydney with an iron fist, while the Gallo's run Melbourne and the Rossi's run the Gold Coast. We have half of the police forces under our thumb, all bought and paid for. But, I already know this information is going to cost me big time, and Enzo knows that I'll pay for it, even if the girl isn't Eleanor. Because the possibility alone is enough to make me do almost anything.

"Nothing," Enzo smirks, sending my entire body into alert mode. "Oh, I find that hard to believe Enzo. You don't give out information for free," I note. My mind already racing through the possibilities. Shit, what is the cunt playing at now? What's his real angle here?

"You're right, I don't. But think of this as a gift," Enzo says without looking at me.

And something in his tone makes my skin crawl.

"You have been searching for this girl for over 10 years now and we need you to take your seat seriously. So, if that means helping you find the girl, then so be it," he continues.

I can feel the trap closing around me even as he speaks.

"What do you mean to take my seat seriously? I've been sitting in it for 10 years now, I see that as taking it pretty seriously," I say, my jaw clenching.

"That's not what I mean, and you know it," Enzo says. His voice is rising. "We need to run more drugs and more girls. But without you on board that's not going to happen."

"I'm not going to traffic girls through Sydney Enzo. Not a chance, it's not happening. That shit can stay down in Gallo's territory," I state, my voice cold and final. "I'm a sadist Enzo, not a psychopath. Also, we run enough drugs through the city already. How much more do we need to push?"

"We need the girls, Matteo!" Enzo yells at me. His eyes gleam with a sickness that makes my stomach turn.

"Think of the cash we could push through the city if we had girls to sell?"

"You really are a psychopath, aren't you Enzo!" I state, no question in my tone; just a statement of fact.

"Hahaha, nope, not even close. I just like money, more than I like people," Enzo says. He stands from his seat, throwing a USB on my desk, "Here is the information we managed to grab. Think about expanding our trade."

And with that, Enzo walks out of my office and down the hall. I watch Spike follow him out, my mind already spinning with the implications of what just happened.

Enzo is seriously insane. I've heard of what happens to the whores who service him and his men. The screams that echo through his building and the bodies that disappear in the dead of night. Only half of them walk back out of the building alive and I'm sure the other half are buried in unmarked graves or dumped in the ocean. There's no way I'm ever trafficking girls for him to maim and kill for his pleasure.

It's clearly the only reason he wants to push them through. He wants girls who won't be missed, girls with no families and no one to ask questions. I'm sure if he had it his way, no girls would leave his goddamn place, at all. As it is, only half do and I'm sure it's just to keep the detectives off his back. We might have some in our pockets but not all of them, because there are do-gooders out there, those who make it their mission to take us down. Bleeding hearts who think they can stop the tide.

Detective Rain Dang, a woman I went to school with, is one who refuses to step over the line and join me. But she's always happy to trade information when needed. We need more like her; I know Spike would be very happy to have her on our team.

I look at the USB sitting on my desk and sigh. I don't know if I have the strength to go on another wild goose chase in search of Eleanor. I Don't know if my heart can take more disappointment. But I also know that I don't have a choice, I'll follow this lead to the ends of the earth if I have to, because she's out there somewhere and I'm going to find her.

"You right Boss?" Angel asks as he walks into the office, sitting in the chair opposite my desk. His presence a steady, grounding force for the chaos swirling in my mind.

"It's just... that man makes Katherine Knight look sane," I exclaim, and it's not an exaggeration. Enzo's capacity for cruelty is almost unmatched.

"I know, Boss. Want me to go through the USB for ya?" Angel asks, I'm grateful for his presence, grateful that I don't have to do this alone.

I throw the USB at him. "Yep, see what info is on there, and arrange a plane to take us to London, leaving today."

"I'm on it, Boss," Angel states as he walks out of the room, already pulling out his phone to make the arrangements.

"Spike!" I yell from my seat, My voice carrying throughout the office.

"Yeah, Boss?" Spike sticks his head around the door, his blonde hair catching the light.

"Double our security, and place extra around the build-ing. We're taking a trip to London and I'll be leaving the building unattended. Who knows what Enzo's real motive for the information is," I command; I'd be insane to leave my empire vulnerable while I chase ghosts across the ocean.

"On it, Boss."

"Oh, and Spike…"

"Yeah, Boss?"

"Travel light. I don't wanna carry 50 bags of crap!" I add.

I can already see the smirk forming on his face.

"Sure thing, Boss," Spike smirks at me and I know, I absolutely know he's going to show up with a minimum of ten bags of weapons. Because Spike and his ever-growing knife collection are a package deal. Honestly though, I wouldn't have it any other way, if we're going to find Eleanor, I'm going to need men I can trust. Men who are willing to burn the world down with me, if that's what it takes.

Chapter 3

Eleanor Wang

It's close to nine in the morning as I walk through the office doors. My heart still racing from the mad dash through London's crowded streets. The damn Tube was running five minutes late today. Which meant the walk from the station to the coffee shop was busier than usual and the coffee shop was absolutely swamped by the morning rush. So, that means I'm running 30 minutes late; a rarity that makes my stomach churn with anxiety.

I'm never late. Not once in 10 years have I ever been late, not a single time. Being late is a luxury I can't afford, not when I'm a PA for one of London's most renowned real estate tycoons. Not when my entire life depends on being invisible and reliable; the kind of person no one looks twice at.

Patrick Murphy is one of London's most successful real estate developers. I have worked for him for around 10 years now. Ever since I ran away from Sydney,. Ever since I jumped on a fishing boat to New Zealand, with nothing but the clothes on my back to run away from

Matteo, in a desperate hope that I could disappear, that I could become someone else; Someone safe.

After leaving Sydney, I was able to pay a shipping company 10 thousand dollars to let me stow away to wherever they were headed. It just so happened to be London, which is how I started working for Patrick and how I began my new life that has kept me alive, kept me hidden and kept Matteo from finding me.

I met Patrick outside a pub in Soho one night, when I was desperate, starving and terrified. I had stopped in quickly to grab some dinner and just so happened to run smack-bang into the chest of a tall, kind-eyed man, who steadied me as I stumbled. After apologising a million times, my hands shaking and my voice trembling, Patrick offered to buy me a drink. I said yes because honestly, I had nowhere else to go.

One drink later, I'd spilled my whole sob story about not only running away from down under, but also from a man who would have destroyed me, if I'd stayed. Patrick offered me a job as his personal assistant for a company he was just starting. He also promised to pay me cash, ensuring I could stay off the grid, so, I could disappear completely and I could keep my son safe.

Fast forward 10 years and here I am, still Patrick's PA, still being paid in cash and never ran a minute late. I owe this man my life, I owe him everything. So, the absolutely least thing I can do to repay that debt, is to be on time every bloody damn day.

I run through the doors, straight into Patrick's office. My apologies tumbling out before I even give myself a chance to catch my breath.

"Sorry, sorry, sorry, oh my god, the Tube was seriously late, the coffee shop was full, shit Patrick, I'm sorry, here is your coffee," I say. The words rushing out as my hands fumble while I try to set the coffee down on his desk.

His hand snakes out, grabbing my wrist before I even have a second to retreat. I freeze. My heart jumping into my throat, I'm still not used to unexpected physical touch, still not used to anyone grabbing me as I still carry the fear that one day someone will recognise me and drag me back to Sydney.

"El, calm down. I don't care if you're late, you know this. Relax," Patrick notes as he grins up at me from his chair. His expression warm and reassuring. I force myself to breathe, trying to remind myself that I'm safe here, that Patrick is safe and that no one knows who I am.

"I know, I know but I just don't like being late," I say as I start to walk out. My anxiety still simmering beneath the surface.

"El," Patrick says.

There's something in his tone that makes me pause.

"Yes?" I ask, turning to face him. My mind already racing through the possibilities, wondering what I've done wrong, and bracing myself for bad news.

"Come sit down and drink your coffee with me, I want to talk to you," he says.

My stomach drops. Those words never mean anything good. Instantly my brains cursing, *shit, shit, shit. What did I do wrong? Maybe he is actually mad that I am late. Maybe, he's finally tired of me, Maybe this is the day that everything falls apart.*

"Oh okay," I say and take a seat in front of his desk,

my hands clasped tightly in my lap to stop them from shaking.

"What's up?" I ask, looking at Patrick, trying to read the expression on his face. Trying to figure out if this is good news, or bad.

"I need you to come to the fundraiser tonight with me," Patrick says.

A wave of relief washes over me, this isn't about me being late or about me failing him.

"I know you hate late notice, but Aela is sick and cannot come and you know I cannot turn up to these events by myself; they smell blood in the water like sharks," he continues.

I laugh at the terror on his face. He absolutely hates these events, hates the way the socialites circle him like vultures and the way they try to seduce him or extract business secrets from him. I normally always attend with him when his wife Aela, cannot make it. He's right. The second he turns up to an event without Aela, the ladies swamp him. That's where I come in; the buffer. The invisible PA who stands by his side, keeping the predators at bay.

"Okay, I'll call Yvonne and see if she can take Niko tonight. Is Aela okay?" I ask. Already mentally running through my wardrobe, thinking about what I need to wear.

"Yes, she is fine. Just a cold, but she refuses to be seen at these events looking weak," Patrick says.

I can totally understand her logic. The last event I went to with Patrick was 4 months ago. I'd just gotten over a bout of food poisoning and lost some weight from all the vomiting. The tabloids the next day announced there was trouble in paradise and Patrick had been seen leaving the event with his 'Skinny and Pale looking PA.' They stated that a stint in rehab would be in my future. The cruelty of it all made me want to disappear even further into the shadows.

I do my best to stay far away from the media, I don't even have Facebook or own a mobile in my name; the one I use is from Patrick and is listed under his name. The bank card I used to pay for everything is also one of his. I owe the man my life and I'm not about to risk it by leaving a digital footprint that could lead Matteo to me.

His wife, Aela, is the first friend I made when I moved to London. I met her at the same coffee shop that made me late today. She'd served me for six months before we exchanged numbers. Then one day, I introduced her to Patrick and the rest is history. They are perfect for each other. They both know about my past, know who I am running from and exactly how dangerous Matteo can be. They both help to keep me off the radar and to keep me safe.

There's not a lot we can do about the media now, though. Once Patrick became the most successful real estate developer in London, I became known to the media, simply as 'El'; a mysterious woman who was always at his side. We've made sure my son Niko never, ever steps foot into the office building, made sure no one knows I have a son; and that's how it stayed.

Because if Matteo ever finds out about Niko, if he ever discovers that I gave birth to his child; he would come for both of us, with everything he has and I know that I will never be able to protect my baby from that kind of darkness.

Yvonne, my nanny is paid for by Patrick. In fact, every aspect of my life is paid for by Patrick; but I earn every single, damn dollar. I work six days a week, arranging both his and his wife's personal and business lives. I run all errands, attend every event Aela is unable to, doing it all with a smile on my face and nothing but gratitude in my heart.

My salary grew as Patrick's business grew. By the time Niko turned five and was ready to attend school, we'd hired Yvonne. She homeschools him while also being his full-time nanny. Niko is completely off the grid. He doesn't exist anywhere. He doesn't have a birth certificate or a social security number or anything that can trace him back to me or to Matteo.

I had a homebirth in my studio apartment with only Aela present and a million YouTube videos on homebirths to get me through it; definitely not something I recommend. Actually, giving birth isn't something I recommend either. The pain is indescribable. The fear, suffocating; But once I'd gotten through it, I knew I needed to keep my Niko safe, to make sure Matteo never finds out about him or about me even being alive.

"Hey, El?" Patrick clicks his fingers in front of my face, Pulling me out of the dark spiral my thoughts.

"Where did you go just now?" he asks.

I realise I've been staring into space; lost in memories of a life I'm desperately trying to forget.

"Sorry, got lost in the past," I admit. It's the truth, I'm

always lost in the past, always wondering if Matteo is still looking for me, terrified that one day he'll find me.

"All good," Patrick laughs at me. "But get your butt to your desk and find something to wear tonight."

"Yep, will do," I say before running back out to my desk to make a quick call to Yvonne. My hands steady now, my mind focused on the present.

"Hey, Yonnie, can you look after Niko tonight? Patrick needs me to attend an event," I say into the phone. Already knowing she'll say yes, because Yvonne is the most reliable person I know, and the most trustworthy.

"Of course, El. Maybe one of these days you will pick up a husband at one of these events too," Yvonne says earnestly, I can hear the smile in her voice.

"Not going to happen. I gave my heart away 10 years ago. But I might find someone for the night," I laugh at Yvonne. Trying to keep things light and pretend that my heart isn't still chained to a man in Sydney, who probably hates me now or thinks I'm dead.

"Well, if you got an itch to scratch, my brother has always said he would love to help," Yvonne laughs right back at me and I can feel the warmth of her friendship in the sound. The safety her presence gives, even through the phone.

"Fuck off, I'm hanging up now!" I say, laughing despite myself.

"Have fun, El," Yvonne laughs back at me.

"I will," I say as I hang up. I immediately pull up my favourite dress shop in the city and give them a quick call; My fingers already know the number by heart.

"Bella Louise, can I help you?" the shop attendant

announces, I recognise her voice immediately because I've been calling this shop for years.

"Morning, it's El here from Murphy's Real Estate. Can I please get my regular sent to the office by 4 pm today?" I ask. Already knowing they'll have something perfect for me.

"Yes of course El. We just got a floor-length, black and gold gown in, with tight long sleeves and a high neckline. Will that do?" she asks.

I feel a surge of gratitude, the long sleeves are an absolutely non-negotiable.

"Perfect, thank you," I say then hung up. I lean back in my chair, my mind already moving on to the next task.

Bella Louise is the best store in town. I've been shopping there for eight years now. They are awesome, they knew my size, dress requirements and my special requests. The ones that keep my identity hidden and keep me safe.

I've always had a massive addiction to getting tattoos, even before I ran from Sydney. I'd already had both arms tattooed from shoulders to wrists. Intricate designs that cover every inch of the skin and after moving to London I added a full piece on my back with some random ones across my belly and ribs. A constellation of ink that tells a story that only I can understand.

Since Matteo tattooed every single piece on my arms himself, marking me with his hands and his art, I have to keep my sleeves long at all times. Absolutely have to. Because if anyone see the tattoos, if anyone recognises them, they'll ask questions, wondering where I got them; someone, may somehow trace me back to him.

Sure, it sucks in summer. But I can still keep cool with

short skirts. As long as I keep my arms hidden. As long as I keep the tattoos hidden, Matteo will never find me. He will never know that I am alive, that I survived and that I've built a life without him.

But the problem with being on the run for 10 years is that you know you'll eventually get caught. The past has a way of finding you no matter how far you run, how hard you hide, or even how carefully you cover your tracks.

Chapter 4

Matteo Ricci

The plane ride to London takes 21 hours, 21 hours of my brain being so focused on the photo of Eleanor, I can barely think about anything else. There's just something about the photo that's screaming at me, "This is it, we've found her this time." Something in the way she's standing, the angle of her face and the light in her eyes that I recognise, even after all these years.

I know, I absolutely know that it is real, this isn't another false lead and I will finally get answers. But I am growing more and more impatient with every passing minute. Every second that ticks by is another second I'm not with her, another second she's out there living a life without me.

Angel gives me the short version of what the USB contains on the flight over. The information makes my blood run cold and hot, at the same time. Eleanor goes by the name of "El" and works for a real estate developer in London. She's been here for the past 10 years; The time-line fits perfectly. The photos we've managed to pull up on social media, sure look like her. She always has her arms covered like she's hiding them intentionally, like she's hiding the tattoos I marked her with.

She's slightly curvier than the last time I'd seen her, but still just as beautiful, still absolutely breathtaking. Her tits have grown too, unless she's had them done; I don't care either way. No matter what they look like, they are mine. All of her is mine. Every inch of her body, every breath she takes, every heartbeat in her chest, belongs to me.

The sleek, black car Angel arranged for us, is waiting and ready by the time we get off the plane. The best thing about flying private is arriving at a private airstrip, and not having to wait around for the traffic or having to deal with the chaos of a commercial airport. The car pulls up the second you walk out the door, no delays, no complications.

But fuck I feel sick. The mixed emotions I have going on are not doing my gut any good. The anticipation, the fear and the rage, all mixing into a toxic cocktail that's making my stomach churn. I need a drink, there better be drinks in the car, because if there isn't I am going to lose my mind.

"Boss, you okay? You're looking a little green around the gills," Angel notes, his eyes narrowing as he studies my face. I can see the concern there. He knows something is wrong.

"I'll be right. I think I just need a drink," I reply, my voice rough and strained.

"I arranged for there to be whiskey and gin in the car," Angel replies.

A wave of gratitude washes over me with his words, this man knows me, knows exactly what I need.

"This is why I keep you around, Cock Face," I smile at the fucker, who is now glaring death daggers at me as his eyes flash with mock anger.

"Lucky you pay my bills, Boss. Any other man would be laid out for a comment like that," Angel admits with a threat in his tone; a promise that he will absolutely beat my ass if I push him too far.

I just smirk at him because I know for sure that Angel will lay me out if it is needed. He's done similar shit in the past, I know he will again in the future, every now and again I need to be taken down a peg; for someone to remind me that I am not invincible. And Angel is the only one who can get away with it and not end up swimming in the harbour, with his body weighed down by concrete.

"We are about 20 minutes from the hotel. From there, we will be able to catch your girl heading to work in the morning," Angel says, laying out the plan.

I just nodded in response, my mind already racing ahead to tomorrow as I am trying to imagine what I will say to her, how I can possibly make her understand that I've never stopped looking for her and that I've never stopped loving her.

Arriving at 6 pm means there is no chance of catching her today. So, I have to wait until the morning. Which I'm certain isn't going to cut it, it's not going to be enough time to prepare myself to finally see her face to face, to hear her voice or to be able to touch her skin.

20 minutes later we arrive at the hotel, the concierge quickly runs out and starts to load our bags onto a trolley,

as Angel heads to the front desk to grab the keys for our rooms. My stomach already churning and my hands already shaking; I know if I don't get my emotions under control, I'm gonna end up vomiting all over the damn hotel foyer.

"Come on, Boss. Let's get up to the room," Spike whispers from my left, His voice low and steady as he ushers me into the nearest lift behind the concierge who has our bags. The small space suddenly feels claustrophobic as the walls begin closing in on me.

"You here for the fundraiser?" the concierge asks, making small talk. His voice is bright and cheerful.

"What fundraiser?" Angel replies, his tone is casual, but I can see the wheels turning in his head. He's already thinking three steps ahead.

"The one down in the city tonight," the concierge replies, looking at us confused, like he can't believe we don't know about this major event.

"And how would one go about getting on the list for such an event?" Angel asks, his voice smooth and charming. I can see the concierge relax, obviously thinking that we're just tourists trying to get into a fancy party.

"Oh, um, it's an invite-only event. Sorry I thought you were going," the concierge looks like he's trying to back pedal a bit; realizing he may have said too much.

"Where is the event?" Angel asks.

I can hear the urgency in his voice now, sensing he's onto something.

"Down at the Natural History Museum, off Cromwell Rd," the concierge says.

My entire body goes rigid.

"Thanks, mate," Angel smiles at the boy, his expression warm and grateful. The concierge practically melts under his charm.

The lift opens up, revealing the penthouse suite. The concierge walks in, drops the bags in the centre of the room before running back to the lift. The way he practically fled from the room, you'd think he could sense the danger wafting off Angel.

"What's the obsession with fundraisers all of a sudden?" I ask Angel, my mind already spinning with possibilities.

"El attends them all with her boss when his wife can't make them," Angel says.

The words stop me in my tracks.

"Get me on that list Angel, NOW!" I command, sharp and urgently and I can see Spike's head snap up, he understands the implications of what Angel just said.

"Hold on, hold on mate. Lemme look it up and make sure they are even attending," Angel replies, already pulling out his phone and working his magic.

I walk over to the mini bar in search of more alcohol. There doesn't seem to be enough in my system at the moment to calm the raging nerves. Needing it to quiet the storm inside me, I pour myself a generous glass of whiskey, the burn as I gulp it down does nothing to ease the tension coiling within my muscles.

"Guest list says Patrick and Aela, his wife," Angel states.

My heart is pounding so hard, I think it might break through my ribs.

I look up to see Spike has already changed his clothes

into full black stealth gear and is now strapping on his million-and-one knives. His movements are quick and efficient and I can't help but smirk at the sight of him.

"Where are you bloody going? Tryouts for Mission Impossible?" I ask, my voice dripping with sarcasm.

"Thought I'd scope out the place, and maybe follow this Patrick back to his digs to see what he knows," Spike states, his tone all business. I can see he's already in full protective mode, already thinking about how to keep me safe and how to make sure nothing goes wrong.

"That's not a bad idea, actually," Angel says, nodding his approval.

"Shit, okay, hold on a sec. Let me get changed into my secret ninja suit," I grimace, already moving toward the bedroom to change as both Angel and Spike chuckle at my expense.

They know how much I hate recon, knowing full well I'd rather be doing something more direct, Something that lets me burn off some of the energy building inside me, something more violent.

30 minutes later we're decked out in all black and I'm strapped with a few weapons; unlike Spike who would sink if someone threw him in the ocean, with all the knives he's carrying. I can't help but shake my head at the sight of him.

"Come on Boss let's go," Spike smiles at me, the excitement clear in his eyes. He's ready for whatever may come next.

"Fuck off cunt, stop looking at me like I'm a fucking fairy," I snap at him, my nerves making me irritable and lash out.

"If the shoes fit, Boss," Spike says, ducking at the same time and narrowly missing the hand Angel sends flying to the back of his head. I can't help but feel a surge of affection for these 2 bastards, they are men who have stood by me through everything.

"Leave the Boss alone, Fuck Face. Just because his vagina is out. Let him be a fucking girl," Angel scolds.

I feel a laugh bubbling up in my chest, despite the tension and the fear.

"You're both fucking fired," I state, before shoulder-barging them to get into the lift first. I can hear them laughing behind me as Spike's calls out something about how I'd never survive without them. He's right; I wouldn't. These 2 are my brothers, my anchors and the only people I trust completely.

Angel organises the car and a driver. 10 minutes later, we're dropped across the road from the museum. Standing outside of a casino of all things; I can't help but think the irony is almost too much. We're about to gamble everything on the chance that Eleanor will be at this event.

"Let's head in there. There's a window seat we can sit at, be able to watch them come in and out," Angel says, pointing toward the casino.

I'm just thankful for a seat, inside with warmth, I'd forgotten just how cold this damn country is; It's a chill that seems to seep into your bones and never quite leave.

Once inside, Spike walks straight to the bar to order us a round of drinks and heads back to the table we've managed to snag that has front row seats to everyone coming and going at the event. I settle into my chair. my eyes fixed on the museum entrance, my entire body coiled and ready to spring into action.

It's well past 7:30 pm now. Everyone arrived for the event 30 minutes ago. So now we're just waiting to watch everyone leave. Waiting for the chance of Eleanor walking out of the building, waiting for the chance to finally see her face again.

"Angel, show me a photo of that Patrick cunt, so I know who to look out for, will ya?" I ask, my voice low and dangerous.

Angel shoves his phone at me so I can see him. He's not what I expected, styled black hair with blue eyes and well over six foot tall; No wonder Eleanors attached herself to him. She would feel safe with this guy. The thought makes my blood boil, causing me to want to murder him slowly, it also makes me wonder if he has ever touched my woman; if his hands have ever been on her skin and that thought instantly makes me want to vomit.

"Boss, you gotta keep your shit together. I've never seen you like this. You're all pale, looking like you're about to hurl into the nearest pot plant," Angel says, his voice laced with concern, the worry evident on his face.

Shit, he's right though. Quickly I stand, vomiting into the planter closest to us, my entire body shakes as I empty my stomach, and the reality of what's about to happen finally hits me. I realise, that in a matter of hours, I'm going to see Eleanor again. And I actually have no idea what I'm going to do when I do.

Chapter 5

Eleanor Wang

We arrive to the fundraiser at around 7 pm. I've always hated these events with a burning passion that never quite fades, no matter how many times I attend them. People thrive on spending thousands of dollars to host these things, just to encourage other people to part with thousands, for things that only receive a fraction of what's actually donated. The whole thing feels like a con to me, a scam dressed in designer gowns and expensive champagne.

Why can't we just cut out the middleman and simply donate the full amount to the charity itself? Am I wrong? Or is it just me who can see the absolute absurdity of it all?

From the second we enter the room, we're bombarded. Patrick would be Britain's most wanted bachelor if he wasn't married. Although, even with a ring on his finger, some still try their luck, circling him like vultures as they whisper propositions in his ear. I do understand it, the wealthy do love to have their side bitches. But not Patrick, the second he laid eyes on Aela, he was a goner;

completely and utterly lost to her. I honestly don't think he's even noticed other women since meeting her. His eyes only ever see her and his heart will only ever beat for her.

I've seen that look on a male's face once before, a long time ago, in another lifetime, in another city. It's a look I try very hard not to think about, because thinking about it, brings back all the pain, the longing and the desperate ache I've spent 10 years trying to bury.

"El, Patrick, so nice you could make it. Where is Aela?" Mrs Brunswick, the host for this event, asks Patrick with a saccharine smile that makes my skin crawl. I can feel the judgment in her eyes, the way she's assessing me, trying to figure out what my relationship is to Patrick.

"At home, unfortunately. We had some paperwork that needed to be finished today so she offered to stay back and get it done," Patrick says with a huge fake smile on his face, it's the kind of smile that doesn't reach his eyes, a smile that screams he'd rather be anywhere else.

"Oh, isn't she just a gem! Well, she will be missed. Thankfully El is here to take her place this evening," she grins at me.

Something in her tone makes my blood boil, something suggesting I'm just a substitute, a placeholder for the real thing.

"Oh, it's such a pleasure to be here, Mrs Brunswick," I say with a heavy smile, my voice dripping with false sweetness. I feel Patrick's hand on my back, a silent warning to keep my temper in check.

"If you would excuse us," Patrick says while waving across the room and I can see the relief on his face as he begins to steer us away from that woman.

Patrick steers us in the direction he was waving. The second we're out of earshot, I lean in close to him and whisper, "Fuck, that woman needs a throat punch!"

"Shhhh El, your green-eyed monster is showing," Patrick laughs back at me as his eyes twinkle with amusement and I can't help but smile at his teasing.

"I can't be the only one who wants to give it to her," I state, as the tension eases from my shoulders.

"Oh, I'm sure there are plenty, like me, for example. But a gentleman never hits a lady," Patrick adds, his English accent thickening and I can't help but laugh at his impression.

It still astounds me that I've been in London for 10 years, Patrick the same but yet, we both still carry the accents of our homelands. Thick and unmistakable markers of where we've come from; reminders of the lives we left behind.

When it comes to Patrick, the more whiskey you feed him the thicker his accent gets; his Irish brogue becoming more pronounced with every drink. But me? I just sound pure bogan all the time. My Australian accent never fades or softens, no matter how hard I try to blend in and disappear into the London landscape.

I might have grown up with wealthy parents and attended private, Catholic schools, but my Aussie accent is pure gutter-trash and I can swear worse than any corner bitch on a Saturday night. I have no idea where it comes from. My parents are all prim and proper, All manners and etiquette. So if anyone says black sheep? Yeah, that's me. The rebel, the one who never quite fits into any mould they try to pour me into.

It still makes me wonder how in the world a man like Matteo had even looked my way. Because Matteo's, well, he is part of Sydney's elite, part of a world that I never had business being in. His father had moved to Australia back when he was a kid. Once situated, He quickly built himself a criminal underworld in the heart of the city, with his 3 best friends. Together, they went on to create what we now call the four seats; The four seats of power, all run by the Italian Mafia. The game's pretty easy, you either do what you're told, or you're killed; simple as that. There's no middle ground, no negotiations, just obey or die.

My family had nothing to do with that world, they had nothing to do with the darkness that Matteo comes from. My father is a science teacher at a private school and my mother is a nurse in the children's hospital. My father comes from old Chinese money made in the gold mines back when the first Chinese arrived in Australia. My mother, on the other hand, came from old British stock that came over with the first fleet. We had a big but modest house in Chatswood. I got good grades at school and had aspirations to be an artist when I grew up, I had dreams of creating beautiful things and of making a mark on the world through my art.

When I left high school after year 12, I went to TAFE to study Art and fell in love with it. Fell in love with the process of creating something from nothing. I got my first tattoo at 18. The Chinese symbol for my last name, Wang. It's placed on my wrist as a way of honouring my heritage. That's where I met Matteo. In the tattoo studio, in that small room is where my entire life changed in an instant.

There I was sitting on the chair, getting inked; the

needle buzzing against my skin, creating sharp and exquisite pain, when in walked this fresh 20-year-old man with slicked back, black hair. Honestly, my undies were drenched just from the sight of him. My entire body responded to him in a way I've never experienced before.

He was well over six foot and Clearly worked out, because his arms were pure candy; all muscle, ink and raw power. With high cheekbones, a square jaw and eyes the most striking shade of blue; like the sky on a perfect summer day. He was wearing a tailored suit and spit-shined shoes. Looking every inch the dangerous man he is. I'd later come to find that the only part of him under that suit that wasn't covered in ink, was a small part on his chest and his dick. He was pure sin and I wanted to lick him from base to tip, I wanted to taste every inch of him and lose myself in him completely.

Yep, I was a goner. Completely and utterly lost from the very first moment.

He walked right up to the till, grabbing the earnings like he owned the place, then waved at the guys working before turning to walk out. That's when his eyes landed on mine and I watched his Adam's apple move as he swallowed. I Watched the way his entire body seemed to shift, acknowledging my presence, before walking towards me with a predatory grace that made my breath catch in my throat.

He held out his left hand and said, "Hi, I'm Matteo. I own this place." His voice was like velvet and gravel mixed together, it was dark, dangerous and utterly intoxicating.

I couldn't even reply. My brain was completely fried.

Did I mention his eyes were the most striking colour of blue? Like super-light blue, like the sky? I couldn't form words. Couldn't do anything but stare at him like an idiot. I was completely mesmerised, my eyes roaming over him, just taking in his features over and over again, like I would never see a man this beautiful again.

He crouched down to my level and spoke again, "Hi, I'm Matteo." His voice was softer now. More intimate and I felt my entire body respond to him.

"Hi, Matteo," I spluttered back. Oh good, my tongue did work after all. Even if it'd felt like it was made of lead.

Matteo stood up and told to the man finishing up my wrist, "Don't charge her. Just make sure she fills out the forms." He turned on his heel and walked out. Leaving me sitting in a daze, completely and utterly undone by a man I'd just met.

"You can wipe your mouth now, Miss," the tattooist said, the amusement clear in his voice.

"Oh shit, fuck, am I drooling?" I asked, while wiping my face. Mortified by the thought that I'd been sitting there with my mouth hanging open like an idiot.

"Nope. But if your mouth stayed open any longer you would have," he laughed at me and I felt my face burning with embarrassment.

Shit. I don't think my face could have gotten any redder. I wanted to disappear into the floor, to sink through the earth and never come back up.

"Hey, Earth to El!" I feel an elbow in my ribs, pulling me back to the present, back to the fundraiser and back to Patrick's concerned face.

"Fuck, shit, sorry," I look at Patrick, the worry in his eyes obvious. He knows exactly where my mind just went.

"What's up with you these days?" Patrick frowns at me, his voice gentle and concerned.

"I don't know. Been thinking of the past a lot lately," I frown at the floor, unable to meet his eyes. Unable to admit to him that I'm terrified, that I'm always terrified, that no matter how much time passes, I can never quite escape the shadow of what I left behind.

"It's been 10 years love. You're going to be okay. If he hasn't found you yet, he isn't going to," Patrick smiles, trying to take my mind off it, attempting to reassure me. But his words do nothing to ease the constant, gnawing fear living in my chest.

"You're probably right," I sigh. But even as I say it, I know he's not, I know Matteo is still out there, still looking for me, refusing to let me go. Because men like Matteo, they don't just give up, they don't just move on, they hunt until they find what they're looking for.

"Maybe, it's time to move on, Love. I can think of many men in this room right now that want to ride your bus," Patrick grins, waving at people as we walk. He's trying to lighten the mood, trying to make me laugh.

"Did you just call my vagina a bus, Patrick?" I ask.

Despite everything, despite the fear and the anxiety, I can't help but laugh at his absurdity.

"Well it did house a child. And it did move with said child inside it, I'd say that's the definition of a bus," he grins and I can see the pride on his face at his terrible joke.

"Fuck, your dad jokes are so lame!" I laugh back at him, shaking my head at his ridiculousness.

"Well, one of us has to be the lame one. And we all know Aela ain't gonna be it. So, I nominate myself," he smiles bright and big, showing the genuine love he has for his wife. You can see it in every gesture, every word, every look.

"And this Patrick, is why you're gonna be stuck with me as your PA for life. I cannot live without your inspirational words of wisdom," I smirk at him, but deep down I mean it. Patrick has become my anchor, my safe place, one of the only reasons I've survived the past 10 years.

"Come on. Let's see what table they have us at today," Patrick steers us over to the table and chairs. We find our names and sit down to the 3-bite, 3-course meal. It looks absolutely pathetic. I know I'll definitely be making 2-minute noodles when I get home because this fancy food is not going to cut it.

We listen to 2 hours of speeches, the amount of money every rich cunt in this room has donated to the evening and by the time it's over, I'm absolutely exhausted, my feet are killing me, my face hurts from smiling and a hefty 40 thousand pounds has been raised for a charity. We can finally mingle or leave. We, being the smart ones, leave without hesitation.

It's around 9:45 pm by the time we walk out of the museum. Patrick calls the car around.

"Come on, Love. Let's get the fuck outta here," Patrick exclaims as he holds open the door for me. I can see the relief on his face as we finally escape the suffocating atmosphere of the event.

"Cheers for the lift home," I say, sliding into the car, grateful as always for his kindness.

"Darling, I've been dropping you home for 10 years now. When are you going stop saying thank you?" Patrick says, his voice is warm and affectionate.

"When the..."

"Weeds stop growing. Yeah, yeah, I know," he smirks at me, I can't help but smile at how well he knows me and the way he finishes my sentences, before I can even speak them.

The rest of the way is in a comfortable silence. The kind of silence that only exists between people who truly know each other, those who have shared so much, And who have become family in every way that matters.

Once we arrive at my apartment, Patrick has the driver wait till he walks me to my front door. ever the gentleman and the protector that he is and I can't help but feel a surge of gratitude for this man, a man who has saved my life in so many ways.

"Ever the gentle fellow, Patrick," I snicker as he walks me to my door.

"Haha. I'll be walking you to your door till I can find you a man good enough to take you off my hands. But until then, you are stuck with my chiselled butt," he grins, the affection lacing his voice, the genuine care shining in his eyes.

"Well, thank you and your chiselled butt," I mock salute. He laughs, a warm and genuine kind of laugh.

I place my key card on the door, unlocking it instantly, before turning back to face him one more time. "See you in the morning Patrick." I Step into my apartment and close the door. My apartment is my safe space in the life I've built away from Matteo, away from the darkness and away from everything that tried to destroy me.

Chapter 6

Matteo Ricci

Angel grabs me a coke and orders us some food. I know he's trying to settle my nerves, trying to keep me grounded, especially after I decimated that poor pot plant; which Spike conveniently moved to a different location, so no one notices the evidence of my breakdown. We sit and eat while waiting for Patrick and his wife to leave the fundraiser and for Eleanor to emerge from the building with them, so I can finally lay eyes on her. Finally confirm that she's real, not just some cruel figment of my desperate imagination.

Honestly, I hate waiting, I'm not good at it, never have been. My father always said good things come to those who wait. Did I listen? Nope, never. Because waiting is a waste of time, a luxury I can't afford. It's been 10 years. 10 fucking years of this torture and I do not want to wait another friggin minute, not another second, not another heartbeat.

2 goddamn, motherfucking hours. That's how long it takes for Patrick to leave the fundraiser. When he finally

emerges from the doors, it is Eleanor with him. Not Aela, Eleanor. My Eleanor, walking beside him like she belongs to him.

I nearly fall out of my chair at the sight, my entire body going rigid as my heart stops in my chest. The food I just ate, threatens to make its way out again as the bile rises in my throat. Because it's her. It's really, actually her. After all this time, after all these years of searching, of hunting, of never giving up, she's finally here; finally within reach.

"It's her," I whisper. My voice is barely audible. My eyes are fixing on her figure as she walks down the steps of the museum. I can feel my entire body responding to her presence, the pull of her gravity, drawing me toward her, like a moth to a flame.

"How can you tell from here?" Spike asks, his voice cutting through the haze of my obsession.

"I just can," I reply, standing from the chair, my movements jerky and uncoordinated as my entire body surges with adrenaline and need. "We need to follow her. Angel, call the car."

"On it now, Boss," Angel says, already moving, understanding the urgency of the situation.

"Quick, let's go. We need to follow her home," I command, my voice sharp and urgent. I'm already moving toward the door before anyone else has a chance to react.

I race out the door and down the steps, Angel quickly following my lead as we watch them get into a car and take off. My entire focus is narrowed down to that one car, my heart is pounding so hard, I feel it might break through my ribs. She's the one woman and this, this is my one moment.

"Fuck, Angel where is the car?!" I demand. My voice rising with the fear and panic. Fear that I'm going to lose her again, that she's going to disappear into the London night and I'll be left with nothing but memories and regret, again.

"Right there, Boss!" Angel yells, as our car pulls up to the curb.

Angel runs forward, opening the door as we pile in. I practically throw myself into the backseat, making sure my eyes never leave the car in front of us. Angel leans forward, telling the driver to follow the car in front. His voice is calm and steady even though I'm falling apart inside.

Thankfully, there is some traffic tonight and the car has stopped just a few cars in front of us at the traffic lights. I can see her silhouette through the rear window, see her sitting beside Patrick. The jealousy that flares up inside me is suffocating, an all-consuming rage threatening to tear me apart from the inside out.

"Shit, Boss, what do you wanna do?" Spike asks from the seat beside me and I can hear the anticipation in his voice, I can sense he's ready for whatever comes next.

"We stay on Eleanor. We'll leave Patrick for another day; I need to see her," I say, my voice hard and final, leaving no room for argument or negotiations because Eleanor is all that matters; Eleanor is all that's ever mattered.

"Alright, Boss," Spike grumbles, clearly put out. I can see the disappointment on his face because he obviously wanted to inflict some violence tonight, wanted to do some cutting, . But that's going to have to wait. Right now, all I care about is Eleanor.

We follow them through the city for a bit, the streets of London blurring past us. Until the car stops at a small apartment block. My entire body on high alert, this is it, this is where she lives. This is where she's been hiding, all these years.

I watch as they get out of the car and Patrick walks Eleanor to the front door. The gesture making me want to spring out of the car and kill the bastard, to rip him apart with my bare hands, because that's my woman, that's my Eleanor and no other man should be touching her, or be walking her to her door, let alone, anywhere near her.

"It's okay Boss. He is just walking her inside," Angel says softly, his voice acting as a soothing balm to my rising fury. I can feel his hand on my shoulder, grounding me, keeping me from doing something I know I can't take back.

The bastard is right. As soon as Eleanor opens the front door, he turns and leaves. I feel a small measure of relief wash over me, but it's quickly replaced by rage. Fuck him and his gentleman shit; I want to slit his throat, I want to make him pay for every moment he's spent in her presence, for every second he's breathed the same air as her. My thoughts are clearly irrational right now, but I just can't get them under control. It's all just too much. 10 years, 10 fucking years of this torture. And now, she's right there. so close I can almost reach out and touch her.

Spike jumps out of the car as soon as Patrick takes off and stands near the front. He's reading the apartment names, trying to figure out which one is hers and just as he is about to press a button, a short old, blonde woman heads out the door to leave. Spike quickly steps aside, holding the door open for her while acting all sweet and gentle-man-like. The action leaves me wondering, what the fuck is going on tonight. Have we all turned into a bunch of pansies? I'm sitting here ready to burn this entire city down and Spike is playing gentleman with some random old woman.

Once the woman jumps into a beat-up old Honda and takes off, we rush out of the car, walking up to Spike, who is holding the door open for us. Angel walks through with a smirk on his face.

"Why, thank you sweet and kind, Sir," Angel says in a southern accent. His amusement clear in his voice.

"Shut up. What apartment is she in?" I snap, my patience wearing thin, the need to find her overriding everything else.

"Apartment 3 is the only one without a name," Spike says as he glances back at the panel again.

"What were the other names?" I ask, my voice low and dangerous.

"Um… Taylor, Jones and Wicket," Spike responds reading the name off the panel.

The moment he says the names, I know with absolute certainty which apartment is hers.

"Wicket, what number is that one?" I ask, a smile forming on my face. She remembers. She's kept the memory alive, even after all these years, she's still connected to me.

"4," Spike says.

"That will be the one," I say with absolute certainty, already moving toward the stairs.

"What? How?" Spike asks, confused. Not understanding the significance of the name.

"Eleanor loved this spin-off series of Star Wars, where they made cartoons of the Ewoks. The main character was called Wicket," I explain, feeling warmth spread throughout my chest.

"Um, okay Boss but that doesn't mean she uses the name now," Spike says, trying to be practical, to keep me grounded in reality.

"Her apartment in the city. The name on the plate was Wicket, it was our inside joke," I smile. I'm happy to see she is still as attached to me as I am to her. The relief that washes over me is almost overwhelming. It means she hasn't forgotten me, she's carried me with her all these years and there's still a chance for us.

We walk up the two flights of stairs to her door. With every step my heart pounds harder. My entire body vibrating with anticipation, fear and pure need. This is it, this is the moment I've been waiting for, the moment that changes everything. She will be coming home with me, today. No more running, no more hiding, no more living without her.

Spike raises his hand and knocks on the door. I hear the sounds of movement inside, hear her moving around. My entire body is coiled tight and ready to spring.

"Coming," comes a muffled answer from behind the door. I register her voice. Actually hear her voice, for the first time in 10 years. It's like music to my ears, every nerve in my body now firing at once.

The door flies open and Eleanor stands there wearing silk pyjamas. She's even more beautiful than I remembered. Even more perfect. My breath catches in my throat. She's real. She's actually real, and she's right here in front of me.

"What did you forget, Yvonne?" she says before she notices who is actually at the door. Her eyes are still focused on something behind us. Then her gaze shifts and lands on me. I watch as her entire world stops, the recognition flooding her features.

"Oh," is all she manages to mutter when her eyes find mine again. I can see the shock, the disbelief, and the fear all warring across her face. I want to reach out and touch her, to confirm that she's real; That this is actually happening.

It's been 10 years, but those eyes haven't changed. I would know her anywhere. Our souls are the same. They're connected in ways that transcend time, distance and all the years we've spent apart. I can feel our connection instantly, feel it pulling at me, drawing me toward her like gravity itself.

"Eleanor," I say as I walk towards her. My voice is rough and raw with emotion. She begins walking backwards. A complete look of shock on her face, With her eyes wide and her mouth open. I see the moment she realises this is real, that I'm really here; that I've found her.

"I found you, Princess," I whisper.

I watch as all the colour leaves her face and she crumbles to the floor. Her entire body giving out; her mind unable to process what's happening.

"Shit," I say, reaching out to catch her. My arms wrapping around her, instinctively, holding her up to keep her from hitting the ground. She's so light and fragile. I'm terrified that if I let go, she'll disappear again.

"Fuck! Angel, find me somewhere to lay her down!" I command. My voice sharp with urgency.

Angel races in front of me. His eyes scanning the apartment quickly. "There is a couch just down the hall," he yells. I'm already moving carrying her toward it.

I lay her down against the grey cushions, with as much care as I can manage. My entire body and hands shake with a mixture of emotions, fear and need.

"Shit, how long does it take for people to wake back up?" I ask. Just as I begin to feel movement under my hands. Looking down, I see her eyelids fluttering as she starts to come back to consciousness.

Eleanor opens her eyes slowly until they land on me again. She reaches up, placing her raised hand on my cheek, her touch burning me, branding me in a way that I've been waiting for. In a dream-like voice, she speaks the words I've wished to hear, "I've missed you."

The words are like a knife to my heart, as everything I've been holding onto for 10 years is suddenly validated; Suddenly real.

"I've missed you too, Princess," I reply. My voice breaking with the overwhelming emotion. I can feel the tears threatening to spill over, but I hold them back, needing to be strong, needing to be the man she's always needed me to be.

With that her eyes round at the corners as she pushes herself up into a seated position, while trying to scoot back up onto the couch. The look of fear on her face worries me and has me wondering what's wrong; what could have suddenly changed. She looks to the left, then the right of her, seeing Angel and Spike. I watch the moment it registers and she realises that she's trapped; there's no escape this time.

"Fuck, fuck, fuck, what are you doing here?" she stammers out, her voice rising with panic, laced with an undertone of fear. I can see her mind racing, trying to figure out what to do and How to get away.

"I've come to take you home, Princess," I explain, calmly, yet possessively as I see the resistance forming in her eyes.

"Nope, not gonna happen. You need to leave. I don't know how you found me, but you've gotta go!" she states firmly.

The rejection in her voice is like a physical blow, sending the anger rising up inside me. The need to understand why she's pushing me away, growing stronger with every word.

"What? Why? Who else is here?" I demand, my voice growing darker, more dangerous as I look to Spike, who takes off to clear the house; immediately understanding my unspoken command.

"No, no, no, no, Spike stop. No, you cannot go down there… Shit!" she says, while trying to climb to her feet. But I've locked her on the couch with my arms keeping her in place, keeping her from running, keeping her with me.

Two minutes later Spike comes back with a kid in tow, a half-asleep kid with black hair and light blue eyes. My entire world stops, as my universe shifts on its axis. I turn to look at Eleanor who's face is a state of pure shock, as she realises that her secret is out.

"Mum, what's going on?" the boy asks. His voice is small and confused. My heart is pounding so hard I think it might explode.

"Eleanor, who the f- f- f- uck is that?" I stammer. My voice is breaking, my mind trying to process what I'm seeing, unable to comprehend what I'm actually understanding.

"That's… your son," she admits, while still holding eye contact with the boy.

The words hang heavily in the air between us; life-changing and absolutely devastating.

Son. Did she just say "son"? Did she just tell me that I have a child? That I have a son? That Eleanor has been hiding my son from me for 10 years?

"Boss," Angel says, clicking his fingers in front of my face. "You still with us?"

I realise my mind's gone somewhere else, somewhere dark and confusing and I can't seem to find my way back.

I can't take my eyes off the boy, The ability to stop staring at him, lost, because he's mine; He's absolutely mine. I can see it in his face. his eyes, in the way he holds himself. I feel something shifting inside me; Something fundamental and definitely irreversible.

"What's his name?" I ask. My voice barely above a whisper.

"Niko," she whispers.

The name hits me like a physical blow. She named him after my great-grandfather, she's kept me with her, the only way she could.

"Niko… as in Niko Ricci?" I turn to her, the answer clear in her eyes before she even speaks.

"Yes, I honoured the bloodline rules for naming your children," she admits, while still only looking at Niko. I see the love in her eyes, the fierce protection and the way she's willing to die to keep him safe.

Niko was my great-grandfather. The family uses the same four names in our bloodline for our first-born son; She remembered my great-grandfathers name.

"Hold on. Hold on. I need a minute," I note as I stand up and walk towards her balcony. My legs feel unsteady and my mind is reeling. I open the door and step outside, the freezing cold wind slaps me in the face, doing its intended job perfectly, Helping to Ground me. Reminding me that I'm alive; And that this is real.

I have a son, I have a fucking son. Why the fuck did she leave? How the fuck has she protected him for so long? How has she kept him hidden from me? From the world? From everyone who would want to use him against me?

I run my hands down my face, before reaching into my pocket for a smoke, only I don't find any, remembering that I quit. Instantly wondering why the fuck I quit? Because right now I need something to do with my hands, something to calm the storm inside me.

A hand reaches out from the balcony doors, holding a cigarette and lighter. I turn to see Spike standing there, something in his expression that tells me he understands; like he knows exactly what I'm going through.

"Thought you might need this Boss," he says, looking out into the night, not meeting my eyes, in a clear attempt to give me the space I need to fall apart without an audience.

"Thanks," is all I manage as I take the cigarette from him with shaking hands.

I light the damn bastard under my shirt. It sure as shit wasn't going to light with the fucking wind. I take a long drag, letting the smoke fill my lungs, letting it calm the chaos inside me.

"I have a fucking son," I say to no one in particular. The words are still not quite real, not quite believable.

"He looks exactly like you," Spike says, the amusement tinging his voice, like he's trying to lighten the mood, trying to help me process what's happening.

I turn to look back through the window, seeing Niko sitting next to his mother while she hugs him tight. The sight of them together, the sight of Eleanor protecting my son and the sight of the family I didn't know I had, is almost too much to bear.

"Fuck, no wonder she ran," I say. Understanding floods through me. Understanding why she left, why she really ran and why she's been hiding all these years.

"She was keeping the kid safe," Spike says and I can hear the respect in his voice. The way he understands what she's done and why she's done it.

"Fuck, what do I do from here? Do I leave and pretend we never found them? Or do I take them home?" I ask, the desperation in my voice clear in the way I'm grasping for answers, for guidance and for some kind of direction.

"Take them home, Boss. Enzo knows about her already. She's already unsafe here. Even if Enzo doesn't know about the boy; he knows about her. That's one too many people knowing her location," Spike answers. I can hear the logic in his words. The way he's thinking 3 steps ahead, seeing the danger that Eleanor and Niko are in, now that their location has been compromised.

"FUCK!" I yell as I kick the closest chair. the rage, fear and need all mixing together into something far more dangerous, as I feel the control slipping away from me; The darkness inside me, rising up.

"We could just kill Enzo…?" I offer, the darkness in my voice letting on all the ways I'm willing to burn the world down, just to keep them safe.

"And start another war? I'm starting to think the reason she left was because of the last one," Spike adds.

His words cause my chest to tighten, because he's right. He's absolutely right and the realisation is devastating.

Chapter 7

Eleanor Wang

"Shit, Niko come here," I say, patting the couch while glaring at Spike with death stares. My entire body is tense from fear and anger. The desperate need to protect my son from whatever is about to happen, overwhelms me. I can see the confusion on Niko's face as he tries to understand what's going on, and to process the fact that the man I've told him about his entire life, is suddenly standing in our apartment.

"That's him?" Niko says while pointing his thumb in the direction of the balcony. His voice may be small and uncertain, but I can hear the mixture of curiosity and fear in his tone.

"Yep, that's him, Baby. Don't be scared. We've talked about this," I whisper into his ear while giving him a hug, pulling him in close to me in an attempt to shield him from the reality of the situation and to protect him from the darkness that Matteo brings with him; Even though I know it's futile, there's no protecting him from his own father, his own blood.

"Does this mean were going to move to Sydney now?" Niko asks while looking up at me.

The question breaks my heart. He's already resigned himself to the reality, already accepting that his life is about to change and understanding that there's no fighting against the inevitable.

"I don't know, Honey. Let's wait to see what happens when Matteo comes back inside," I offer, the uncertainty lacing my tone. The way I'm grasping for time, for some kind of reprieve, a moment to figure out what the hell I'm supposed to do, now that my worst nightmare has become our reality.

I turn to look at the balcony, at the exact same moment Matteo turns to look inside. It's like our eyes are magnets; Always finding each other in a crowded room, always drawn to each other; no matter how much time has passed; No matter how much distance separates us. Nice to see that even 10 years later it still happens, our connection still exists and the inevitable pull is still there, burning as bright as it ever has.

Taking him in, I notice he has aged since I last saw him. He's grown a lot more bulk. His shoulders are broader, his chest is more defined, and a few extra frown lines mar the corners of his eyes; Lines that speak of a life lived in darkness, of decisions made in the shadows and a burden that's too heavy for one person to bear. There are no greys peppering his hair yet, but he's only just 32 now, still young to the rest of the world; Still in his prime.

I can't imagine life being the head of the Ricci's is a relaxing job, plus, being a member of the four seats; The pressure must be immense, the weight of it crushing on the soul. Maybe, some part of me wants to see some greys there, to know that life has been hard on him since I left. Wanting him to suffer the way I've suffered, for him to understand the pain of losing everything. It was hard on me, only fair he went through the same hardships, right?

Even though I know that's not how life works, that karma doesn't always balance out the way we want it to.

I watch as Matteo flicks his cigarette butt off the balcony. The gesture is casual but yet, dismissive. Before he walks back inside, his movements controlled, almost Predatory as the danger radiates off him in waves. I can feel my entire body going on high alert.

"Ever heard of saving the environment?" Niko bravely and sarcastically jabs at his dad. The shock on Matteo's face evident with the way he's taken aback by his son's boldness. By the fact that Niko isn't intimidated by him and isn't cowering in fear, the way most people do.

Matteo looks like his son just slapped him and for the briefest moment I see something soften in his expression, something almost vulnerable. Then in the blink of an eye, it's gone; Replaced by the hard mask he wears so well.

"Sorry, Son. I won't do it again," Matteo replies, frowning back at Niko. I can hear the genuine apology in his voice, the way he's trying to connect with his son, to establish some kind of relationship. The sight of it is both beautiful and terrifying.

"Right, you both need to pack a bag. We're flying back to Sydney tonight," Matteo announces calmly, like he is making a cup of tea and not just casually rearranging my entire life, making decisions that affect not only me but my son too. The casual way he says it, mixed with the absolute certainty in his voice, makes my blood boil.

"No," I state. The word hangs in the air between us, like a challenge, a declaration of war.

"What?" Matteo asks and I can see the shock on his face. He's not used to being told no, not used to anyone defying him or to anyone standing up to him.

"I said no," I turn to face Matteo fully, my entire body coiled and ready to fight; Ready to do whatever it takes to protect my son and our life here. "I'm not going to just pack a bag and leave right now. I have responsibilities and a life here. You're welcome to go back to Sydney. You don't need us to come with you," I declare as I stand, preparing to face Matteo down.

I watch his expression change. watching the moment the decision is taken from me completely. His eyes darken, his face losing all emotion and I can feel the shift in the air. The way the temperature drops, even our surroundings give a sense that I've crossed a line, I know I shouldn't have crossed.

"Do you honestly think you have a choice here, Eleanor?" Matteo questions, his voice now low and dangerous, the underlying threat in every word clear to all around. He's not asking me, he's warning me to back down, to surrender and accept my fate.

"Yes. Yes, I do have a choice. I'm a person who can make choices. I chose to leave you 10 years ago, and now I'm choosing to stay here, without you," I spit out, lifting my chin, I stare Matteo down. My eyes blazing with defiance.

He straightens, and I see the moment he decides that I

don't get to have a choice anymore. His eyes darken even further and his face loses all emotion. becoming a blank slate; The face of a man who runs an empire; The face of the man who gets exactly what he wants.

"Go pack a bag now, Eleanor, before I throw you over my shoulder and walk you out of here," Matteo says. His voice is cold and final, leaving no room for negotiation or even an argument. Just the absolute certainty that he will do exactly what he's threatening to do.

"Fuck you," I spit at Matteo, my anger overriding my fear and my defiance overrides my common sense. I watch his jaw clench and his hands curl into fists.

"You clearly haven't changed," Matteo states as he walks towards me. His movements slow and deliberate, making my entire body respond to him. The fear, the anger and the attraction, all mixing together into something I can't quite name.

"Spike, go pack a bag for Niko. Angel, go throw some clothes into a bag for Princess over here," Matteo commands, the authority clear in his tone. The way his men immediately jump to obey, moving without question, without hesitation, shows they are more used to this side of Matteo.

"Nice to see you still boss the Buffy boys around like your own personal lap dogs," I remark, my sarcasm dripping from every word. My snark hit the mark as Matteo's eyes flash with something dangerous.

"Keep it up, Eleanor, and I'll spank that ass of yours back into submission," Matteo declares. His voice is low and threatening, causing the heat to rise in my cheeks. my body betrays me, responding to his threat, his promise of dominance and the raw power he's radiating.

"Mum, just do what he says," I feel a small tug on the back of my top, turning to see Niko looking up at me with pleading eyes. The sight of my son asking me to surrender, asking me to give up, is almost too much to bear.

Fuck. What do I say to that? How do I explain to my son that I'm terrified? That I'm angry? That I'm heartbroken? That the man standing in front of us is the love of my life and the reason I had to run?

I turn completely, hugging my son, I pull him in close to me, breathing in the scent of him, trying to memorise this moment and feeling, because I know that everything is about to change.

"I'm sorry," I whisper in his ear. I can feel my tears threatening to spill over. The weight of my failures, my mistakes, and my desperate attempt to protect him from a life he was always going to have to live.

"It's okay, Mum. You said this would happen one day," Niko offers.

His words are like a knife to my heart; I did tell him. I tried to prepare him for the possibility that Matteo would find us, warning him that one day his father might come looking for him. I thought I was being strong, thought that I was just being practical, but really I was just accepting the inevitable; waiting for the other shoe to drop.

"I did. I just didn't think it would be today," I mumble into Niko's hair, before turning to face Matteo with a desperate last attempt to buy us some time to find some way out of this situation.

"I can't just go back. I got here illegally, and Niko has

no records whatsoever," I try my last attempt at pleading with him. My eyes searching his face for some sign of mercy, some sign that he might understand and give me a chance to figure this out.

"All good, El. I've already arranged for documents for you. I'll just simply add Niko to them," Angel states.

My heart sinks. Of course Matteo has already thought of this, of course he's already planned for every contingency; he's already won the battle before it even began.

"I just need an updated photo of Niko and yourself," Angel states, walking over towards us and snapping a photo of our faces, before I even have a chance to protest or even have a chance to refuse. I can see the finality in his actions, the way he's already moving forward with the plan, treating us like we're already his.

We're screwed. Completely and utterly screwed and there's nothing I can do to stop it. Nothing I can do to protect my son, nothing I can do but surrender to the inevitable.

I turn to look back at Matteo, but he isn't here. Where the hell did he go? My question is very quickly answered when I see him walk out of my bedroom wheeling a suitcase. My suitcase. The one I keep packed for emergencies. The one I've kept ready for the day when I might have to run again.

The sight of him with it, hits me hard. H0im taking control of my life, making decisions for me, it's almost too much to bear. The suitcase looks fuller than it was, now bursting at the seams as Matteo struggles to finish doing up the zipper.

Well, this is shit, I think to myself. I realise that I'm

going to have to call my boss from the road. Tell him that I won't be coming in tomorrow, let alone be coming in ever again. That my life in London, my safe and hidden life, is over.

There's nothing I can do to stop it. Nothing, but accept that I'm going back to Sydney, back to Matteo and back to the life, I'd so desperately tried to escape.

Chapter 8

Matteo Ricci

"Angel, arrange for all of Eleanor's belongings to be packed up and shipped back to Sydney," I command as I look over at Eleanor. She looks defeated, completely and absolutely, defeated. I see it in her eyes, the moment she realises that no matter what, I'll win this fight; There's no escaping me. She and my son will be coming back home with me today.

The relief that washes over me with the situation is almost overwhelming. After 10 years of searching, 10 years of never giving up, and of holding onto the hope that I would find her, she's finally here; finally mine again. the knowledge settles something in my chest. Something that's been wound so tight for a decade, but is finally beginning to loosen.

I turn and see Spike walking toward the front door, holding a large bag bursting with stuff. I'm assuming it's the kid's belongings. A surge of something I can't quite name washes over me, It's like pride mixing with fear. I have a son, a child that I didn't know existed. The weight of that responsibility finally starting to sink in. This is now more than just a mission to get my woman back, I'm going to have to learn how to be a dad.

"Come on then, Princess, let's go," I announce.

I watch the way she turns to the boy and kisses his cheek, the tenderness in the gesture and the love that radiates off her. I feel a pang of something that might be jealousy or it might be fear. What if she doesn't love me anymore? What if 10 years has changed her feelings for me? What if I've lost her completely? What if I'm going to have to spend the rest of our lives trying to win her back?

"Come on, Honey, let's go follow the big bad wolf," she says to Niko.

I hear the resignation in her voice, the way she's accepted her fate. I want to tell her that I'm not the big bad wolf, that I'm just a man who's been lost without her, a man who's been searching for her across the entire world. But I don't. I need her to understand that I'm serious, that I'm not going to let her go again; she's mine and she always will be.

She turns, pushing Niko towards the front door in line with her and we all walk out of her apartment. Angel quickly making sure all the lights are turned off and the door is locked; After all, we don't want her burgled before we can ship her things home. The way Angel is taking care of her belongings, he's treating her like she's already part of our family, the domesticity in his gestures makes me realise that everyone knows. Everyone understands that Eleanor is mine, she always has been and she always will be.

Spike is standing outside, next to the car we hired

holding the door open. Quickly taking a glance inside the vehicle from where I am standing, I can see the way he's arranged it. There's only one seat left and it's on my lap. A surge of anticipation flows through me with the realisation that I'm finally going to have her close to me, finally going to have her within arm's reach and be able to touch her.

With my hopes up, I watch as Eleanor slides in after Niko, lifting him up and placing him on her lap.

I feel a flash of disappointment. She's managed to avoid me even now, managing to put distance between us, to maintain some kind of control. I realise that she's not as complacent as I thought. In her own ways, she's still fighting, still resisting as she tries to maintain some kind of agency.

I was looking forward to some forced closeness, to having her pressed against me, feeling her body against mine. But I suppose, I can be patient, waiting for the right moment to claim what's mine.

We drive the whole trip in complete silence, I swear I feel like I'm going to bust out of my suit. The tension in the car is suffocating, overwhelming in a way that threatens to consume me whole. I can't stand the quiet and Eleanor knows it. She knows that silence drives me crazy and that I need to fill the void with something, anything.

I see the way she's using it as a weapon, to punish me, to maintain some kind of control and I hate it. I hate the way she can still manipulate me, the way she still has this power over me after all these years.

After what feels like an hour, we finally arrive at the private airstrip and file out of the car. Angel had arranged with the hotel for our bags to be brought directly to the plane. The last thing I need is some nosy hotel employee asking about the arsenal we're carrying; So, I'm hoping all of Spike's knife collection is strapped to him, and the other stuff was prepacked before they grabbed our bags from the suite..

"Come on, Darling," Eleanor says to the boy, the warmth in her voice clear, like she's trying to make this easier for him; Trying to keep him calm and safe.

"Let's get on the Mystery Machine and hope they have Scooby snacks!" she continues.

I hear Spike laughing up ahead, clearly he missed Eleanor's humour as much as I have. The sound of his laughter with the sound of her voice making him laugh, makes me realise just how much I've missed her, missed her presence while she has been absent from my life. I need her to be okay, to be happy and to be mine again.

We all get onto the plane together. Eleanor takes the seat furthest away from us all with Niko. I see what she's doing, trying to put distance between us, to maintain some kind of separation. I know that putting distance between us isn't going to be how it works. She is mine and she is going to act the part, whether she likes it or not.

Nope, She can't just decide to have a child with me and not be my wife. So, while we're at it, she will marry me. I'll get Angel to arrange the quickest wedding possible, I just need it official, making sure that the entire world knows, she belongs to me. She's mine and no one else's.

I watch Eleanor strap herself and the kid into the seat, before walking over to them and taking the seat in front of them. She sees me sit and lets out a long sigh, the sound of her sigh and the resignation in it makes me wonder, have I already lost her. Has she's already moved on. Is there any part of her that still loves me, the way I love her.

The fear that rises up inside me is suffocating and threatens to pull me under. What if I can't win her back? What if she's spent the last 10 years learning to live without me? What if I'm too late?

"You can't avoid me forever, Eleanor," I tell her, the desperation in my voice clearer than I'd like, but I'm begging her. Pleading with her in the only way I know how, to just give me a chance.

"So it seems," she replies. The resignation in her voice is like a knife to my heart.

"Why don't you start with why you left?" I say while looking Eleanor straight in the eye. I'm searching her face for some sign of the love that used to be there, for some indication that she still cares about me, still feels something for me.

"This is both not the time, nor the place for this conversation, Matteo," she replies. I can hear the wall she's putting up, the way she's trying to shut me out, to keep me at a distance.

"I disagree," I state. I can feel the anger rising up, the frustration from 10 years of searching, 10 years of wondering, of not knowing if she was alive or dead, finally beginning to boiling over.

"Well, you can disagree all you want. I'm saying, I'm not having this conversation with you right now. If you plan on sitting with us, get used to the quiet. We're going to be sleeping," Eleanor clarifies as she grabs the blanket off the seat next to me and throws it over Niko's legs.

With the finality in her voice, the way she's shutting

me down and refusing to engage with me. I know that this is going to be harder than I'd originally thought. Winning her back is going to take more than just finding her. It's going to require me to prove to her that I'm worthy of her love, of her trust. More importantly that I'm worthy of her.

"Get some sleep, Honey. Hopefully, Matteo will feed us in the morning," she tells Niko. The sarcasm in her voice clear, she's mocking me.

I can't help but to roll my eyes at Eleanor, I'd forgotten how snarky she could be. Forgotten how sharp her tongue is and how much I love that about her. I watch as they snuggle up and go to sleep. I'm struck by how beautiful she is; How even after 10 years, even after she's spent that time running from me and after everything that's happened. She's still the most beautiful woman I've ever seen.

She might be 10 years older, but even sleeping, she is perfect. There is no way I'm going to let her go this time. No way I am going to let her run away again; Not a chance.

I wonder if Angel can chip her, like a dog. That way, even if she does manage to run, I'll be able to find her. Thinking about it makes me smile, because I know Angel will understand, he's probably already thinking the same thing.

I look up at the other seat, finding Angel looking right at me. He nods at me and says, "Already on it Boss."

I wonder if he can somehow read my thoughts or just predict my thought patterns. I suppose after 20 years of friendship you would expect it. A surge of gratitude washes over me with the thought, for the man who's been by my side through everything, he's the man who's helped me search for Eleanor and never questioned my obsession with finding her.

I turn back to look at Eleanor, who is curled up with Niko. The sleeve of her silk pyjama top has ridden up a bit allowing the hint of her tattoos to peek through. My work, that marks her as mine. I still remember the first one I gave her. Still remember the way she looked at me when I told her I was going to mark her, still remember the way she submitted to me and remember the way she became mine in that moment.

After my eyes had locked with hers at the shop, I knew even then she was mine. My heart crashed to the floor the second I'd seen her golden eyes; Those light amber eyes that I'd never seen on anyone before. They drew me in like a Christmas beetle to a front porch light. I'd known instantly she would be my undoing and that she would change my life in ways, I couldn't have even imagined.

Two hours later, I'd gone back to the shop, just to grab the information form I'd demanded she fill out. I'd needed to know everything about her, to find her and to make her mine.

It had her name, date of birth and an address. She had listed an apartment in the city on Bridge Rd, in Glebe, just across from Foley Rest Park. I honestly didn't have a plan, I'd just jumped in my car and headed straight over; I couldn't wait. I couldn't stand the thought of not seeing her again, couldn't bear the idea of her being out in the world without knowing that she belonged to me.

Her apartment block was old, with a single unlocked front door to enter the building. I remember thinking it wasn't very safe, she needed to be protected, needed me to keep her safe. She had listed apartment 5, so I took the stairs two at a time to her door. The nameplate read Wicket, which I found interesting as her last name was Wang.

I knocked on the door. Fuck. The girl had made me sick with nerves, right from day one. I'd always had a crazy sensitive stomach and would hurl at any given moment. Since I was a child, my father had taken to keeping vomit bags in his back pocket. It didn't change much as I'd gotten older. I remember him throwing one under my nose after my first kill and drilling me to carry one on me at all times from that day onwards. He was worried I'd leave DNA evidence because I couldn't wrangle my stomach into submission. It had taken until my 10th dead body for it to stop protesting.

But standing at her door had caused a reappearance, but before I could even consider grabbing the bag from my pocket, the front door swung open and there she stood. "Fuck," was all I managed. She was even more beautiful than she had been in the tattoo shop. Even more perfect. Even more mine.

"Matteo?" she said while tilting her head to the left; like a dog did when you talked to it. The gesture was so innocent, so pure and so perfectly her. I'd felt my heart skip a beat.

"Hello, Princess," I smirked. I could see the confusion on her face, the way she was trying to figure out why I was at her door.

"Umm, what are you doing at my door?" she asked. Her face gave off a small hint of fear; I loved that fear, loved the way she was uncertain and the way she was vulnerable.

"Came to claim what is mine," I stated. She was mine now, whether she wanted to be or not. I'd meant every word of it, with every fibre of my being and every breath in my body.

"Um ok, I'm a little confused. We only met 3 hours ago in a tattoo shop, that certainly doesn't make me yours," she remarked as she slowly started to close the door on me. I'd felt a flash of panic, I couldn't let her close the door. I couldn't bear the thought of her being separated from me, I wouldn't let her shut me out.

I stuck my foot out to stop it from closing. "It's okay, Princess. You're not mine yet, but you will be." I'd meant it. Meant it with every ounce of my being, because I'd known, with every fibre of my being, that she was my forever, she was the one I'd been waiting my entire life for.

"Okay, you're starting to freak me out now. I would appreciate it if you left before I call the police," she'd said, while trying to push my foot out of the way, so she could close the door. I could see the fear in her eyes. The way she was trying to protect herself. I'd wanted to tell her that she didn't need to be afraid, that I would never hurt her and instead, I would spend the rest of my life protecting her.

"Oh, Princess you can try, but they don't usually come running for a Ricci," I admitted.

With that, all the colour had drained from her face. She'd known the name, known who I was and had known better than to fight me. I saw the moment she'd understood, the moment she'd realised that she was mine and there was no escaping me; she belonged to me.

"Shit," is all she said before her mouth hung open. I'd felt a surge of satisfaction, She knew, she understood. And now, she was finally accepting her fate.

"Well, are you going to let me in, Princess?" I replied.

She pulled the door open, before turning to walk into the apartment, showing me her back. I remember thinking that she was so submissive. So perfect and so absolutely mine.

"In future, Eleanor, don't show anyone your back. You don't know what they will do," I observed as I closed the door behind me.

It was right there, in that moment I'd given her my heart. She was beautiful, submissive and totally all mine. I was a man who didn't share his toys. Being an only child to a billion-dollar empire had made me that way. But there was one thing that would be new to me, monogamy. Being a 20-year-old male in Sydney with cash to splash meant I could have any girl I wanted, when I wanted it. I'd done it so many times. But now, I would keep my dick to myself and Eleanor.

And I had. For the whole two years we were together I'd only ever touched her. Even now, 10 years later, I still hadn't fucked another cunt.

But what about her? Shaking off the memories, I mentally scold myself. Fuck. Now I am spiralling. I need to know, I need to understand if she's been with anyone else. I need to know if I've lost her completely. The fear that rises up inside me is suffocating. Threatening to pull me under.

I lean forward, tapping Eleanor's leg till she wakes.

"Come with me. NOW."

Chapter 9

Eleanor Wang

"Come with me. NOW." Matteo growls at me, his voice cutting through the cabin like a blade.

His eyes are pitch black, the light blue I remember from this morning is gone. Replacing it, is his demon within. I know those eyes, I've seen them before. He's mad, furious and barely holding himself together. My heart jumps into my throat because I know what this means. I know what he wants to talk about, I can feel it radiating off him in waves.

"Okay," I mumble, getting to my feet and following him into the bedroom at the back of this insanely luxurious plane he happens to possess. My stomach churns with anxiety, fear and with something else I can't quite name.

I step into the room, taking in the opulence of it all; Silk sheets, mahogany furniture and floor-to-ceiling windows showing nothing but clouds and sky.

"Fucking rich cunts," I grumble under my breath as I

walk further into the room. My way of trying to lighten the mood. Attempting to ease the tension that's suffocating me.

"Nice to see you haven't lost that potty mouth, Princess," Matteo smirks at me. His eyes have lightened a little, thankfully losing some of the dark. But there's still fire in them, that dangerous edge that makes my pulse race.

"We need to talk Eleanor. My mind is going a thousand miles an hour and I can't make it stop. I need answers and I need them now," he states. I can hear the desperation in his voice, he's barely holding it together. I can see the way he's trying to maintain control, when everything inside him is screaming.

"I'll answer what I can," I say honestly as I perch on the end of the bed with my hands clasped tightly in my lap as I try to prepare myself for whatever comes next.

"Have you touched any other man since you left me?" Matteo asks, his eyes darkening once again.

Clearly, this is the reason we are here. He's worried someone has touched what belongs to him. He was always a possessive fucker; Clearly, that hasn't changed. The intensity of his need to know, mixed with the way he's looking at me is like the answer will determine whether he lives or dies. It's overwhelming.

"Matteo, I left you 10 years ago. What I have done between now and then, isn't any of your business." I explain, before watching as Matteo whips out a bag from his pocket and vomits straight into it.

Shit. I'd forgotten how sensitive this tyrant can be and how his stomach betrays him when he's overwhelmed. He ties the top of the bag into a knot and throws it into the bin next to the bed. Makes me wonder how the bin stays in place and doesn't roll around during take-off. Oops. Getting off topic. I know my mind is doing that thing where my train of thought wanders when I'm nervous.

"You belong to me, Princess. Don't you get that? No one else is allowed to touch what is mine," he growls. His voice is raw, possessive and Dangerous, sending a shiver down my spine.

"Like you didn't touch anyone after I left?" I imply, raising my brows. "So don't get all high and mighty and up in my face. Take a look in the mirror before coming at me, cunt," I add in my loud, whispering voice. I'm trying to stand my ground to show him that I'm not going to be bullied into submission. But inside, I'm terrified. Terrified of what his answer will be. Terrified of how much it matters to me.

"I didn't touch a single cunt while you were gone," he glares at me.

"Wait… what? I find that hard to believe," I say. My voice is sharp. Sceptical. But even as I say it, I can see the truth in his eyes. The absolute certainty with the way he's looking at me, like this is the most important thing he's ever said.

The truth must be written on my face, because Matteo snaps his arm out and grabs my chin while crouching down in front of me. His touch is firm, possessive and demanding. I can feel the heat and raw power radiating off him.

"I said… I didn't touch another cunt the whole time you were gone, Princess. Not a single one. Yes, I got blow jobs, but even then I stuck a condom on top. I promised you that my cum would belong to you, and you only, and I meant it. Ricci's keep their promises," he glares straight into my eyes. His gaze is intense. Burning, like he's trying to brand this moment into my soul.

"Really?" I whisper, barely getting the word out. My throat is tight, my heart is pounding so hard, I think it might break through my ribs.

"Really, Princess. I told you. You belong to me, and I belong to you. That was never going to change. Not for 10 years. Not for a hundred years. You are mine. Forever," he insists. His voice low, Intimate. Filled with a longing that matches my own.

"I haven't touched anyone since I left. Not even a damn kiss. I've been too busy being a mum. Staying under the radar," I admit, the words tumbling out of me before I can even think about what I'm admitting and before I can stop them to protect myself.

The second the words are out of my mouth Matteo leans in, gently placing his mouth on mine.

It's like not even a second of time has passed. It's all coming back to me in a rush. My heart explodes in my chest at. the taste of him, the feel of him. The way he makes me feel like I'm the only woman in the world. All the longing, the pain, the love I've been trying to bury for 10 years. His kiss is soft, tender, almost like he's afraid I'll break; like he's afraid I'll disappear again if he holds too tight.

But just as quickly as his lips touch mine, he pulls away.

"That's enough for now, Princess. I just vomited. I don't want to turn you off just yet," he says as he rises and walks right out the door. His voice is rough, strained. Like it cost him everything to pull away from me.

One simple touch and my undies are drenched. I'm not even kidding, I'm pretty sure I've got a wet spot on my pyjama pants. My entire body has responded to him; My heart is racing, my skin is burning and I feel like I'm going to combust from the inside out. I can still feel the ghost of his touch on my chin.

I get off the bed and walk back out to my seat. My legs are shaky. My mind is spinning. I need to get back to Niko, needing to ground myself, to remember why I'd left in the first place.

"How far away are we?" I ask Matteo as I settle back into the seat next to my sleeping son.

"We have been in the air for five hours, Buffy," Angel responds from somewhere behind me. I can hear the grin in his voice.

I turn and give him the finger. For fuck's sake. How am I back here again? How am I back in this world? How am I back with these men who feel like family and danger all rolled into one?

"Leave her alone, Angel," Matteo mutters from his seat across from me. His eyes are still dark, still watching me like I could disappear at any moment.

"Oh great, guess we're back to "Princess" being the favourite again," Angel states looking right at Matteo. There's amusement lacing his tone; A teasing quality that suggests this is an old argument.

"She never stopped," Matteo says looking at Angel and shrugging his shoulders, like it's the most obvious thing in the world and there was never any question about it.

"Great to see you still bicker like old ladies at bingo on a Thursday," I mutter while getting settled into my seat again. I'm trying to deflect, trying to ease the tension that's still crackling between Matteo and me.

"Oh Princess, you have no idea," Spike jabs from his resting place up the back. I thought the man was asleep, but clearly he's still using his good old ninja skills. It's seriously like no time has passed, like these men have been waiting for me, they never moved on.

"Shhh, Dickheads, the kid is sleeping," Matteo whispers loudly. His eyes are on Niko, watching him sleep with an intensity that makes my heart ache. He's looking at his son as if he's the most precious thing in the world.

"The kid has a name, and Niko could sleep through a tornado, so don't stress," I point out. I'm protective of Niko, defensive in a way. I don't want Matteo thinking he can just waltz back into our lives and take over.

"He clearly gets that from you," Matteo remarks with a warmth in his voice, almost like pride, like he's pleased that his son has inherited something from me.

"Well, he didn't get his looks from me, so he had to get something," I mutter, looking at Matteo, who is smiling at Niko's sleeping form. It's the kind of smile that transforms his face, making him look younger, less dangerous and more human.

"He really does look like me," Matteo says, his voice filled with wonder. Like he still can't quite believe that Niko is his. That he has a beautiful son, that shares his blood.

"He is you. Walks, talks and acts just like you. Clearly, the Ricci DNA is strong," I frown at my son. I'm worried., terrified that Niko is going to grow up to be just like his father, that he's going to be drawn into the world of darkness, violence and crime.

"You say that like it's a bad thing," Matteo looks at me. His eyes searching mine, like he's trying to understand why I would be upset that Niko is like him.

"Well, I've spent 10 years trying to make sure he was different, and it clearly didn't work," I say. The frustration, exhaustion and the weight of trying to protect my son from his own nature, evident in my voice.

"Why would you not want him to be like me?" Matteo asks, frowning at me. He looks hurt, like I've just told him that I think he's a monster; that I think being like him would be the worst thing that could happen to Niko.

"I don't ever want my son to be a killer. Let alone a head of the four-seats; A Mafia leader," I glare at Matteo. "I might be coming back to Sydney with you. But you will not be inducting my son into your world. I ran to escape that shit. The last thing I want is for you to ruin that." My voice is fiercely protective. I'm drawing a line in the sand, making it clear that there are boundaries and Niko is off limits.

"No sugar coating with you, is there now," Matteo states. But there's something in his tone, respect maybe or admiration; Like he appreciates that I'm not backing down instead I'm standing up to him.

"Never have and never will Matteo. You just don't like the truth," I answer. I'm exhausted and emotionally drained. I just want to sleep, want to stop thinking about what comes next.

"You would be surprised with what I like coming out

of your mouth Eleanor," Matteo smirks at me. His voice is suggestively low, filled with an innuendo that makes my cheeks burn.

I roll my eyes and snuggle back into my son. "Goodnight, Matteo," I reply, closing my eyes in an attempt to go back to sleep. But I'm acutely aware of his presence, the way he's watching me and Niko, the way he's looking at us like we're his entire world.

And despite everything, the fear, the uncertainty and despite the fact that I ran from him for a reason, I can't help but feel like maybe, just maybe, Coming back to Sydney wasn't the worst thing that could have happened; Maybe, it was inevitable. Maybe, it was always going to end this way. Maybe, we were always going to find our way back to each other.

But I push those thoughts away, burying them deep because hope is a dangerous thing. I've learnt the hard way, loving Matteo Ricci comes with a price.

A price I'm not sure I'm willing to pay.

A price that might just cost me everything.

Chapter 10

Matteo Ricci

The plane ride took forever, or it felt that way. Eleanor pretty much slept the whole way, only waking for food or to read a book on her phone, while Niko played games on some new age Gameboy. I watched her sleep, watched the way her chest rose and fell, the way her face softened when she was unconscious; She looked peaceful and safe. Like the weight of the world wasn't pressing down on her shoulders anymore.

I wanted to reach out and touch her. To run my fingers through her hair and trace the line of her jaw, but I didn't; I let her sleep. let her have a final moment of peace before everything changes.

With the time difference, we arrive to the hangar around 7 in the morning. The sun only just starting to rise, painting the sky in beautiful shades of pink and gold. we were home.

Walking off the plane, the bright hot heat of an Aussie summer hit, like a slap to the face. it is definitely what England had been missing. That place was an overcast grey, with a miserable cold most of the year. Ugh. I'd forgotten how good it felt, the familiar smells of the tarmac mixing with the sounds of the city in the distance, and how alive the heat seeping into my bones made me feel.

I turn, watching Eleanor tilt her face up to the sky, like she's welcoming the sun and heat back into her bones. She looks like she has come home, like she's finally where she belongs. Her skin glowing in the morning sun and Her face almost peaceful. In this moment, she looks like the girl I'd fell in love with, all those years ago.

"You look beautiful like that," I admit. The words tumbling out without notice, the woman has always gives me a case of word vomit.

She closes her eyes, tilting her head down and bites her bottom lip. I watch her turning to Niko and helping him down the stairs and onto the runway. I know she's avoiding me, avoiding the compliment and the intimacy of the moment.

"Come on, Darling. I'm sure Matteo has a car ready for us," she states as she walks right past me toward the building that leads to the front. She's using that professional, distant tone that tells me she's putting up walls, she's trying to protect herself.

Clearly, she has decided to take the "let's just ignore Matteo" route and that's fine. My house is only 40 minutes from here. And yes, she's right. I do have a car waiting for us, I just didn't organise it, Angel did. That man thinks of everything.

I trail after her, watching her walk in her silk pyjamas towards the waiting car. How she knows it's the one for us, I don't know. But she climbs into the back with Niko and waits for the rest of us. Niko is a very quiet kid, I'm not even sure if he knows what's going on, but he follows his mother's orders without question. There's a discipline there, a respect that makes me proud. It makes me wonder what kind of mother she's been, what kind of life she's built for him.

Angel and Spike load up the back of the SUV with our bags, before slipping in with us. Angel arranged a much bigger car this time, making sure it seats us all. Cars have never been my thing. I don't care what model, what shape or what horsepower a car has, as long as it is bulletproof and gets me from A to B, I'm happy. Function over form; that's always been my philosophy.

The drive ends up taking us over an hour, the traffic is heavy. After all, Sydney traffic is always a nightmare, especially in the morning.

"I definitely did not miss this kind of traffic," Eleanor states while looking out the window. There's a hint of a smile on her face, like she's remembering something, like she's remembering what it was like to live here and to be a part of this city.

"It's only gotten worse since you left," Spike states, watching Eleanor with an intensity that suggests he's missed her; he's been waiting for this moment, just as much as I have.

"Half the roads in the city have been made one way. So you gotta go round to get to where you wanna go. If you miss one simple turn off..." Angel grimaces. The man is known to miss turn offs all the time, hence why he never gets to drive. Eleanor laughs at that, it's a real laugh too.

Not forced, or polite, but a genuine laugh that fills the car and makes my chest tighten.

"Still live in Potts Point?" she asks, her eyes on me now, like she's curious. Wondering what I've done with my life, where I've been, how I've survived without her.

"Nope. Sold my parent's place after they died. Bought our house in Double Bay instead. You'll love it, I bought it with you in mind," I respond. Her eyebrows rise with my confession. The shock on her face clear that she's processing what I just said; I bought a house thinking of her and have never given up hope that she would come back.

I want her to understand that this house, this space. It's been waiting for her. That I've been waiting for her. So, I lean over, my voice low, intimate and possessive as I whisper into her ear. "Not one woman has ever stepped foot inside our house.".

She stares me down with my admission, her eyes searching mine as if looking for the truth; Looking for proof that I'm not lying. Yep, I think she likes it, I think she likes knowing that I've kept the space sacred and I've kept myself for her.

As we turn the corner onto our street, I watch her expression as she sees the house. Recognition flares in her eyes, I knew it would. It's the house she'd always wanted, the house she'd dreamed about.

When I was 20, I used to do the money pick-ups and she would come with me. We used to drive out past here, past this street, past this exact house and she used to say, "That's it, that's the one. We can retire and live out our lives in that house right there!" Her voice was full of hope, dreams and of a future that I was going to give her.

The second I'd sold my parent's place, I walked right up to the house, knocked on the door and offered 3 times the retail price. The owner had been more than happy to part with it and the amount of money and time that was put into restoring the house, was well over what it was actually worth. But I didn't care, I would have paid 10 times that. Because this was Eleanor's dream, this was the house where we were supposed to build our life together.

And right now, looking at Eleanor's face as the gate opens, I know it was all worth it. Every penny, every hour, every moment I've spent thinking about her, while I was restoring this place; It has all been worth it.

Her jaw hangs open, catching flies and even Niko is looking out the window at the house. His eyes wide, filled with wonder. That's when i realise, I never set up a room for a child. I turn, looking at Angel who just winks at me. Yep, that fucker is already onto it. Fuck, he deserves a raise after the last 4 days, the man has been invaluable, my rock through all of this.

"Whatever payment you're thinking of, Boss, don't. I've got something else in mind," he smirks at me, mischief filling his eyes. I know that look, I know exactly what he's thinking.

"Whatever you want, Angel, just say it," I reply. I owe him, I owe him everything and more.

"Won't be saying it in the car, Boss, but thanks. I'll just charge it to the card," he laughs as he jumps out, clearly planning his reward. Already thinking about what he wants from me.

I mentally laugh, knowing full well that fucker is gonna call Candy and charge me for the visit. Oh well, he can have her now, I no longer need her. Eleanor is here, she's mine, and I'm never letting her go again.

"Come on you lot, let's go inside and I'll give you the tour," I announce as I climb out of the car. My heart is pounding, my hands shaking. This is it, this is the moment where I get to bring her home. Where I get to show her that I've been waiting for her, building a life for us.

Eleanor and Niko follow me out. Eleanor still has her mouth hanging open. So, I reach out and gently push up on her chin, closing her mouth for her. My touch is gentle and intimate; A reminder of what we had and what we could have again.

"Close that mouth, Princess. Before I fill it with something else," I say suggestively, keeping my voice low and full of promise and threat all rolled into one.

Her cheeks bloom red instantly as she looks at the ground. She's blushing, the same beautiful blush that I remember from all those years ago; The one that tells me she's thinking about me, and what could happen between us.

I chuckle. "Come on, you two. Let's go inside."

I lead them toward the front door. My hand hovering at the small of Eleanor's back, not quite touching, but close enough that she can feel my presence, close enough that she knows I'm here and I'm not going anywhere.

She's finally home.

Chapter 11

Eleanor Wang

What the ever-loving fuck?

He bought the house, The. House. The one I'd wanted for us. The one I dreamed about for years, the one I'd thought was just a fantasy, the beautiful dream that would never come true.

I am speechless, I mean I knew he loved me, but this is a whole other level. What the actual fuck. This man has spent 10 years building a life for me, a life I'd run away from, a life I'd thought I could escape.

I follow after Matteo as he walks up to the front door. My heart is pounding while my mind spins, trying to process what I'm seeing and what this all means.

"Normally I use the garage door to get in. But seeing as we took a car today, let's use the front door and I'll give you the proper tour," Matteo suggests as he presses his finger to a panel on the front door, which makes a clicking noise a second later.

"I'll get Angel to add you both to the lock panels on the

house. All you have to do is touch the panels with your fingerprint and It will unlock for you. Every single door that leads inside and outside has to be unlocked with a fingerprint," Matteo states, his voice all matter of fact; Like this is just normal and Fort Knox style security is standard for a home.

"Bloody Fort Knox," I grumble, trying to lighten the mood as I try to process the fact that he's locked us in, reality is we're trapped here with him.

"Yes, Eleanor it is. And you will do well to remember that this is OUR safe haven. No one can touch you within these walls," Matteo glares at me while I just stare him down. I'd forgotten how protective he can be. His obsessiveness with how he views me as something to be guarded, something to be kept safe and to be possessed.

"Sorry," I grumble back. I'm not really sorry, but I've learnt that sometimes it's easier to just agree with him and just let him have his way.

"That's okay, Princess. It's been 10 years. I'm sure we all need to remember a few things," he mutters as his eyes narrow with a warning in his gaze. A subtle reminder that he's not the same man I'd left behind, he's become something darker, more dangerous.

Oh, don't you worry. I've not forgotten how much of a psycho he really is under that suit. Matteo may hide it well, but I know he is borderline insane. I've always known it, It's always been part of what drew me to him. The danger and unpredictability, the way he makes me feel alive.

I'm actually shocked his family never had him committed, but I suppose his father loved that his son was a little crazy. Must have made handing his seat down easier, knowing his son would burn the whole city to the ground in a temper tantrum. It was what drew me to him to start with. I wanted to revel in his fire and bury myself in the ashes, but that was 10 years ago and without a child in the mix. Now, I have a child to protect, one I don't want sitting on the Ricci seat, A child I don't want becoming his father.

As we walk through the front door, it becomes very obvious that Matteo has styled the house for us. Everything is dark, antique furniture. The all-black painted walls are, crammed full of paintings and pictures, with minimal furnishings and trinkets. The wooden floors are done in a rich, dark stain with beautiful black and white cowhides scattered about. It's my dream home and Matteo knows it. He's remembered every conversation, every dream I'd shared with him and every vision I'd had for our future.

I wipe a stray tear that's suddenly fallen onto my cheek. This was the future I had dreamed of for us 10 years ago; The future I'd taken away from us both when I'd run. It's the life I'd thought I could never have.

"I'm going to take that tear as a win and assume you love it Eleanor," Matteo utters, looking at me with hope filled eyes. In this moment, he looks vulnerable, like he's terrified I'm going to reject him, that I'm going to reject the house and I'm going to run again.

"It's very beautiful, Matteo," I manage to whisper. I'm overwhelmed, emotionally exhausted and I don't know how to feel about any of this.

"Well, come on now. This is just the lounge room. Let's move on to the rest of the house," Matteo says before taking my hand and leading me deeper into the house.

Matteo has done well, I'll give him that. The whole house is similar to the lounge with dark timbers, black walls and lots and lots of art cramming the walls. Matteo knows how much I love art and minimal furniture. He has gotten the balance just right. Even the kitchen is amazing. The whole room is painted in my favourite forest green with black cupboards and black appliances; He has taken my verbal dream and built it into a house. Taking every conversation we've ever had and turned it into reality.

"Just down here will be Niko's room," Matteo says as we reach the end of a hallway, he opens the door revealing a massive room, that's completely empty and my heart sinks. He didn't know about Niko. He didn't know he has a son until a few days ago.

"As you can see, Niko. I did not know about you. So I'd never created a room just for you. However, Angel will arrange it all and you can create something super cool and we'll have it fixed ASAP," Matteo states. His voice is warm and welcoming, like he's already accepted that Niko is his and he's already planning a future with him.

"This room has its own bathroom and a balcony overlooking the bay. Otherwise there is one other room downstairs you can use, if you would prefer that one," Matteo states.

"I'd like to see both please," Niko replies politely. My son is curious and practical. He's assessing his options like a true Ricci.

"Of course you would," Matteo laughs. "Come on, let's go."

We exit the room, heading back towards the lounge room where Matteo then leads Niko down a set of stairs. Going down we enter straight into what looks like a second lounge room, but it's unfurnished. Empty and waiting.

"I never come down here," Matteo admits lifting a shoulder. "So, I've never gotten around to doing it up."

To the right of the room is a door, leading into a smaller empty room and to the left is another door which leads to a small bathroom.

"Yep, I'll take this one downstairs, thanks," Niko declares, clearly he's already made his decision and already chosen his space.

I just laugh at him. "Of course, Honey."

"Well, it's big enough to have a school desk and a computer system set up down here too. Plus, the door down here opens up to the pool," Niko excitedly grins at me.

"School desk? Computer System? You sure this is my kid?" Matteo observes. The pride and amusement clear in his voice.

"Niko has been homeschooled his whole life. He feels the most comfortable behind a computer system," I respond looking at Matteo. I'm defensive and protective, waiting for him to judge me, to judge my choices.

"Homeschooled, his whole life?"

"Yep. How was I meant to enrol him into a school with no documentation to prove that he even existed?" I shrug. It's a fair question. I did what I've had to, in order to keep him safe, to keep him hidden.

"Okay, that makes sense. But now that you're home,

we will get him his documents. Which I'm sure Angel has already arranged, so we can get him into a great school," Matteo states. He's already planning, thinking about Niko's future.

"Nope, no thank you. I like being homeschooled, I don't want that to change. Can't you just get a teacher that will come to me?" Niko suggests. His tone firm and resolute; He knows what he wants.

Matteo starts laughing, a full-on belly laugh. "Yep, you were right. He definitely is mine. Sure thing, Buddy. We'll get you a teacher," Matteo says, turning to start heading back up the stairs.

As I turn to walk back up, Angel walks down. "Hey, Niko. Can you stay down here with me for a moment. That way we can go through some ideas of what you will need and actually want down here, yeah?"

"Is that okay, Mum?" Niko asks. He's checking in with me, asking for permission and making sure I'm comfortable with the arrangement.

I look Angel right in the eyes. "Sure, Darling. Just come, find me when you're done." I trust Angel, I always have. He's always been like a brother to me. And if he's the one helping Niko set up his room, then I know it's going to be perfect.

I start walking back up the stairs and see Matteo standing there, his expression soft and inviting, with his hand outstretched towards me; Like he's offering me a lifeline, offering me a way back to him.

"Come on, Princess. Let me show you our room."

"Our room?" I stammer at him, my heart racing, palms sweaty. The thought of sharing a bed with him, of sleeping next to him, Is terrifying and exhilarating, all at the same time.

"Yes. If you think you will be sleeping anywhere but next to me at night, you have another thing coming," he asserts, his tone firm, non-negotiable. He's made his decision and he's not backing down.

Fuck, I'm so screwed. I've not slept next to anyone in 10 years, let alone Matteo, well except Niko. I'd dreamt of it nearly every night, but actually living it is a very different thing. The reality is so much more intense, so much more overwhelming. I watch as his eyes darken a little as I reach out, allowing him to take my hand.

Matteo guides me up the stairs and around to the other side of the lounge, where another set of stairs ascend. His hand in mine is strong, warm and possessive; like he's afraid I'll disappear if he lets go.

"We're up here?" I ask, trying to process what I'm seeing.

I follow along behind Matteo as he leads me up. And holy shit, it's perfect. The stairs open into a room that could only be classed as a library, with floor-to-ceiling bookshelves lining the walls and a small fireplace along the back wall, complete with huge plush-looking day chairs in front. The whole room, including the ceiling is painted black, with a massive clear skylight in the middle. It's like stepping into a dream, a dream I've had a thousand times.

"I always told you I would build you a library, Princess. It might be 10 years late. But I still built it for you," Matteo admits while looking at my tear-streaked face. I turn, looking him in the eyes, all I can see is love.

It's the same look he'd given me every day, for two years. This man owns my soul, and he knows it.

"Thank you," I whisper. It's all I can manage, my voice is broken. My heart is shattered. I'm falling back into him and I can't stop it.

"Don't thank me yet. You haven't seen the rest," Matteo laughs, the joy and pride clear in his voice, he's been waiting for this moment, planning this reunion for years.

He points to two doors that reside on either side of the stairs,

Matteo points to the right side. "That's storage. Mainly guns and ammo, also some cash. But to the left here is our room," he says as walks over and opens the door.

It's a dream. The room is painted a deep, deep red and in the centre is a massive four-poster with curtains. The bedside tables are made from the same timber as the bed with intricate carvings on them. To the right is two open doors. The first, into a massive walk-in wardrobe that is only full on one side. The other remains empty, like he's kept it just for me. The other door revealed a stunning bathroom, with a huge clawfoot bath and an open shower and 'his and her' sinks along the opposite wall; 'His' side clearly used and full of Matteo's products, The other left empty and waiting; just like the closet.

"Matteo... I... I don't know what to say..." My voice and hands are shaking, overwhelmed by the enormity of what he's done, the fact he's kept this space for me, that he's been waiting for me and the love he's showing me.

"You don't need to say anything, Princess," Matteo states as he walks closer to me. "Just don't run away on me again." His voice is soft and pleading, he's terrified that I'm going to leave, that I'm going to run again.

Matteo slips his arms around my neck and shoulders, pulling me in close to his body. This man smells just as good as he looks, even after a 21-hour plane ride; He smells like cedar and pine. It's nice to see his signature cologne hasn't changed. He smells like my safe place, like home. The scent alone hits me, crashing down my walls, and I break, crying.

"Shhh princess, it's ok. You're home now, where you belong," Matteo utters into my hair. His voice is tender and protective, like he's going to shield me from the world, to keep me safe.

I pull back, looking into his eyes. "That's the thing, Matteo. I don't belong here. My son isn't safe here."

"There is nothing I won't do to keep you both safe." His voice is fierce, determined; Like he's making a vow, promising me something he intends to keep.

"I know. And that's the issue." Because his idea of keeping us safe, and my idea of keeping us safe are two very different things. He wants to lock us away inside this fortress and I want to run, to disappear and to protect my son from this world.

"Come on. I'll grab your bag so you can shower and change. You bloody stink, you know," Matteo says with a chuckle, before turning on his heel to go find my bag. I know he's trying to lighten the mood, attempting to ease the tension between us.

I don't follow him, there is no point. Instead I strip off my clothes and step right into the shower. Once I'm in, I turn it on, allowing the cold water to rain down on me. The shock from the cold water helping me think, to process and to understand the gravity of my situation.

I'm so fucking screwed. We will all either be dead in a week, or I'll be so deep in love with him again, that I won't care anymore; letting him consume me and own me completely, because I have never been able to resist the man.

Chapter 12

Matteo Ricci

I walk out of the bathroom in search for Eleanor's bag. I find it sitting on the floor in the library. Clearly, Spike has brought it up for her, he's always been good at reading the room and knowing what needs to be done without being asked.

I turn, heading back towards the bathroom, when I hear the shower turn on. She hasn't even closed the door; Leaving me wondering if it's an invite to join, or am I reading too much into it.

Is it wishful thinking? But if I do join her, am I ready to walk back in there and see her naked? My dick, which has been at half-mast since I'd walked into her apartment back in London says, "hell yes, we do." But my heart knows I need more time. I don't even know the real reason why she ran. I mean, I know it was to keep our kid safe, but I could have done that with her by my side, here in Sydney. I need to know why, I need to know it all.

But before I can mentally make a decision, my body makes one for me. My legs quickly propelling me forward into the bathroom, towards the siren. Towards the woman who owns my soul.

"Holy shit!" I say as I step into the steamy bathroom.

The water cascades down her body as she turns at my words, her skin glistening under the bathroom lights.

"What?" she responds, covering her body with her hands, she's shy and modest. It's endearing but it's also infuriating because she's mine; I want to see every inch of her.

"Turn back around, Princess," I request, allowing my eyes to run all over her back. Her back is completely covered in tattoos that weren't there before, I step closer to get a better look. It's a whole piece, with smaller ones around it. In the centre is a huge castle, with a dragon flying above it. Accompanied by giants and wizards all battling at the base; It's the end battle of Hogwarts. She's had the final battle tattooed on her back.

I mean, I knew she loved Harry Potter, I'd tattooed the death mark on her arm 10 years ago. But this is amazing work. Around the sides, she's had quotes, small pictures and symbols placed that I don't understand. It's like her entire back is a canvas of her soul, a map of everything she loves and everything that matters to her.

"They are all from the books I love," she offers, her voice is soft, vulnerable as she continues, "Every quote, every symbol, is from a book that's stolen a part of my soul."

"It's beautiful," I say. "Now, turn around so I can admire the rest."

She turns around, removing her hands from her breasts and there is nothing I can do to stop the overwhelming surge of emotion that crashes through me, nothing I can do to stop the tears running down my face.

Her ribs and stomach are all covered in more quotes and symbols, but between her breasts is a heart, and inside is a quote. Our quote, the one quote that has always defined our entire relationship.

"Whatever our souls are made of, his and mine are the same," I repeat, tracing my finger gently over each word. This is us, this is the quote she used to say to me all the time. The one that's haunted my dreams for the past 10 years. The one that's kept me going, even when everything else has fallen apart.

I strip my clothes off, so I can stand bare before her. I need to show her something too, need her to know that I've been waiting for her, that I've always kept her close to my heart.

I hear a small gasp as I finish removing my clothes and I know she has seen it the second I straighten; knowing the moment she finally understands.

Tattooed over my heart, is the same quote. Except mine is under a crown that has her name on it., Written in beautiful script is Eleanor, permanent, and forever.

"You remembered..." she whispers, her emotion filled voice coming out broken.

"Princess, I remember everything you've ever said to me. Every word, every moment, every promise we've made to each other," I admit, I'm pouring my heart out to her. Showing her the depths of my obsession, the extent of my love.

I reach out, drawing her into my arms under the spray of the water. "This is where you belong. Right here with me. We fit together perfectly." I grab her chin with my thumb and finger, tilting her head back so I can claim her lips. I feel her body relax into me as her tongue searches mine; Her body responding to me like it always has.

Her arms reach up, snaking around my neck and pulling me closer. Her hands glide through my now-wet hair. My own arms crushing her into me. My dick is so God damn hard, I can feel it pressing into her belly. I reach down with both hands, grabbing her ass and lifting her up, so her legs wrap around my waist.

Fuck, it feels good to hold her again. I feel her hot entrance at the tip of my dick, but I don't want this to end too quickly; I want to savour it. I want to make love to her slowly and tenderly. To show her that I've been waiting for her and no one else has ever compared.

I walk us right out of the shower and straight to our bed. The water dripping from our bodies onto the dark red sheets as I lay her down flat on the bed. I trail my hands down her chest, playing with each nipple as I go. I hear her gasp, feel her squirming under my touch. She's still so responsive to my touch, sensitive and still mine.

I run my hand between her legs, finding she's neatly trimmed but not bare, I like her bare; we will need to fix that later. I lightly touch her clit and she moans loudly, the sound echoing throughout the room.

"Shit Princess, I need to close the door. I'm not used to having a kid," I say. The last thing I need is Niko hearing his mother's moans and for him to know what's happening in here.

I quickly dash to the door and close it, flicking the lock

just in case. I need privacy, need to claim her without interruptions.

I turn around, seeing that she's moved up the bed a bit and spread her legs for me to see. She's gently rubbing her clit, likely sating the growing want. The sight of her touching herself, of her pleasuring herself, is almost too much. It's almost enough to make me lose control.

"Who said you could touch what's mine?" I growl. My tone dangerous and possessive. Every inch of her, every sensation, every pleasure, belongs to me.

"Well, hurry up and touch me before I explode," she whimpers. Her voice desperate, needy and filled with want.

I climb back up onto the bed, batting her hand out of the way as I start circling her clit for her. using my other hand, I slip two fingers into her drenched pussy; She's so wet, so ready for me.

"Fuck baby, you're so tight and wet. My hand is dripping with your juices," I say. I pull my hand to my face and lick my fingers. "You taste just how I remember. Sweet like honey. Look how creamy you are," I say as I shove my fingers back into her cunt and then into her mouth so she can taste herself.

She sucks on my fingers, tasting herself off me. The intimacy and the rawness of it, is almost too much.

"I'm not gonna last more than two minutes in that pussy. You're gonna have to cum for me now, Princess," I say, shoving my fingers back in and out of her. I twist my hand slightly, ensuring I hit that sweet spot inside of her, while rubbing her clit in slow, small circles. I watch her face as it transforms, her legs beginning to wriggle as she fists the doona with her hands.

I can feel her pussy getting tighter and tighter, strangling my fingers. I know she's about to explode. So, I shove a third finger in as I pinch her clit and I know it's all over.

I watch the pleasure rolling over her face as her legs shake. The moan that leaves her lips is pure bliss and ecstasy. It's the most beautiful sound I've ever heard.

"That's it, Princess cum all over my hand. I wanna be able to smell your cum on my hands," I encourage. Fuck, I wanna kiss her mouth, devour those moans and consume her. I want to make her mine, in every way possible.

Once she comes down from her high, I slip my hand from her core, climbing up between her legs. I grab my dick, lining up with her entrance, before sinking into her slowly. The feeling of her wrapping around me, of her pussy accepting me, is like coming home.

"Oh Fuck, Princess, this is gonna be our quickest fuck in history. You're so wet and so tight!" I pull back out and slam myself home. "Fuck, I've missed this sweet cunt." I start up a quick, yet brutal rhythm. This is my happy place, this is where I belong, inside her. Claiming her, Reminding her, she's mine.

"Fuck Matteo!" I hear her yell as another orgasm hits her. Her pleasure is my pleasure, I smile to myself as her body convulses beneath me.

Her pussy tightens to the point of pain, that's all it takes. I explode inside her. The sensation of her pussy milking my dick, is overwhelming, it's too much but yet, it's everything.

"Fuck princess, I love you," I declare as I look into her eyes. I need her to know, I need her to understand the depth of my feelings, the intensity of my love.

"I love you too, Matteo," she gasps out. "I've never stopped."

"I've never stopped either, Princess," I reaffirm, leaning over to kiss her. "Not for a single second, or a single moment. You've been mine since the day I met you. And you always will be."

I pull back to look at her. Her face is flushed, her hair is wet, but she looks absolutely beautiful, she looks like she belongs here; with me.

"Now, get that ass back into the shower, so we can go find our son," I say.

Chapter 13

Eleanor Wang

"Shit," I say jumping up and running back into the shower. I'd forgotten I told Niko to come and find me, once he was done telling Angel what he wanted for his room. Safe to say, I have the quickest shower known to man, I shove some shampoo in it to clean out the dirt. My mind is still spinning from what just happened, the intensity of being with Matteo and the way he claimed me, the way I let him.

As I'm rinsing the shampoo out, Matteo jumps into the shower behind me. Turning on the other shower head, the water begins to cascade down from above.

"That has to be one of the best features rich people seem to get," I say, pointing to the second showerhead. I hate fighting for the hot water in a shower, I'm a selfish shower bitch, the water is all mine. If you get in with me, you better be prepared to only get it once I get out.

Matteo laughs at me. "I remembered your shower rule. So, I had an extra one added, that way I don't have to freeze my ass off."

"Smart. 'Cause I'm never ever gonna share," I say with a shrug. I don't even bother with conditioner, as I jump out and begin towelling off. My skin is flushed, my body is still tingling from his touch. I feel like I'm floating, like I'm in a dream that I'm terrified of waking up from.

"Hopefully you grabbed my toothbrush and beauty products," I mention as I open my bag. I'm trying to ground myself, attempting to focus on practical things, rather than think about what just happened between us.

"In the drawer on your side of the sink, is a new toothbrush. I don't know what products you use these days, but if you give a list to Angel, he'll have it all delivered by the end of the day," Matteo states as he jumps out of the shower himself.

"Is there anything Angel can't get in a day?" I grumble, while searching for my face wash and creams. Angel is like a magician, making things appear out of thin air.

"Nope, not really. He is a tech genius. Can get just about anything I need, when I need it," Matteo says with a shrug as he wraps a towel around his waist. Water drips from his hair, making him look dangerous and beautiful, all at once; like a Greek god.

"Great," I sigh. "Niko has probably racked up a million-dollar list of items I can't afford," I grumble as I shove on a long-sleeve black top and tartan mini skirt.

"Princess, I'm a billionaire. I can afford anything you or Niko need. Just ask and you shall receive," Matteo says with a bow. He's being playful and charming, like he's trying to win me over with his wealth and humour.

"Matteo, I would believe you if you had pants on," I note, throwing my hand out wide to point out his state of undress. He's standing there in just a towel with all his tattoos on show.

"Pants or no pants, you have full access to my accounts," Matteo shrugs while continuing to get dressed. He's serious about this, giving me access to his money, his resources, to his life.

"What? Why? Are you insane? Hang on, don't answer that, I already know the answer," I retort, holding my hand in the air like a stop sign. "I don't want your money. I have a little of my own and I can find a job to work for the rest," I protest. I know saying this is going to piss Matteo right off. And I'm right, I watch as his eyes instantly darken and he steps slowly towards me.

"Do not, for one second think you have a say in this Eleanor. You ran away from me. You left me," he says while pointing at his chest. His voice is soft and danger-ous, like a predator circling its prey. "I've just got you back. And there is no way in fuck, you're walking out that front gate, unless it's with me. Understand?"

"Matteo, I understand you need to control everything in your life. But you can't expect to control everything in mine. If I want to work, I will. If I want to walk out that gate without you, I will. I understand that I can't run again, but you need to stop thinking you can control me. If you try to, you will lose me forever," I reply. I'm standing my ground, drawing a line in the sand by telling him that I'm not going to be caged; Not even by him.

I watch as a full-body shudder rakes through Matteo's body, his eyes going blank, completely blank, like no one is home, like the lights are on but nobody's answering.

This is what I have been afraid of, this is the darkness I've been protecting Niko from.

"Shit. SHIT!" I say, backing out of the bathroom, towards the bedroom door. My heart is pounding, hands shaking. I know I need to get away from him, I need to get help.

I remember not to turn my back to Matteo as I go, slowly creeping my way to safety. When I reach the door, I unlock it and open it slowly. As soon as I have it open enough to step through, I yell out, "Angel! Spike!"

I don't let my eyes leave Matteo's the whole time. I can't help but feel like a mouse, caught under a lion's paw; one small move and I'll be lunch. One wrong word and I know he'll snap, one mistake and he'll lose control completely.

I feel Spike behind me, before I hear him; stealthy fucking ninja, he moves like smoke, like a ghost.

"Boss," Spike says as he slowly steps into the room. His voice is calm and controlled, like he's done this a hundred times before.

"Eleanor, why don't you go downstairs and see if Niko needs help with Angel," Spike offers, while holding eye contact with Matteo. He's taking control of the situation, giving me an out and protecting me.

"Okay," I nod, backing right out of the room, until I can no longer see Matteo. I turn, running down the stairs. When I reach the bottom, I see Niko sitting on the floor cross-legged with Angel, looking at a laptop screen. My son is safe, he's here, he's okay.

"Hey Eleanor, Niko is just designing his room using

the blueprints here on my laptop," Angel says, glancing up from the screen.

"Spike might need you upstairs," I say to Angel as his eyes meet mine. I'm trying to keep my voice steady. Trying not to alarm Niko.

"Fuck already?" Angel says while quickly getting to his feet. He knows what it means, he knows exactly what's happening upstairs.

"Yep," I say. I'm trying to stay calm, to be strong for Niko.

"What set him off?" Angel asks as he moves toward the stairs.

"I told him I wanted to work. And that he can't control me. And if he tries, he will lose me," I whisper to Angel once he gets closer. I'm admitting my mistake, acknowledging that I've pushed him too far.

"Shit, Eleanor, not a good thing to say to someone who's spent well over 10 million dollars searching for you, for the last 10 years!" Angel growls, before running up the stairs, two at a time. He's right. I shouldn't have said it, I should've known better.

"What's wrong with Matteo?" Niko asks as I sit down on the floor with him. His eyes are filled with concern and worry. I'm unsure of how to approach this with Niko. How Matteo can get is something I've never filled Niko in on, but now is as good a time, as any.

"Your father, he has these blackout episodes, every now and then. His eyes will darken and go completely blank, like no one is in there. Sometimes he will go blank and just stand there for ages, doing nothing at all. Other times he will go crazy and kill anyone in his path," I state.

I'm being honest with him, preparing him, trying to help him understand his father.

"Has he tried to hurt you before, Mum?" Niko asks, a hint of worry in his voice. My son is protective. He's always been concerned about my safety. It breaks my heart.

"Thankfully, no. Spike, Angel and I are the only ones who haven't been hurt by his rage. I'm not sure we ever will, but I don't know if it will be the same for you. He doesn't know you," I sigh, admitting the uncertainty, and trying to acknowledging the risk.

"What should I do if it happens when I'm around?" Niko asks, a look of complete fear filling his eyes. He's terrified, but trying to prepare himself, trying to be brave.

"Nothing Niko. You need to do nothing. Stay still and don't move. I'll try to make sure you're never alone. That either Angel or Spike will always be around," I say. "But if for some reason we're not, just stay still, like a statue and wait it out. Kind of like if you were to see a snake, you don't move, don't react. And it will be okay. He only seems to respond to movement," I press, knowing I'm giving him the tools he needs to survive, teaching him how to navigate his father's darkness.

"Mum..."

"Yes?"

"Is Dad a killer?" Niko questions, his tone small and uncertain. He's asking the question I've been dreading.

"Yes sweetheart, he is and a very good one at that. And I don't think he has ever been caught or suspected of it." I'm being honest with him, not sugarcoating it, or lying to him.

"Cause he is head of the Mafia?" Niko questions.

"Yes, because of that. But also, just because he is a very dangerous man. I suspect we will never know that side of him fully. He keeps it well hidden. It only comes out when he's working. He's never treated me badly or scared me at home," I say, trying to balance the truth with reassurance, to help him understand that his father is complex. Yes, he's dangerous, but not to us.

"So, even you don't know how dangerous he really is?" Niko asks.

"Nope. And I don't want to. I'm happy knowing the nice side of him. And that's all," I say. "Now, that's enough of that talk. Show me your plans for this space!"

"Oh, mum you gotta check this out!" Niko says angling the computer screen my way. He's eager to show me, excited about his project and trying to move past the fear.

He has completely transformed the room on the screen, decking it out with computer monitors, TV screens and even lounges. What a little legend. The walls on the screen are even a different colour. It's perfect and exactly what he needs.

"This is amazing."

"Yep! Angel showed me how to create each room and write the algorithms for each item I wanna place in it!" Niko's face lights up as he talks. He's engaged and passionate about this. He's happy.

"I think Angel might be able to teach you even more about tech stuff," I admit. "Angel is Matteo's tech nerd, his resident hacker." I laugh, trying to keep things light, to move past the fear.

"Really?! That's SO cool. Do you think he can teach me how to hack?" Niko's eyes are wide with excitement.

"Hang on a minute, matey. I didn't say you can learn to be a hacker." I elbow Niko while laughing at him.

I hear a rustle on the stairs, looking up I see Matteo sitting a few steps up, listening to us. His eyes are clear now. He's back, he's present, he's himself again.

"Hey," I say softly, relieved to see him and yet, terrified of him at the same time.

"Hey," he says back looking at his hands. He looks ashamed, broken, like he hates himself for what he is.

"You okay now?"

"You know I would never hurt you, Eleanor," he says. His voice laced with desperation, need and the desire for me to believe him.

"I know," I say. And I do know, I know that he will never intentionally hurt me. But I also know that when he's in that state, he's not in control, he's not himself; He's something else entirely.

"So why do you always leave and get Angel or Spike to help?" He asks, turning his head to face me. There's pain and confusion filling his eyes, like he doesn't understand why I'm running from him even now.

"It's been 10 years Matteo. I wasn't sure if things have changed with your blackouts," I say, being honest with him, admitting my fear.

"Nothing has changed. They are just more frequent than they used to be," Matteo says. "Look, no matter what, I'll never hurt you or Niko. Just don't leave me when it happens," Matteo pleads, his voice raw, vulnerable. He's begging me to stay, to trust him and believe in him.

"Okay," I say. I'm making the promise. I'm committing to him, choosing to stay.

"Niko, has your mother explained what happens if I blank out?" Matteo asks, turning his attention to my son.

"Yes, Sir," Niko responds, like Matteo is a stranger.

"Sir?" Matteo says, taken aback. He looks hurt, like the formality of his answer is a rejection.

"Sorry, what did you want me to say?" Niko looks at me for guidance, his tone uncertain.

"You could call me, dad?" Matteo offers, his voice tentative and hopeful, like he's asking for permission to be Niko's father.

"Um, okay..." Niko replies, though he's uncertain, trying to process this.

"I don't mean all the time, but maybe every now and then. I know I've only just met you, but I would love to get to know you," Matteo says looking back down at his hands. "I know your mother ran away to keep you safe. But you're back now and it's my job now to keep you both safe. Please, just give me a chance to do that."

"Okay, Dad, we can try. Can't we, Mum?" Niko asks, looking up at me, seeking my reassurance and approval.

"Yep, we can try," I reply. I'm giving them both a chance, choosing to believe that this can work. That we can be a family.

Matteo blows out a deep breath, before clapping his hands together. "Okay, let's see this list you have for your little spot down here and see what we can get done today!"

Chapter 14

Eleanor Wang

It turns out we really can get a lot of stuff done in one single day. Angel arranged for a painter to arrive just after lunch with colour samples for Niko to choose from. The painter will be back in the morning to paint the rooms for Niko, a bed has been delivered and is being set up as we speak and his computer and TV will be delivered later this afternoon. It's like watching a machine work. Everything in Matteo's world runs like clockwork, everything is coordinated, perfect and I shouldn't be surprised..

"Niko, please remember to say thank you to Matteo for all this. I know he is a wealthy man, but I don't like spending his money like this," I say to Niko, trying to teach him not to take things for granted.

"Mum, Matteo said it's your money too."

"Did he now?" That cunt is gonna get a word from me tonight. He's trying to make me complicit, attempting to make me feel like I have a stake in this. "Either way Niko, we're not spending it all okay?"

"Okay, Mum. When's dinner? I'm starving," Niko asks

as his stomach rumbles. His stomach is like a bottomless pit, I swear he's grows a foot every day.

"Dude, it's like two pm. You just ate lunch 20 minutes ago!" I'll never understand kids and their bellies. I can go all day without eating anything at all. Yet, Niko cannot go half an hour, It's ridiculous.

"Hey, Niko," Angel walks halfway down the stairs. "Hungry? I just ordered a few pizzas to tide us over till dinner. They'll be here in 20." It's like they're twins. They have the same energy and the same bottomless stomachs.

"Heck yeah!" Niko jumps up off the floor and follows Angel upstairs. He's already bonding with Angel. Already comfortable with him. It makes me feel less guilty about bringing him here.

"Eleanor, Matteo was looking for you. He is in his office."

"Ok, thanks. And Angel…. where is Matteo's office?" This place is a rabbit warren. It's massive. It's overwhelming. I'm still getting lost.

"It's the first door on the right after walking in the front door," Angel yells back down the stairs.

Right. Let's go see what's in store for me now. I've only been back in the country for what, 8 hours and already it feels like I've lived here a week. I walk back up the stairs and find the door Angel mentioned. My heart is pounding, nervous about what Matteo wants, about what he's possibly planning now.

I knock and wait, I can hear rustling inside. "Come in," I hear mumbled from inside. So I walk right on in, only to stop halfway.

Matteo is sitting at a desk piled high with paperwork

and boxes. The floor too is littered with piles and piles of it to. It's a chaotic disaster. It's overwhelming.

"Um Matteo, what the fuck?" I say, pointing to the desk and floor, trying to process what I'm seeing.

"Princess…" he says smiling at me. "You wanted a job. Well here it is," he says, spreading his arms wide. He's so pleased with himself, so confident that he's solved all my problems.

"Ummm, yeah I did. But what is all this?" I indicate to the mess we're standing in. There's so much paperwork, so much organisation needed.

"This, my sweet, is my paperwork. I normally hire an admin Officer three times a year to come into the city office and organise it for me," he sighs. "But to be honest, this year I haven't got around to it."

"So, what is it exactly you want me to do?"

"Well, seeing as you're so good at being a PA, I thought you could perhaps be mine. It then solves the need for a job issue, helps me out, and keeps you safe," Matteo smiles at me. He's thought it all through. He's found a solution that suits him.

This motherfucker has an answer for it all.

"This clearly isn't your main office, is it?" I ask in disbelief, because this is way too much paperwork for a standard home office.

"Nope. I have a high-rise down on Elizabeth St," Matteo says.

"So, why can't I just do the paperwork at the office in the city?" I ask. "Am I not allowed to go there?"

"You can, but only when I'm there. Plus this is only the

back log of everything, it will need to be sorted fairly quickly," Matteo states. "Just tell…"

"Angel, what I want and he will have it delivered to the house?" I finish for him, starting to understand how it all works. Matteo clicks his fingers and Angel gets it sorted.

"Yep! That!" Matteo snickers at me, clearly amused by my frustration and the fact that I'm starting to understand his system.

I had been secretly hoping Matteo was going to demand that I stay at the house office to work. That way I could keep an eye on Niko and not have to meet any of the other four seats. The thought of meeting the other mafia families terrifies me. The thought of being introduced to his world in that way makes my stomach turn; Plus, it would give me some time without him. It's only been a day and I'm already so wrapped up in him, consumed by his presence again, just like I was before. Every time I turn my head, he pops up. I'd loved it during the two years we'd spent together, I loved the all-consuming feeling of him, but now it makes me feel a little suffocated.

I've spent the last 10 years being independent, making my own choices, and now, now I'm stuck with a man who does everything for me. The worst part is I know I'll let him, I might push back and say no, but I will give in, I do every time, I've never had the ability to really say no to this man.

"Princess," Matteo says softly as he wraps his arms around me. I didn't even hear him move. Let alone, walk across the room to stand in front of me. He moves like a predator, silent, deadly and precise. "You really need to tell me what's going on. There is only so much I can do with the limited information I have." I take a deep breath, inhaling cedar and pine.

"Later. We'll talk later. Today, I just want to breathe," I respond. I'm know I'm not ready to open up. I'm Not ready to tell him everything that's weighing on me.

Matteo kisses the top of my head, resting his chin a top it. "Okay princess, but the next time I ask, you're going to answer me." It's not a request, it's a command, a promise, and a threat.

I pull away from him gently and look at the mountain of paperwork surrounding us. It's chaotic, overwhelming, and exactly what I need right now. Something to focus on, something to organise, to be able to control when everything else feels like it's spiralling.

"You know what? I might as well start now," I say, moving toward the desk. "No point putting it off."

Matteo watches me for a moment, his blue eyes studying my face like he's trying to read my mind, trying to understand what I need from him in this moment. I can feel the weight of his gaze, the intensity of his attention. But I don't look at him, I can't. If I do, I'll break. If I do, I'll tell him everything and I'm just not ready for that yet.

I sit down on the floor, pulling the first box toward me. The papers are a mess, invoices mixed with receipts, business documents tangled with personal correspondence. It's going to take days to sort through this, days to organise; days where I can lose myself in the work.

I hear Matteo move, hear his footsteps as he walks toward the door. I'm grateful for it, grateful that he understands, that he knows when to push and when to give me space.

"I'll leave you to it, Princess," he says softly from the doorway. "Let me know if you need anything."

"Thank you," I whisper, not looking up from the papers in front of me.

The door closes quietly behind him and I finally exhale. A long, shaky breath that I didn't know I was holding and rest my forehead on the box in front of me for a moment, just a moment, just enough time to gather myself, enough time to remember who I am.

Then I sit up, roll my shoulders, crack my neck, and I start to work.

The papers blur together as I sort them into piles, invoices here, receipts there, business documents in one stack, personal correspondence in another. My hands move mechanically. My mind starts to quiet as the constant anxiety that's been humming through my veins since I arrived, begins to settle.

This is what I need, this is what I've always needed. The ability to organise chaos, to take something broken and make it whole, to control at least one small part of my life.

I don't know how much time passes, could be minutes, could be hours. But eventually, I hear Niko's voice from downstairs, hear Angel's laughter and the sounds of life happening around me.

I stand up and stretch. My back is sore, my neck stiff, but my mind is clearer. And when I hear Niko calling out that he's starving, I can't help but smile.

Angel rounds us all up to ask what we want for dinner. "I need some carbs, please Angel. Pasta of any form, noodles even," I say with a yawn. "Is my favourite Italian place in the city still open?" I ask. After COVID-19, god only knows what restaurants survived.

"Fratelli's? Baby my family owns the restaurant. We have used it for years to launder money. Of course, it's still here," Matteo laughs as he walks into the room. "We'll put in an order and have Antonio hand-deliver it himself, seeing as the restaurant doesn't open till 6." He's so casual about it, so open about the money laundering, clearly comfortable with his criminal enterprise.

I raise my eyebrows at Matteo. "Since when are we so open about the family business?" I ask, concerned, worried about Niko hearing this.

"Princess, how many times do I have to tell you? You are mine. You will not be leaving again. So that means you will be told everything and anything you want to know relating to the business. You are also my PA. So, you're gonna have to learn how to hide the money," he smirks at me. He's making it clear that I'm now a part of it all, that I'm complicit and that there's no going back.

"Fuck, Matteo," I say looking at Niko. "I want him kept out of all this." I say, drawing a line to protect my son.

"I plan on it. He can train under Angel to be the next tech-savvy nerd. But he won't be taking my seat," Matteo declares as he walk's back out of the room. He's making a promise, letting me know that Niko won't be forced into the family business, that he has a choice.

"This has to be the longest damn day I've ever lived," I

mutter, running my hands down my face. I'm emotionally, physically and mentally exhausted.

"I'll have a prawn linguine," I say to the room, before turning and heading up the stairs to our bedroom. This fucker better have some sweats I can steal. "I need to have a bath." I declare over my shoulder. I need to freaking relax, to decompress and to process everything that's happened today.

I walk into the bathroom, checking all the cupboards and drawers, there has to be salts and bubble bath somewhere. Sure enough, under the sink, I find a box of Epson salts and a bottle of men's body wash. That'll do, donkey, that'll do.

I turn on the bath and start the super-long process of filling it up. While I wait for the bath to fill, I go on the hunt for some sweats, I know Matteo has to have a pair in his wardrobe. And he does. In fact, he has about 10 pairs, all grey. I swear all hot men have a thing for grey sweats. Next, I go through his drawers, looking for an oversized t-shirt, which again I find like 10. What is his obsession with 10 of everything? I knew he had an OCD issue before with his clothes, but it was mainly having them all hung up in colour order and being folded a certain way; Not the amount. Pfft, whatever.

I stand up to walk out of the wardrobe and nearly wet my pants when I see Matteo standing in the doorway, his arms crossed and a smile on his face. He's been watching me, watching me rifle through his things and steal his clothes.

"Shit, Fuck Matteo, don't do that. My bladder is fucked since having Niko, I just peed a little," I admit as I cup the damp undies beneath my skirt. I'm mortified and embarrassed.

"Sorry, Princess. I was just watching you snooping through my side and was wondering if you needed any help," he smirks, amused and enjoying my discomfort.

"Fuck off. I wasn't snooping. I needed some sweats and a top and seeing as you only packed all my uncomfortable shit, I thought I would just steal yours instead."

"What's mine, is yours or so they say," Matteo laughs as he walks back out of the room, not bothered by me taking his clothes. He's not bothered by anything I do. He's just happy to have me here.

Fuck, that cunt really is crazy.

I walk back into the bathroom to find the tub nearly full. Shit, that's a good tap. My last apartment took close to 20 minutes to fill the bath halfway, I'll need to remember that in the future. Don't want the bath to overflow and flood the whole house.

I strip out of my clothes and sink into the bath, sighing as I lower myself down. It's the perfect temperature, just this side of scalding hot, enough to make my skin red, but not leave me with burns; Just how I like it. The heat seeps into my bones, relaxing me. Soothing me. Healing me.

This time, I hear Matteo's footsteps as he walks into the bedroom and then into the bathroom. He's making sure I hear him coming, making sure he doesn't scare me.

"Did you purposely make your footsteps heavier just so I could hear you?"

"Yes, Princess. I didn't want to scare you and have you leaking again," Matteo chuckles while handing me a glass with a finger of whiskey in it.

"Oh God, yes," I say, grabbing the glass. "Thank you." The whiskey burns as it goes down. It's perfect. It's exactly what I need.

"All good. Dinner is about 10 minutes away. Want me to bring it up?" he asks. He's giving me options, allowing me to have control.

"Nah. It's okay. I'll just heat it up if it's cold when I get down there. Can you please organise Niko to have a shower and get his PJs on?" I ask Matteo, before a look of concern crosses his face. "What's wrong?" I ask.

"Nothing. I'm just shocked you asked me to do something for our son." His voice is soft, vulnerable, like he's been waiting for this moment, hoping I would trust him with Niko.

"Why would that shock you?" I ask, genuinely confused by his reaction.

"Cause you have only trusted Angel to be around him so far. I wasn't sure if you trusted me." He admits, insecurely. Allowing me to see his fear that I don't believe in him, that I don't trust him with our son.

"Well, I trust you enough to tell him to have a shower and get his pyjamas on," I laugh, giving him a small piece of trust, a small piece of responsibility.

"Thank you," Matteo utters, before kissing my head and leaving the room. He's grateful, honoured and is taking this seriously.

I mean, what choice do I have? We are gonna have to live here now. Matteo is gonna have to be in his life and I am gonna have to give him some responsibility towards Niko. Doesn't mean I am gonna trust him with the big things, but I can still delegate some smaller roles to him and see how he goes.

I lay my head back onto the lip of the bath, closing my eyes, just needing to take a moment to relax before the food arrives. Ah, just a moment to breathe. Just a moment to be.

I FEEL THE COLD AIR HIT MY SKIN AND THE WATER receding, before I realised I must've fallen asleep in the bath. I open my eyes to see Matteo leaning over to scoop me up.

"Come on, Princess. You've turned into a prune. Let's get you dressed and reheat this pasta," he says. His voice is warm, but amused; like he's enjoying taking care of me.

"Shit, sorry," I mumble, still trying to get the fog of sleep to recede. I'm groggy, confused and disoriented.

"Nothing to be sorry for. Can you stand long enough for me to get your clothes on?" he asks.

I bat Matteo's hands away. "I can get dressed myself. I'm not that old, yet." I retort, trying to maintain some independence.

"Could've fooled me. We could hear your snoring from downstairs," Matteo laughs, teasing me.

"Fuck off. I don't snore." I snipe, as I feel heat lick across my cheeks, I'm embarrassed.

"Bullshit. Niko heard it and I quote said, 'That would be Mum asleep in the bath again. So, clearly this is a regular thing for you. He even offered to come up and help get you out.'" Matteo manages to get out while laughing a full-on belly laugh.

"Shit, cats outta the bag." Dam Niko ratting me out. My secret is out.

"Big time. Now come on, Angel's just heating up your pasta for you." Matteo says with a shit eating grin on his face.

Chapter 15

Matteo Ricci

Watching Eleanor snore in the bath is possibly the cutest thing I've ever seen. The woman is perfection personified. To see her actually snoring, with her mouth wide open and drool pooling, just made her cuter. She grumbles her way through her pasta, before walking Niko down to his room and putting the kid to bed at 7 pm. On her way out he states his bedtime is usually 8 pm but with the time difference and being jet-lagged, it will be early to bed for us all.

She grumpily says good night to us all as she walks back past the kitchen and up the stairs to our room. Fuck, she is cute, even grumpy.

"Now that we got her back here, Boss, what are we going to do about Enzo?" Spike speaks up first. His voice is serious, thoughtful; like he is already three steps ahead of the problem.

"I don't know, Mate. He's gonna want something for the info he supplied, I can feel it in my bones. I also wanna know how he found her in the first place, when Angel was unable to, Even with his facial recognition software," I say. There's something off about it all, something that isn't adding up.

"Considering how often she was photographed with Patrick, you would think the software would have picked her up," Angel huffs in frustration. He's annoyed that his technology failed him. "I need to check it out, something must have been blocking it from working across the UK. There is no way it wouldn't have picked her up earlier if it was working properly."

"I feel like Enzo might know the answer to that one," Spike states, and I think he might be right. Enzo is too smart, too connected and too aware of everything that happens in our world.

"What if Enzo knew where she was this whole time?" I suggest, the thought making my blood run cold. "What if he was just waiting on this info for the right time? Right when he knew he'd need me for a vote at the table or something?"

"I think you're onto something there, Boss," Spike says, nodding like he's been thinking the same thing.

"Shit, that's exactly what we don't need," I huff. "I'm going to assume he doesn't know a thing about Niko. Otherwise he would have been used against me a lot earlier."

"Fuck, I think you've gotta be right on that one, Boss. Eleanor did a real good job keeping him under wraps this whole time," Angel says, impressed with the fact that she's managed to hide our son from the entire underworld.

"That she did," I mutter. She's stronger than I'd given her credit for. She's survived on her own for 10 years, while raising our son alone and keeping him safe from this world.

"You okay, Boss? I mean with her being back? You don't seem as happy as I thought you would be," Spike asks. He's reading me, seeing through my facade.

I take a huge breath in. "I am bloody ecstatic, but I know she is still keeping shit from me. She won't talk to me, won't tell me why she left or why she didn't trust me to keep her and Niko safe." The frustration of not knowing is eating me alive and driving me insane.

"Our son," I confess. "If the kid didn't look like my clone, I would have questioned if he was mine."

"She's just gonna need time," Spike offers, while finishing off his whiskey. "Look, we just turned up, grabbed her from her place and pissed off back to Sydney. I can't imagine anyone wanting an interrogation after that."

"Fuck, I know you're right, Mate. But that doesn't make me feel any better. I've never been good not knowing the whole story, let alone waiting on someone else's time-line for it," I grumble. "I don't know how much longer I can wait nicely without losing my goddamn mind. I've had 10 years of scenarios running through my head. I need answers."

"Have you asked her?"

"Yep, and she said she needed time. How the fuck is 10 years not long enough?" I gripe; the irony is not lost on me.

"One step at a time, Boss. Let's just be happy she's

back and that you've got a son," Angel smiles at me. He's right, I know he's right. But knowing something and feeling it, are two different things.

"Fuck, that's another thing. Shit, mate, it's like looking in a mirror at myself," I laugh. The kid is my spitting image, it's both terrifying and amazing. "Speaking of Niko, Angel I want you to teach him as much tech as possible. He seems to be wicked intelligent and we could use another techie."

I'm already planning his future, already thinking about how he can help the family business, without being pulled into the darkness.

"Sure thing, boss. But to be honest, I think Niko will be teaching me, the kid is insanely smart and already knows his way around," Angel grumbles. He's actually not bothered by it, he's impressed.

"Alright, cunts, that's enough sweet talk, I'm out of here. See you in the morning," Angel announces as he stands from his seat and heads for the front door. He's exhausted; We all are.

"Need me on watch, boss?" Spike asks as he stands.

"Nah, you're right. Fuck off home. I'll see you at 6," I respond, clasping him on the shoulder. "I'm gonna head up to bed too."

With that, Spike heads off, leaving the kitchen in a state of disarray. Fuck I hate mess. I roll up my sleeves to get to the task of cleaning up. For me, it's therapeutic, calming and helps me think.

Thankfully, we only ordered takeaway, so it's mainly just me throwing out containers and loading the dish-washer. Still, it took me a good 30 minutes before I was walking up the stairs to bed. Opening the bedroom door and seeing Eleanor curled up on my side of the bed settles some of the unease I have been feeling.

She's finally home.

I can finally touch her again.

Stripping off my clothes, I climb in behind her, gently slipping one arm under her pillow and my other around her waist so I can pull her closer into me. Her body fits with mine perfectly. The shape of her round ass fitting against my waist, like a puzzle piece, while her head tucks under my chin. She smells like soap and my body wash, she obviously found my stuff under the sink and used it in the bath as bubble bath.

I'm enough of a possessive cunt that my dick twitches at the thought of her smelling like me. She's mine, and she knows it.

I run my hand down her belly, towards the top of my sweats, wondering if she's wet. Was she thinking of me before going to sleep? I push my hand down and cup her pussy, it's still too hairy for my liking, but I can fix that with a trip to Woollies in the morning to buy her some razors.

I slip a finger between her folds, inching lower until I find her hole. Yep, she is wet. Back in the day, she was always wet. I don't think there was ever a time when she wasn't wet, always ready for me and it seems that hasn't changed.

I pull my hand out of her pants, using it to push the sweats down off her hips. I can tell she is starting to stir from all the movement. But I don't stop. I lift my leg up, tucking it into the back of her sweats, so I can push them down. I can feel she is awake.

I lean forward, softly kissing her neck. A tender reminder of what we can have again, before slipping my arm under her leg and lifting it up so I can line the head of my dick up to her hole. Fuck, I can feel the wet, warm heat of her.

I feel a hand snaking into my hair, before it pulls my head forward. She turns around enough to kiss me. She tastes like peppermint, clearly having brushed her teeth before bed. I slowly sink the head of my cock into her, feeling only a slight bit of resistance. Which is quickly fixed by her curving her back forward for a better angle.

"Fuck, Princess, I've missed this. I've missed you," I say into her mouth. The words are raw and desperate, filled with 10 years of longing.

"Oh, geez," she moans, as I sink right to the hilt. She's tight, so tight, like her body is made just for me.

"That's it. You remember how my dick used to feel? You remember how much your pussy craves my dick?" I tease. Reminding her of what we had.

"Yes," she says. Just one word, but it's everything.

Fuck, that one word is all I need. I start to move in and out quicker, feeling her wetness coating her pussy lips now. She is singularly the best thing in my life. Right now, this moment is all I need. Being balls deep in her cunt is where I feel the most at home.

"Fuck, Princess I can't hold it any longer. I need you to cum for me," I say as I use my fingers to circle her clit. There is no way I'm coming first, I need her pussy to squeeze me dry.

Ever the responsive one, I feel as her legs start to shake as her breathing gets quicker and her body tightens around me.

"Oh, fuck, Matteo," she moans. I pinch her clit and she explodes around me. Right at the perfect moment, my balls draw up and I let her cunt squeeze my dick dry.

"Fuck, Princess, that's it. Strangle my cock. This cum is yours and only yours," I say. I can feel her fluttering around me as my hot cum coats her walls. I want her pregnant. I need to put another baby in her, wanting to see her belly round with my child. I need to find out what contraception she is using, so I can throw it out.

I relax into her, pulling her back in close to me as my cock softens inside her. "Princess, I need you to marry me. I want you to carry my last name. I cannot lose you again," I whisper into her ear. The words tumbling out, before I can stop them, before I can think about what I'm asking.

"Okay," is all she says.

"Really?" I say confused. I thought there would have been a struggle to get her to say yes. I thought she would fight me on this.

"Really, Matteo. I'm not going to fight you over it. I've wanted to be yours for 12 years, Just don't break my heart," she says as she closes her eyes and snuggles into me. Her words settle something inside me, something that's been broken for a decade.

"Baby, we'll talk more about me breaking your heart another time. But you gotta get up so we can clean you up. I don't want you getting a UTI," I say uncurling my arms from her, while also pushing her forward. I'm being practical and protective. Being the man she needs me to be.

"I forgot how bossy you are," she complains, but there's no heat in it. She likes it, she always has.

"I remember that you like me bossy," I smile into the dark.

"Tomato, tomarto," she grumbles, climbing out of bed and heading to use the loo.

I forgot how grumpy she gets when she's tired. It's like all the nice pleasantries just evaporate from her the less sleep she gets. I wonder how grumpy she must have been when she was sleep-deprived with Niko at first. That reminds me.

"Eleanor, what are you using for birth control at the moment?" I ask, watching as she begins climbing back into bed, only to freeze halfway,

"Fuck, shit, goddamnit," she splutters. Her reaction is telling, She's panicking, obviously worried about something.

"What?" I sit up, my protective instincts kicking in immediately.

"I don't use anything. And I totally didn't even think of it. Shit, sorry, Matteo. I'll get Angel to take me to the docs tomorrow and grab the pill," she says while climbing the rest of the way into bed. She's apologising, like she's done something wrong.

"No need. I want you pregnant again," I say as I pull her back towards me. The thought of her carrying my child and her belly swelling with my baby, is intoxicating.

"Not a chance, Matteo. One and done. This shop is closed. I'm not going through that again," she states firmly. Attempting to draw a line, setting a boundary.

Laughing I say, "Okay, Princess let's just shelve this

conversation for later." She can shut that shop all she wants, but I'll be opening it back up for business. I'll convince her, I'll make her see that we need this.

"Go to sleep. We'll talk more tomorrow," I mumble into her hair, pulling her closer.

I always get what I want in the end.

Chapter 16

Eleanor Wang

I have been back in OZ for over a week now, and every day is like Groundhog Day. Wake up, get dressed, make breakfast, go through mountains of paperwork, tell Angel what I want so he can order it and have it delivered to the house the same day, eat dinner, go to bed. The routine is suffocating. The monotony is crushing, but it's also safe and predictable.

Matteo is back working at the office in the city, leaving Angel here with us at the house. Matteo supplied me with a phone on my second day of being back. So I've been able to send an email over to Patrick and explain everything that happened. He'd threatened to go to the police if he doesn't get an email from me every few days to confirm I am alive. We'd talked about it in the past. What to do if Matteo did ever find me and what would happen. So he wasn't completely shocked when I emailed him after being missing for 4 days.

It's safe to say he wasn't happy, but he did understand. Which says a lot, cause I wasn't sure how well it would go down if Matteo found out I was emailing Patrick. There has never been anything between Patrick and me, but Matteo is a very, very jealous and possessive man. I know it would either end with Patrick being murdered or me losing my phone privileges. I hope to avoid that situation and have arranged for my emails to be sent to Aela only. My best friend and the only person who's always known where I was, the only person I've ever trusted with all my secrets.

Matteo has hardly spoken to me since he's gone back to work. He is gone when I wake up and back after I've fallen asleep. He wakes me up every night with his dick between my legs; but that's it. It is like he's avoiding me, like he's giving me space, but also not trusting himself around me, and I can't work out why. The distance is killing me, the silence between us is deafening.

I plan to stay up tonight to confront him and find out what is happening. I've also prepared myself to tell him the truth as to why I left. I feel like it is time to air everything out. I need to keep Niko safe, and I can't do that if Matteo doesn't understand, if he doesn't know the real threats, what I was really running from.

I set myself up in the library with a book, fully prepared to stay awake for however long it takes Matteo to come home. Naturally, of course, I don't make it. I wake to find Matteo lifting me from the chair I'd fallen asleep in. Since having Niko I never make it past 9 pm without falling asleep, My body, my mind, everything about me is exhausted.

"Hey, Princess, let's get you into bed," I hear him

whisper into my hair. His voice is soft, tender; like he's handling something precious.

"Matteo?"

"Yes, Princess?"

"Are you avoiding me?" I ask through a yawn. I need to know, I need to understand what's happening between us.

"Why do you think that?"

"Cause you get home when you know I'm asleep and you're gone when I wake up," I look up at him as he places me on the bed, trying to read his expression, trying to understand what he's thinking. I watch as she slowly strips out of his suit, leaving it crumpled on the floor, and him climbing onto the bed with me.

"Princess, if I was avoiding you, I simply wouldn't come home at night. I've got some drama with the four seats going on and I've been trying to deal with it. I only come home 'cause you're here. Otherwise I would just stay at the office," he admits. His words settle something inside me, he's not avoiding me, he's just working.

"I tried to stay awake so I could talk to you," I say, pouting up at him. "But I can never seem to make it past 9 pm anymore. I'm only 30, for Christ's sake. But 9 pm seems to be the magical number."

He chuckles at me. "Princess, you were never a night owl. You used to fall asleep in the taxi on the way home from the club when you were 19. So I'm not surprised that you're a nanna now."

"Fuck off. I'm not a nanna. I just like my sleep," I grumble back, trying to lighten the mood, to ease the tension. "Anyway, I want to talk to you, so stop distracting me." I say, slapping his chest lightly as he settles into the bed next to me.

"What did you wanna talk about?" he asks, while running his hand up my leg, towards my pussy. He's trying to seduce me to avoid the conversation.

"Enough of that," I say, sitting up in bed. Drawing my legs up to my chest, I continue, "I want to talk about a few things." I state, putting my foot down. I won't let him distract me this time.

"O.K," Matteo says, spelling each syllable separately. "What did you wanna talk about?" He sits up in bed and flicks on the bedside table lamp. His expression shifts, his face becoming serious, more focused and intense.

Okay, shit. Now that I have his attention, I don't know if I want it. When Matteo has his serious face on, it's either a thing of beauty, or a thing of death. After this conversation, I know it's gonna be death.

"Ok," I say, taking a deep breath. "I have two things I need to address."

"Well now, don't you sound all professional. All that PA work must have rubbed off on you," he says with a slight smile. I know he's trying to lighten the mood.

"Fuck off, cunt," I quip, shaking my head.

"Argh, there she is. My little gutter mouth. I was wondering where it went," he laughs.

"Seriously, Matteo, you're the only person I know who doesn't seem to mind my gutter trash voice," shaking my head. "Okay enough of that," I pause, holding up my hand as I take a breath. "First, I need you to get fake paperwork for Niko's schooling in the UK, so I can get him a teacher."

"I have Angel already working on it," he says. Of course he well ahead of me.

"Thank you," I say with a nod. I'm grateful and relieved that he's handling this.

"And I want to tell you why I left," I say, looking down at my hands. The words are heavy, they've been sitting in my chest for 10 years, I know this will be difficult. "I know you said you would look after us and keep us safe, and we have been fine since we've been back. But I know, once I step one foot out that gate it's gonna be a whole different ballgame." I'm trying to go easy on him, to explain and to make him understand. "I can't stay locked up here forever. I know that and you know that. So, you need to know the real threat before I can go outside the walls."

Matteo reaches out, placing his finger under my chin and lifting my head up to look into my eyes. "Princess, no matter what it is, I'll deal with it, okay." His voice is firm.

"Okay," I say, leaning forward to kiss him; It's not a romantic type of kiss, just one to steal a little bit of strength from him, in an attempt to ground myself before I tell him the truth.

"You know the war you were in the middle of when I left?" I ask.

"Yes," he says. He remembers, knowing exactly what I'm talking about.

"One of the four seats murdered my parents. The day before I ran away, there was a letter slipped under my door with photos of their bodies. Stamped on the back of it was the four seats symbol."

I feel Matteo stiffen next to me, his entire body going rigid, like he's been turned to stone.

"There was a note attached that said I was next if I didn't disappear," I continue. The words tumbling out. The truth finally out there.

"Why didn't ya tell me? I could've kept you safe," Matteo exclaims, his tone sharp and angry. I know he's furious that I didn't trust him, that I didn't come to him.

"There is more," I admit, taking a deep breath, knowing full well this is going to change a lot. "I ignored the photos and just threw them in the bin. I mean, they had died over 6 months before. So, I'd thought it was just someone messing with me. Plus, this wasn't the first time I'd gotten threats sent to me, the truth is I actually got them a lot."

If I'm confessing one thing, then I've decided it's time to, lay bare all the things I've been hiding.

"They started the second I'd met you. It was notes left in my car or slipped into my mailbox. I knew it was something that went hand in hand with being with you. At first, I thought it was just a jealous ex or someone you'd fucked once. So, I just threw them away, every time I got one. I didn't even read half of them before trashing them." I say, my voice steadier now as the words flow free.

"Princess, I don't understand why you didn't just tell me," Matteo says, shaking his head with a massive frown; He's hurt.

"Well, as I said you were in the middle of a war and I didn't want to add to your burdens at the time. Also, I'd just thought it was something I was going to have to live with if I wanted to keep you," I reply, as I reach out and run my hand down his cheek. I'm trying to make him understand, to help him see that I was just trying to protect him too.

"I never took them seriously," I offer with a shrug. "Until that day," I say looking back down at my hands, that day changed everything, that was the day that made me run.

"Fuck Matteo, this is hard to say," I stumble, a single tear running down my face. I feel his hand instantly wipe it away, before he lifts my chin back up to meet his eyes.

"Princess, it's okay. I'm not going anywhere. There is nothing on this planet you could do or say to make me leave you," he states with a slight grin on his face.

Blowing out a breath, I press on. "Okay, so I threw the pictures in the bin and didn't think anything of it. Now, by this time, I'd known I was pregnant with Niko. I had known for about 5 days. I was just working up the courage to tell you and ask if the offer to move in with you was still on the table." I shrug, admitting that I was actually going to tell him, I was going to give us a chance.

"But as we know, I'm a chicken shit when it comes to talks like this," I say, gesturing between us both. "The next day, 30 minutes after you had dropped me home, I had a knock on the door. I'd assumed it was Angel or Spike as they were the only two who ever knocked, but when the door swung open, I found 3 men standing there. They pushed me inside my apartment and shoved me into a chair. I'd never seen these men before, but they were definitely Italian."

At this point, I have a stream of tears running down my

face. The memories flooding back, as well as the fear, the pain and the terror.

"They did what they'd came to do," I say, my voice breaking. "And just before they left, one of the men said if I stayed any longer and didn't disappear, I would end up like my parents. So I ran. I ran to save our baby, and to save myself."

The room is dead quiet. Matteo is so still I'm sure Rigor Mortis has set in. I know if I look up into his eyes, I'll find them blank and soulless. Except this time, I'm not going to creep out of the room or call for help. I slowly lower my head down into his lap and cry silently, prepared to wait him out. He asked me to stay, So stay I will.

Chapter 17

Matteo Ricci

The last words Eleanor said repeat over and over in my mind, they'd assaulted her, hurt her, threatened her and made her run; they took her from me. I know she has triggered me. I just don't know how to get back out of my own head. I want to let go, to let the haze take over and burn the whole damn city down, to find every single person responsible and make them suffer the way she suffered.

But I also know this happened 10 years ago now, so finding the 3 assholes isn't going to be happening right now. The rage is consuming me, eating me alive from the inside out. I can feel my hands clenching so tightly that my nails have drawn blood from my palms. My jaw is locked so hard, I'm afraid my teeth might crack. Every muscle in my body is tense, coiled tight and ready to explode.

I feel a slight pressure against my cheek, and what sounds like crying. Suddenly, the pressure on my cheek disappears and two light amber colour eyes come into view, they're red from tears, filled with pain and fear. She's looking at me like she's terrified of what I'm going to do, like she's afraid of my reaction.

The pressure on my cheek comes back, except now it's on both sides. I can register her hands cupping my face, an attempt to ground me, to bring me back. The amber eyes peer right into my soul, the sadness in their depths clear. I know I need to reach out to her, but I can't seem to get my arms to move. My body is frozen, locked in place by rage, shock and the overwhelming need to protect her.

I watch as she leans in and kisses my lips. The feeling of it so grounding to my mind, like her kiss is chasing the fog away, like she's pulling me back from the edge of the abyss. I can feel my mouth starting to move with hers. My arms no longer feeling heavy or foreign. It's like her touch alone has drawn me back out, like her love is the only thing that can save me from myself.

I lift my arms, cupping her face with my hands. She's so beautiful, strong and so brave for telling me the truth. For trusting me with this and letting me in. I slowly kiss her back Tenderly showing her that I'm here, I'm not going anywhere because I love her more than I love my own life.

She is my forever, all I need to do is show her that.

"Eleanor," I whisper onto her lips. Her name is a prayer, a vow and a promise all rolled into one.

"Matteo," she whispers back. Her voice is vulnerable, small and broken.

"I love you," I remind her as I capture her lips with mine. My arms wrapping around her waist before pulling her onto my lap. If anyone is able to pull me out of the fog, it was always going to be this woman. She's my anchor, my light, and my reason for breathing.

I grab the hem of the t-shirt she's wearing and drag it up over her head, making sure her body is bare to me. Perfect. I pull the top of my boxers down, freeing my cock. I want them off, but at this point, I don't want to break the connection I have with Eleanor. So I settle on pulling them down just enough to free myself so I can grab my shaft.

I hold my dick straight, allowing Eleanor to sink herself down on me. She's so hot and wet. A moan escapes her as she slides down. "Oh Matteo…" Her voice is breathless and needy, like she needs this connection just as much as I do.

We stay kissing and not moving for several moments, the connection perfect like this. Us moulded together, our souls connected by our intertwined bodies. This is what love is, what our forever feels like.

Eleanor is the first to start moving, sliding herself forward and backwards, creating friction on her clit. We aren't fucking tonight, we are making love. Our mouths fuse together once more as Eleanor grinds down on my cock. Each movement is deliberate, intimate, like she's pouring all her love and trust into me.

I run my hands down her back, feeling every curve, every muscle; very part of her that belongs to me. I kiss my way over her neck, shoulder and collarbone. Showing her with my body what my words can't express, worshipping her.

"I've got you Princess," I whisper against her skin. "I've always got you. No one will ever hurt you again, I swear it on my life."

She whimpers against me. Her movements becoming more urgent, more desperate, like she needs to feel me, needs to know that I'm here, that I'm real and I'm not going anywhere.

It doesn't take long for her pussy to clamp down on my cock, causing her to cry out "Fuck Matteo, this is it!" Her orgasm washes over her like a wave. Her entire body shakes as her walls squeeze me so tightly, I can barely breathe.

Her orgasms always milk my cock dry. Her inner walls squeezing me so tightly, I can't help but explode inside her. "Take it all baby. Everything I have. It all belongs to you," I say into her mouth. I'm pouring myself into her, my love, my devotion, my entire soul.

Once we both catch our breaths, I wrap my arms all the way around her back and pull her into my chest, my cock softening inside her. Tonight, I won't make her move, won't make her go clean up. Instead I lean back against my pillow and hold her close. She needs to feel safe, needs to know that I'm here, that I'm in it forever.

Eleanor is quick to fall asleep, she's always been an easy deep sleeper. Her breathing becomes steady as her body relaxes against mine. She looks so peaceful, so innocent and o beautiful.

I don't move. I just lay here, with her in my arms, holding her, protecting her, loving her.

I may be physically still, but my mind is working overtime, planning, already three steps ahead of the problem.

I need to find those men, the fact that they are Italian is a big issue. Killing them is going to be complicated, doesn't matter if they are members of my crew or Enzo's. I know finding them is going to be even harder.

It happened 10 years ago. I don't know who they are or

if they are even still alive, but I'm going to find out. I'm going to hunt down every single person responsible for hurting her, threatening her and for making her run.

And when I find them, when I've finally tracked them down, I'm going to make them pay, to make them suffer and make sure they understand what it means to hurt something that belongs to Matteo Ricci.

But that's for tomorrow. Tonight, I'm going to hold my woman, I'm going to cherish her. Tonight, I'm going to show her that she's safe, that she's loved and that she's mine, and I will burn the world down to keep her.

I run my fingers through her hair, breathing in her scent, committing this moment to my memory. The feel of her in my arms, the sound of her breathing and the warmth of her body against mine.

This is what I've been missing for 10 years, it's what I've been searching for, what I've needed to survive.

She stirs slightly, pressing closer to me, like even in her dreams she's seeking me out, even unconscious she knows I'm her safe place.

"I love you princess," I whisper into her hair. "I'm sorry I wasn't there to protect you. I'm sorry I didn't know. But I'm here now, and I'm never letting you go again."

Chapter 18

Eleanor Wang

I wake in the morning to an empty bed and sticky thighs. Shit, I didn't clean up last night. I thought Matteo would have stayed, I hate waking up alone. The bed always feels cold without him, and the silence feels deafening. I reach over to his side, feeling the sheets are still warm, he obviously hasn't been gone long, but it doesn't matter; He's not here and that's what hurts.

I climb out of bed, jumping straight into the shower, because if there is anything my romance novels don't mention, it's that cum-covered thighs the next day are not easily washed away with water. Cum itself isn't easily washed away, it turns into clag glue, unless you use large amounts of soap and we all know that regular soap versus a vagina, is not a good mix.

If I end up with thrush or a UTI from this, I'm gonna be pissed.

I quickly shower and get dressed, noticing it's nearly 10 am. What the fuck? I never sleep in. I mean I do press snooze a good 6 times every morning, but I never actually sleep in. I didn't even hear the alarm this morning and Niko hasn't come to find me either, which is unusual, and not like him.

I quickly run down the stairs, only to discover Matteo sitting at the table drinking a coffee with Niko and Angel sitting on the other side, working on something tech related together, while Spike sits by the window drinking tea from a teacup with matching saucer, The sight is interesting. Glancing out the window I notice the weather is crap and it's clearly gonna rain all day.

I slow my steps as I walk in, the scene is so domestic, so normal; everything I've been dreaming about for 10 years. "Um, what's going on here? I thought you would have been at work," I say, looking at Matteo. My heart is racing, something feels different, like somethings shifted.

"Princess, every time I leave the house from now on, you will be with me. I'm not leaving here anymore without you by my side. If that means I have to wait every morning till you wake up, then so be it," Matteo says, his voice firm, almost resolute, like he's made a decision and there's no changing his mind.

"I'm confused, why do I have to come?" I ask, frowning, not sure how I feel about this, about being attached to him at all times.

"After last night, I've realised that if I had have kept you with me at all times, none of this would have happened. So, I'm not leaving you alone from now on," Matteo rationalises like it's the simplest answer, and the most obvious solution in the world. He's protecting me, claiming me, making sure I'm never hurt again.

"Well, I think that might be a little bit impractical. And

I don't think it is something that can be established for a long period of time. But hey, I do need to get out of the house before I get cabin fever. So fuck it, why not?" I mumble, trying to convince myself just as much as I'm trying to convince him. The truth is, I want to be with him, to be by his side and to be his. "Lemme me go get changed; I can't be seen out in public wearing sweats and a t-shirt," I laugh.

Matteo laughs. "Of course, you can't. I can't imagine you in anything less than a power suit when out of the house."

"Matteo, you think you're whipped now, just wait until you see me in a skirt and blouse," I laugh back at him, fully meaning it.

30 minutes later I've wrangled my body into a skirt and blouse, slapped some makeup on and slipped on some new heels. Given how tight they are, I know I'm gonna have to hunt down some Band-Aids. There's no way I'm going to last wearing these heels all day without some. But I know I look good, I feel powerful, like myself, like the woman Matteo fell in love with all those years ago. My side of the wardrobe is now over-flowing with unpacked bag's from online purchases, as much as I didn't want to spend Matteo's money, I needed clothes and so did Niko. And an online, unlimited budget shop is something no woman can refuse.

Walking back into the kitchen in my business gear, I'm not quite prepared for Matteo. Down on one knee, with an open box lying on his palm. My heart stops, my breath catching in my chest as my entire world shifts.

"I told you I was going to marry you, Princess. So I

think it's about time to adorn my ring," Matteo smirks, so confident, and so sure of me, so sure of us.

"Shit," I exclaim, looking at Matteo, I'm overwhelmed and emotional. I'm so in love with this man it hurts. "Alright, give it here," I say, holding my hand out in the 'give me, give me' sign.

Matteo smiles wide and grabs my hand. "Hey, at least let me do the honours, Princess." he laughs at me. His eyes are so blue, so full of love, so full of promise. I know he's savouring this moment, making it special.

The cool metal glides onto my ring finger perfectly, like it was made for me and everything about this moment was meant to be. The ring is beautiful, elegant, timeless; Just like our love.

"Let me guess. You magically knew the right size to buy?" I state, eyebrow raised, teasing him. But I'm also genuinely curious, how could he have possibly known?

"Nope, I put a piece of string around your finger while you were sleeping," Matteo admits, tapping his nose and smirking at me. He's so clever, so thoughtful and so completely obsessed with me. The fact that he did it while I was sleeping, that he was so careful as not to wake me, It's the most romantic thing I've ever heard.

"It was actually my idea," Niko says from the table, not even looking up from the screen. "Matteo was wondering how to get it right. So, I just googled it, because Google always has the answer," Niko states, matter of factly. My son. My beautiful, brilliant son, is helping his father, bonding with him, and accepting him. My heart swells with pride and love.

"Right well, okay then. Did someone make me a coffee

while I was gone? I think today is a coffee kinda day," I say, looking at the floor, trying to process all of it.

"Nope, we'll grab one on the way," Matteo says. "And some food. You're too skinny." He's always trying to take care of me. Always trying to make sure I'm fed, safe and loved. It's one of the things I love most about him.

"Mum doesn't eat breakfast, Pa. If you feed it before you give it coffee, you might as well sign your own death certificate," Niko mumbles to Matteo. I smile at my son. He's right. I'm not a morning person. Always, coffee first, food later.

"Pa? What's this Pa business?" Matteo frowns at Niko. "You're making me feel like an old man."

"You are old, but I'm playing around with names till one feels right," Niko announces, with a grin on his face.

"Well, Pa doesn't feel right, try another," Matteo laughs. He's so patient with Niko, completely smitten with our son.

"Come on princess, let's go," Matteo says, swinging his arms in the direction of the front door, like a bell boy.

"Okay, okay, let's go," I say, walking over to the table.

"Love you, Niko. Give Angel hell for me," I suggest as I kiss Niko on the top of his head. "Wash your hair today too. It smells." I pull a face at Niko.

"I washed it yesterday." Niko grumbles.

"Well, wash it again. You did it wrong," I throw over my shoulder as I walk towards Matteo who is holding the front door open for me, he's always holding the door open for me.

"You want cafe coffee or drive-through? They opened

up a drive-through Starbucks, which is on the way to the office," Matteo states.

"Starbucks please. They have Pumpkin Spice Lattes at the moment, they are to die for," I smile back.

"Ask and you shall receive," Matteo opens the car door for me. "In you hop, my lady." He jests, being chivalrous and playful.

"Keep this shit up and I'll end up sucking your dick to say thank you," I say softly as I take my seat. And I would too, the man's dick makes my mouth water. Honestly the more chivalrous Matteo is, the more I want the weight of it on my tongue. Yeah, I'm no feminist. I get wet from filthy words and doors being held open. I love it when Matteo takes care of me, when he shows me that I'm his priority, that I'm his everything. The combination of his dominance and his tenderness is intoxicating.

Matteo walks around the other side of the car and jumps in. while Spike slides into the back seat. Where the fuck does the Ninja come from? I need him to teach me some of those skills; Never know when stealth will come in handy.

"Spike?"

"Yes, Eleanor?" Spike responds, sarcastically.

"Wanna teach me how to be stealthy like you?" I ask, turning around in my seat. I'm curious, intrigued. I want to learn, to be strong, I want to be able to protect myself.

"Nope," Spike says, popping the 'p'.

"Why not?" I say with a frown, genuinely disappointed.

"Matteo was the one who taught me. So he can teach you," Spike points at Matteo with a grin on his face.

"Wait, what? Really?" I look at Matteo. "I feel like Spike is a lot stealthier than you. But..." I say, teasing him. Pushing his buttons and testing to see how he reacts.

"Well gee, thanks, Princess. Is this your way of saying I need to update my skills?" Matteo laughs at me. "You asked me to stop being so quiet, but now I'm not stealthy enough cause you can hear me, when I'm purposely making noise, so you know that I'm coming." Matteo says with his eyebrow raised. He's got a point. He's been making himself known so I don't get scared.

"Well, when you put it that way..." I say pouting at Matteo. "Well, will you teach me?"

"Princess, as I said before, ask and you shall receive," Matteo grins at me. He's so generous, willing to give me everything I ask for.

"Thank you," I say smiling back.

50 minutes later, with one super-large Pumpkin Spice Latte in hand, we arrive at the Office. We park in the underground parking and take the lift up to the 20th floor. My heart pounding as I'm about to see Matteo's world, his empire, his life, the inner workings of the place where he rules from.

"Give me that coffee," Matteo states.

"Nope," I say, popping the 'p.' "If you wanted to try it, you should have gotten one." I jest playfully, teasing him.

Matteo turns to face me, pouting his lips. "Please?" He looks so cute when he pouts, so vulnerable, not like the scary mafia boss everyone else sees. This is the Matteo that only I get to see, the Matteo that belongs to me.

"Fuck, you look cute right now," I say, handing over my cup. Matteo takes a sip, immediately pulling a face.

"What in the ever-loving fuck is that?" he asks, looking like he's just drunk cats piss. I can't help but laugh at his expression, his face is priceless.

"Pumpkin Spice Latte, with two sugars," I state back, taking a big sip.

"No, I know what you ordered, but that is gross. It smelt amazing from over here, but that tastes horrible," Matteo pulls a face again at my cup, genuinely disgusted. It's hilarious.

"Good. Means I don't have to share it with you," I say in a sing-song voice, sticking my tongue out at Matteo as I step out of the lift and take a good look around.

The office is a very-grand, open-plan style. The colour scheme is clearly plain white and glass. The receptionist's desk is massive with 3 girls manning it, all wearing headsets and typing away at the computers. Ricci is written across the wall behind them in gold lettering. I look down the hallway, comprised of rows of doors on either side. This is his empire, his kingdom. This is where he rules over it all.

The 3 women look up, greeting him in unison, "Good morning, Mr Ricci." then turn back to their computers. I have to smother the laugh bubbling in my chest at the sight of it. I'm clearly doing a shit job of it as Spike pokes me in the ribs and whispers in my ear. "Good morning, Angels." Then whispers into my other ear, "Good morning, Charlie." And I'm done. The giggles take over, and there's no way I can stop them. I'm laughing so hard, I can barely breathe.

"What are you two laughing about?" Matteo turns to

face us as he starts walking down the hall, clearly trying to figure out what's so funny; He's suspicious.

"Nothing," I'm quick to jibe back. I can't tell him, he'll be mortified.

Spike just continues to laugh. He's not helping, he's making it worse.

"What have I gotten myself into?" I hear Matteo mutter to himself before he opens the last door at the end. He knows we're laughing at him.

We walk into what is clearly Matteo's office. It's all dark furniture and white walls, with a brown leather Chesterfield on the right wall. But what catches my attention the most, is the massive picture on the wall behind Matteo's desk.

It's us.

In black and white.

10 years ago.

I remember the moment the photo was taken. We were sitting on a hill in Wollongong, with the lighthouse in the background. We had taken a day trip down to see the lighthouse. We stopped to eat some fish and chips while looking out at the ocean. The trip had gone to plan, but the weather hadn't and I'd refused to let it affect the date. So, Matteo and I sat on the wet grass, in the rain and ate soggy fish and chips while looking at the water. Spike and Angel sat in the car, watching us act like 3-year-old children. Angel had taken the photo. It was taken the moment Matteo had pulled me up from the grass, and demanded we dance in the rain. There we were in each other's arms, dancing, getting soaked, smiling at each other; A mobster's son and a penniless wannabe artist.

My heart breaks and heals all at once. He's kept the photo, kept the memory, kept us alive in his heart for 10 years, while I've been running, hiding and trying to forget; He's been remembering, holding onto us, waiting for me.

I am snapped back to reality as droplets of water splash across my face, "What the fuck?" I snap. I see Spike standing in front of me with water dripping from his fingertips, making it obvious he's just shaken water on to my face.

"What the fuck was that for, dickhead?" I growl at him, my eyes wet with tears but I'm trying to hide it.

"I could see the picture had transported you back to that day. So, I thought if I threw some water on you, it would be even more realistic," Spike offers, laughing at me, he was trying to recreate the rain.

Motherfucker has a death wish. "Can you believe this cunt?" I point at Spike while addressing Matteo, which is clearly pointless cause he is smothering laughter of his own. "You're both a bunch of dickheads," I say as I take the seat behind Matteo's desk, before he even has a chance to sit in it.

"Princess, what are you doing?" he asks, lifting an eyebrow at me.

"Oh, Matteo, sorry didn't see you there. Please take a seat," I say, gesturing to the seat on the other side of the desk. "I'm glad you could join me," I smirk at him as I lean back in his chair, making myself more comfortable and steepling my fingers like a bond villain does.

"Why, thank you," Matteo replies, actually taking the seat, playing along.

"Seeing as you're in my seat today, would you mind

starting up my computer and pulling up the calendar, so I know what is planned," Matteo suggests from his seat.

"Sure," I say, flicking open his laptop. "What's the password?" I look over at Matteo, knowing full well I've never once been given access to his computer or phone before.

"Wicket," he states, putting all his cards on the table, giving me access and trusting me. He's showing me that I'm his, there are no secrets between us anymore.

I type it in, wondering how long he is going to let me play this game before he stops it. The laptop opens up and for the second time today I am stopped in my tracks. His wallpaper, again, is us. This time it's a photo from when Matteo was tattooing my arm, in the tattoo shop where I'd first met him. I haven't seen any of these photos in 10 years. When I ran away, I'd left every single thing I owned in the apartment.

My eyes fill with tears. He's kept these memories, kept me alive in his heart, never letting me go. All this time. All these years, he's been holding onto us.

Matteo had done a money pick-up the day before and left 30k in cash, in a bag in my bedroom. That was all I'd grabbed when I ran. I had wondered what happened to everything in my apartment after.

"Matteo, what happened to my stuff from my apartment?" I ask, looking up into blue eyes, that always managed to see right into my soul.

"It's in storage. I had it all packed up and placed into a storage unit. At first, I'd thought if I went through it then I would find a clue to where you had gone," he said softly. "But as we now know, there wasn't one. So, it's been sitting in storage ever since. Did you want me to have it emptied and brought to the house?" Matteo asks. He's been keeping my life preserved, keeping me alive in his world, just waiting for me to come home.

"Yes please. I'm feeling nostalgic now, I'd love to be able to dig up some golden oldies to show Niko," I smirk at him. I want Niko to see our history, to understand how much his father loved me, how much we'd loved each other back then. Stories are one thing, photos are another.

"Matteo…"

"Yes, Princess," Matteo says with a half grin.

"Do you still own a tattoo kit?"

"Yes," he says simply.

"Wanna use it on me again," I ask, looking at his laptop screen. I want to mark myself, to show the world that I'm his, to carry him on my skin and to be permanently marked by him again.

"What did you have in mind?" he asks, interested. His voice is low, like he's already imagining what I'm going to ask for.

"An M with a crown on top of my ring finger," I state, looking up from the screen. I want to wear him, to carry him with me always. I want everyone to see that I belong to Matteo Ricci.

"And that's my cue to leave," Spike says, quickly heading to the door, knowing what's about to happen.

"Ask and you shall receive," Matteo replies, clearly touched. His eyes slowly growing more predatory.

"Thank you," I tell him softly, looking back at the keyboard of Matteo's laptop.

"Thank you for what, Princess?" Matteo questions, as he rises from his chair and walks over to where I'm sitting.

"Thank you for not giving up on us, for not falling out of love with me. I know, I ran away, and I know I didn't want to be found. But the whole time I was gone, I've always felt like I was missing a piece of myself, and since I've been back, I feel like I've found it again," I admit. "I feel like I'm whole again, like I'm home. Even though I'd hoped you would never find us, I always secretly wanted you to."

I feel Matteo's hand grab my chin, lifting my face up, so my eyes meet his. "Princess, you're mine. I'd told you that day on your doorstep that I had 'come to claim what is mine.' And I did. Nothing has changed since that day," Matteo leans over me, pressing a button on the intercom. A girl named Becky answers. "What can I do for you, Mr Ricci?" she purrs down the line, her voice dripping with desire and want.

"Hold all my calls and appointments, until I say otherwise. Do not disturb me in my office," Matteo states with a flare of authority in his voice.

"Of course, Mr Ricci," she purrs back before the line goes dead.

"Well, she clearly has some wet undies for you," I grumble, jealous.

"Princess, she can change her undies 20 times a day for all I care. I've never touched my employees, and I never will. Plus, they are about to hear why," Matteo remarks, his eyes darkening.

"Stand up," he demands, and I do. Call me weak, sure.

But this man just knows how to make me obey. His dominance is intoxicating, his control is addictive.

"Sit on the desk," he orders as he moves his laptop into one of the drawers, before sweeping the rest of the desk off with his arm. Oh, I see where this is going. Kinky office sex, others might get worried about people walking in or overhearing. Me? Nope, not even a little bit. Auditory exhibitionism is a kink of mine, always has been. Matteo might not like other people seeing me, when he fucks me. But he has no issue with them hearing it. The thought of everyone in this office hearing him make me scream, hearing him claim me, is thrilling.

I sit on the desk, scooting my ass back a bit. "Spread those legs and let me look at what's mine," he growls, so I do. I didn't wear undies today on purpose, I'd been planning on teasing him with it. Now it looks like my idea has come in handy. He's going to see that I've come to work ready for him, ready to be his.

"Fuck me, I've forgotten you like to tease," he says, sinking to his knees. Positioning his face level with my cunt, he leans in and licks me, ass to clit. His tongue is magic, his mouth is heaven, I'm already losing my mind. The feeling of his mouth on me is intoxicating.

"Oh, God," I run my hands into his hair. He's so good at this, all the practice before he meet me was well done.

"Oh Matteo, that's it. Fuck yes," I feel his little finger starting to push into my back entrance, while his others are pumping in and out of my cunt as he licks me. God, it feels amazing. The sensation is overwhelming, it's everything I need. Matteo pulls his hand away, leaving me empty. I lift my head up off the desk, looking down at him wondering what he is doing, I let out a little whimper.

"Don't worry, I'm not done with you yet," he says as his free hand reaches up, squeezing my breasts over my shirt. My breasts feel heavy, aching to be released, but Matteo clearly wants what's under my skirt more as he pushes it up higher and pulls my ass off the edge of the desk.

He licks me from ass to clit again, making me moan and squirm. "Please Matteo," I don't even know what I'm asking for.

He pushes just the tips of his fingers back inside me, before letting saliva drip from his tongue onto the base of his fingers. I watch it run down, until it hits my entrance. Completely ensnared by the sight I don't notice his hand moving before I feel it. He pushes his little finger back inside my back entrance, inserting it to the first knuckle this time. The sensation is incredible, pushing me closer to the edge.

"Fuck that feels good," I moan, my entire body is trembling, my mind spinning, completely lost in sensation.

He starts fucking me with his fingers faster, while flicking my clit with his tongue. I feel a second finger push into my back entrance, and I know I'm about to explode. The moment his teeth pinch my clit, I know I'm done. Reaching up, I grab my tits and pinch my nipple as my inner walls clamp down on Matteo's fingers.

"That's it, princess. Strangle my fingers," he demands, speeding up, pushing me higher, taking me to the edge and making me lose control.

"Oh fuck," I scream as my first orgasm morphs into a

second. Except this time, I feel the flood of cum gushing out of me. Matteo seals his mouth around me, drinking it up like a man in the desert, consuming all of me.

As I come down from seeing stars, I feel Matteo stand and lean over me. He grabs my cheeks with one hand, squeezing them until I open my mouth and he dribbles my cum back into my mouth, before leaning down to kiss me, so the taste combines between us. It's filthy, but I love it.

He stands up, dragging me off the desk and turning me around, so I'm bent over with my ass in the air. "Princess, I'm gonna fuck your ass now, you're gonna cum all over me and my desk, so I can smell you in here for days," he states as he lines up with my cunt and pushes in, coating himself in my cream. Once he has coated his dick in my juices, he pulls out, adjusting slightly as he gently pushes into my ass.

"Oh God, Matteo," I whimper, gently pushing back to help him in. He's so deep, so thick, everything I need. The feeling of him inside me is indescribable.

"That's it. Push back onto me like the whore I know you are," he commands, sinking all the way to the hilt. "Your ass looks perfect swallowing my dick." His filthy words setting me on fire.

Matteo grabs my hips and starts to piston in and out of me. His movements are deliberate, controlled, and power-ful. He's fucking me like he owns me, like I'm his property and I belong to him.

Moaning, I push back on him, meeting every thrust. I want everyone in this office to hear him come undone for me, to hear his balls slapping on my clit, to know that he's mine.

My breasts rub against the desk with every thrust, heightening my pleasure even more. I know I'm about to cum again. I can feel my legs starting to shake as the pressure builds up. I'm so close, right there.

"Harder," I demand, and he does, always giving me what I ask for.

"You like that? You like feeling my dick in your ass? Scream, so they can all hear you out there, claiming your man," he growls. That's all it takes, A few simple words and I explode, my cum gushes out, all over my legs and Matteo's floor.

I've always been able to squirt, but never by my own hand. Matteo knows how to make me gush down my legs. And by God, do I love it. I hope his office smells like me for days. I wanna rub my cum into the carpet, so the smell never comes out. New kink unlocked? Maybe. Definitely.

I feel Matteo stiffen behind me and I know he is about to explode. So I push my ass back hard, taking him in as far as I can.

"Shit Princess, that's it," and that is it. Matteo explodes inside me, filling me with his cum. "God, Baby, that was freakin amazing," he exclaims, collapsing onto my back. His dick still in my ass as his arms wrap around me and he kisses my shoulder. I can feel his heart pounding against my back.

We stay close for a moment. Just breathing and existing together.

Our bubble popped when there is a knock on the door and Spike's voice from the other side. "Boss, Enzo's just arrived at the desk downstairs." His voice is apologetic.

"Motherfucker," Matteo snaps, frustrated. Obviously

wanting more time with me, not wanting to deal with business just yet.

"Okay, give me 5," he calls back.

"Princess, there is a bathroom behind that door there. Go clean up. You're about to meet the man who sits in the second seat," he grimaces. "He is a complete lunatic, so get your game face on," he sends me a pleading look.

Ok, sure. I'll just go push the cum out of my ass, freshen up, and be back in 5 for mobster politics 101.

Welcome to my new life.

Chapter 19

Matteo Ricci

Why the fuck is Enzo even here? We usually make appointments to see one another, or we call, like normal people. But this cunt loves to just pop up unannounced, like a weed between the cracks in the pavement, useless, annoying and immune to weed killer.

I walk into the bathroom behind Eleanor, wash my dick in the sink and tuck myself back into my pants. I notice how wet they are and smirk at Eleanor. "There is cum on my pants and shoes," I say, holding my foot out for her to see.

"Are you complaining?" she asks from the toilet.

"Nope, but I might get you to lick it off my shoes later," I deadpan. The thought of her on her knees, licking my shoes clean, makes my dick twitch all over again.

"You wouldn't," she narrows her eyes towards me.

"Oh, I would Princess, and you know it," I say as I wet a hand towel and rub my pants clean. "I'll save you the hassle today, but if you think teasing me with no undies won't end in a punishment, then you don't know me very well." I turn, looking at her as she straightens her skirt and begins fixing her hair in the mirror. She turns, walking towards me with a huge smile on her face.

"If multiple orgasms are punishment Matteo, I can guarantee I'll never wear undies again," she offers leaning up to kiss me and making my dick twitch in my pants. She's so fucking perfect and so fucking mine.

"Be careful what you wish for, Eleanor," I say, slapping her ass as she walks out of the bathroom door. "You can sit in my seat," I state as I grab the chair from the other side of my desk and pull it around to sit beside her.

She scoots the chair over a bit so we both sit on the correct side of the desk facing out. We look fucking ridiculous, but I couldn't give a flying fuck. What matters is that she's here, she's beside me, and she's mine.

I grab my laptop, pulling up Spider Solitaire and place it in front of her. "Here princess, you can go through the paperwork while I chat with Enzo Morelli." She looks at me with the cutest confusion lines between her brows.

"Sure, no worries," she says.

A knock comes on the door and Spike voices, "Boss, Enzo is in the waiting area."

"It's alright Spike, come in," I sigh, already irritated and Enzo hasn't even walked in yet.

"Want me to escort him in, Boss," Spike's head pops in the doorway.

"Yeah mate, go get him." I turn to face Eleanor. "Just sit there and do the paperwork Princess and only speak when spoken to, alright?" I say raising my eyebrows. I need her to stay quiet, for her to be safe and to not draw attention to herself.

"When spoken to hey?" she says with a sly grin on her face, and I know why. Eleanor, while she might be submissive to a point, is also headstrong and bitchy to a fault. Telling her what to do is more than likely to result in the opposite happening. She's going to do whatever she wants, she always does, and I love her for it.

"I mean it, Princess. I know you hate it when I tell you what to do, but this time you need to listen." She bristles at my comment, I can see her jaw tighten as she fights with herself.

"Okay, Matteo," she replies, relenting and looks at the desk. She's compromising with me, showing me that she trusts me.

I take my seat next to her and lean her way, grabbing her chin between my thumb and finger. "Hey, Firecracker, I love you."

"I love you too, Cocksucker." She's teasing me, calling me out, she's really perfect.

Enzo laughs as he walks into the office. "Nice to see my information paid off, and you got Eleanor back," he says pointing a finger in Eleanor's direction. His tone is congratulatory, but there's something else underneath it, something I don't like.

"Yes, it did mate, thank you for that," I say, snapping into mobster mode. Some days being a mobster feels like having two personalities, today is definitely one of those days. In fact, since Eleanor has come home, the feeling has become more and more apparent. I'm two different men.

The man who loves Eleanor with every fibre of his being, and the man who runs this empire with an iron fist.

"What can I do for you today, Enzo? I actually have a fully booked day, but making an appointment seems to be beneath you lately," I say crossing my arms, irritated. I want him out of my office. I want to get back to Eleanor.

"We all have a business to run, Matteo," Enzo laughs at me. "But I was actually popping in to talk about the girls I want to run through the city."

"Ah, this is a conversation I believe we've had already, and I voted NO. What makes you think I'm going to change my mind?" I stare Enzo down. I'm not going to budge on this, I've already told him no. I won't support human trafficking. Not now, not ever.

"Sure, this isn't a conversation we need to have in front of the lady," Enzo points to Eleanor who continues to play solitaire on the laptop, not acknowledging that Enzo is talking about her.

"Eleanor has taken on the role of my personal assistant," I smile at him. "So, she will be present for many of our conversations from now on," I state raising my brows.

"Okay, so be it," Enzo says, raising one shoulder in a shrug. "I want to traffic women through the cross, using the velvet to stage the auctions down in Melbourne."

"I've already told you, I won't be voting towards trafficking women Enzo. Leave that to Gallos. We sell enough pussy through the clubs, we don't need to traffic them on top," I say, getting more and more irritated with the conversation. The thought of women being trafficked, of what happens to them, makes my blood boil.

"I know you think that way Matteo, but we can get up to 500K per piece, and we only need to hold one to two auctions a year, we'll walk away with millions. I'm fucking over peddling drugs and pussy," he says with more vitriol in his voice.

"Enzo, I know what happens to the girls who visit your side of town. I'm not stupid, the girls all talk and I wouldn't wish that on my worst enemy. So no. No way am I going to vote yes on pushing unwilling girls into this city," I sigh, running a hand down my face. I'm done with this conversation, done with Enzo.

"We shall see about that," Enzo states, turning to his men standing outside the office. "Tino!" Enzo yells at his crew, holding his hand out. I feel Eleanor stiffen beside me her eyes glued on something outside the door, as a bald man walks into the room. He hands Enzo a yellow envelope and walks back out.

"Take a look at these and get back to me soon, Fratello," Enzo says as he walks right back out the door, like he hadn't wasted 10 minutes of my day and he hadn't just threatened me.

"Fucking cunt," I spit. I look over at Eleanor, noticing she's as white as a ghost. Something is wrong, something has scared her.

"It's okay, Princess. He is a complete fuck tard. I'm never going to vote yes to him pushing girls through," I say, leaning down to kiss the top of her head.

"He isn't the issue," she whispers, so softly I hardly hear her. Her voice is shaking, she's terrified.

"Princess, what's wrong?" I feel my stomach start to gurgle as I notice just how white she is. My protective instincts kicking in. Something has happened, something has scared her.

"Who uses the office, two doors down?"

"Um, no one at the moment. It's empty. I think…" I answer confused. "Why?" My mind racing. Why is she asking about the office?

"One of the…. Ummm, the three men who just walked out of the room…" she says so softy I have to strain my ears to hear it, but I do.

"What?!" I gasp, jumping up from my seat and grabbing my gun from the back of my pants. "Stay inside my office, Eleanor. Lock the door behind me, and only open it when I come back," I yell, taking off down the hallway toward the elevator. I run into Spike on his way back from escorting Enzo to the lifts.

"What's up Boss?" he asks, going on high alert and grabbing a knife out of his pocket.

"Eleanor told me one of the three guys just walked out of office three." Spike knows already who I mean. I'd informed both him and Angel the second I'd climbed out of bed this morning. Safe to say they were just as murderous as I had been about the information. Angel has been pulling any and all surveillance from Eleanor's old apartment, anything he can get his hands on. Spike has been calling all his contacts to gain as much information as he can get. With them being Italian, we have to assume they run in the Ricci or Morelli groups. Even though there is a lot of us in the Sydney area, there isn't a lot we aren't associated with.

"I'll go check outside and get Angel to comb the

surveillance in the office now," Spike states, taking off in a run as he pulls his mobile out to call Angel.

I thought I'd stay and check out the office, see what I can glean from it. Walking back down the hall, I open up the empty office, finding it completely deserted, nothing actually inside it at all. Confused, I take off towards the front desk, stopping to ask the girls about what's happening with the room.

Walking behind the reception desk, Stacy turns around and smiles at me. "What can I do for you, Boss?"

"Can anyone tell me why office number three is empty, and what it's currently being used for? And who was last in it, they walked out about 10 minutes ago?" I query, raising my eyebrows.

"We asked if we could turn it into a lunchroom for just the girls, remember?" Becky states from her seat, while typing out an email.

"Boss, we asked you about it last week," Lisa adds, turning in her seat to face me.

"Okay, but why is it empty then?" I ask.

"We had all the furniture moved to down the other hall, for Peter to use in office 4," Stacy says as she pulls up the visitors log. "And the man who went down there was… Mr Venchetti, Tony Venchetti," she says, reading the name on the screen. "He's the contractor we hired to fit out the room, to change it into a lunchroom."

"Do we have contact details for Mr Venchetti?" I sternly ask the girls, my mind working overtime. Who the fuck is Tony Venchetti?

"Yes, Boss," Stacy says, writing his name and number on a pink Post-it and handing it over.

"Thank you, girls. I would appreciate it if you would hold off any more renovations for the room, until I say so," I utter as I walk off. I need to check this guy out.

"Yes, Boss," Becky says in a husky voice, which just pisses me the fuck off. She's trying to seduce me, trying to get my attention. It makes my skin crawl.

"Oh, and girls," I add, turning back around. "Ms Wang will be joining us as my personal assistant. She will also be joining me as my wife, so I would appreciate it if you showed her the respect she deserves," I declare, staring Becky right in the eyes. I want them all to know, I want the entire office to know, Eleanor is mine, she's my wife.

"Congratulations, Boss," Lisa beams at me.

"Yes, congratulations Boss," Stacy smiles at me. Becky on the other hand, just glares at me, before turning around back to her computer. Becky may have to go, but I'll let Eleanor make that choice, I have a feeling she won't last the week.

I walk back to the office, knocking on the door, announcing it's me. Eleanor opens the door with a gun cocked towards my head.

"Shit sorry, I'm a bit jumpy," she states, placing the safety back on and walking back over to my desk. The gun shaking in her hand as she sits in her seat.

"Princess, as much as that image made my dick so hard, it might bust out of my pants, like the Hulk does his clothes, I wanna know where you got the gun from?" I say, while rearranging my hard-on. Even scared, even in danger, she turns me on.

"Bottom draw," she says, pointing to the desk.

"How did you know I had one there?" I ask raising a brow.

"You've always kept a second gun in the bottom drawer of everything, safe to say the habit has kept up," she comments, rolling her eyes. She really docs know me to well.

"Nice to see you pay attention," I note, snorting a laugh.

"Yes well, I haven't touched one since I left Sydney, but it's definitely like riding a bike."

"To which I'm glad," I comment as I lean down, wrapping an arm around her neck, I pull her close, before using my other hand to take the gun from her hand.

Placing the gun on the desk, I grab the back of her neck and angle her to face me, placing small delicate kisses on her lips, showing her I'm here, that I'll protect her and not let anything happen to her.

"Are you okay, Princess?" I ask into her mouth.

"Yes, I am now," she says, melting into my body.

Chapter 20

Eleanor Wang

It's been over a week now since I saw who I've come to know as Tony Venchetti. A man under the employ of Matteo, who has gone underground since he'd locked eyes with me in the office. I've been in and out of the main office with Matteo every day since, and nothing else has happened, but there is always a calm before a storm. And right now, I feel like I'm sitting in it.

Enzo also hasn't been back in for any more impromptu chats, it's both a relief and a concern. Matteo has a four seats meeting coming up in two weeks, which will be held here in Sydney. They like to hold meetings every 3 months, alternating between the city's. Sydney always gets two, but they like to break it up between them. Thankfully, the fact that it's here in Sydney this time means Matteo won't be leaving me behind, the thought of him leaving terrifies me.

Since seeing Tony, I've found myself completely dependent on him, a place mentally, I just don't like being in. I've always been independent, always taken care of myself and Niko. But now I'm relying on him for every-thing, and it's making me crazy.

I feel like I was a lot safer in London, than I am being in the city I grew up in, it's a strange realisation. Sydney should feel like home, but it doesn't. It feels dangerous, like there are threats around every corner.

I still locked my door at night in London, but now I'm double and triple checking the locks. Knowing full well we're guarded at all hours of the day and night. Since telling Matteo how I feel, the guards have doubled. I now see them walking the border of the house, and out the back beyond the fence line. They're everywhere.

You would think it would help calm my nerves, but it's doing the damn opposite. It's like I can actually see the danger now, clearly. I know it's a mind-over-matter issue, but still. The fear is real.

Niko finally has a teacher who comes over daily. She had been a teacher at the Catholic school Matteo attended as a child. Her husband works for the Ricci's, so she is well ingrained into the Mafia world and understands how it works. She is down on the payroll as a cleaner, just in case anyone ever comes across her and asks questions. So, we can keep Niko well and truly away from the limelight, safe and hidden away from the world, making sure no-one knows he exists, for now.

Niko hates her. She's old-school and teaches with an iron fist; a real take-no-shit attitude. I on the other hand love her. If she was allowed, I'm sure she would use the old school cane too. Yvonne was way too soft on Niko back in London, allowing him to get away with a lot. I didn't mind so much as we lived a different life back then, but now that we're back and Niko is learning all about what it takes to be a Mafia Leader's son, I feel like a much harder approach is needed.

If I had my way, Niko wouldn't be involved in this world at all. But every day it looks more and more like I won't get a say in it. He's Matteo's son, a Ricci, and that means he's destined for this life, whether I like it or not. I just wanna delay it as much as possible.

Angel and Spike have been working hard trying to pull up as much information as they can from 10 years ago, while I've been doing the paperwork. Matteo isn't a paper-work man, at all. He had a lady who'd come in every three months to sort it all out for him, but as I dig deeper and deeper into the mess, I'm finding it's actually more of a mess than I'd thought; There might even be a tax audit in the future with the mess I'm discovering.

At the moment, I'm just working on arranging the paperwork into corresponding years. Turns out there is 10 years' worth. I swear the number 10 is out to haunt me, 10 years since I'd left, 10 years of paperwork, 10 years of memories and even the paperwork that was done for him is not organised the way I like.

I had to place an order with Officeworks to have a million boxes and filing cabinets delivered. Thankfully, Matteo had one of the guards put the cabinets together for me, before moving them into the home office. I've got no patience for building furniture. I mean once upon a time that shit was delivered whole, built nice and sturdy, but now it's all delivered in a flat cardboard box, with a million screws and instructions that might as well be in Swedish for all the sense they make to me.

Fuck that shit.

"Hungry, Princess?" Matteo asks, leaning against the office door frame. Yep, he has set up a makeshift office on the dining table. He'd taken one look at the mess of papers thrown all around the office and ran away with his tail between his legs. No problem, the next time I need a breather from him, I'll just bring up the paperwork. I know that'll send him running.

I look up at him from my spot on the floor. He looks so good standing there, so strong and so completely in control. "Yes actually, I am. Please tell me it's late enough that I can have pasta from Fratellis?" I ask, hopeful, right as my stomach starts rumbling. I've been working through paperwork for hours.

"Sorry, Princess, it's only 3 pm. It doesn't open for another two hours. Wanna hold on till then or want me to cook something?" he asks.

"Cook? For me?" I look up confused. "You have time to cook still?"

"If you keep frowning at me, you're gonna end up with wrinkles," he jibes back, a shit eating grin consuming his face.

"Matteo, they created Botox for a reason you know," I reveal, looking back down at the paperwork on the floor.

"Didn't think you were into that stuff Princess." Matteo laughs at me.

"If you think there isn't Botox in my face and filler in my lips Matteo, then maybe you don't remember how I actually looked before," I quip, raising my eyebrows at him. "Come to think of it, I'm due for more..." I mentally add a sticky note to my brain to find someone in the area. Aging isn't something I like to do.

Shaking his head at me Matteo asks, "Anyway Princess, as I said, do you want to wait or do you want me to cook."

Taking a gamble, I say, "You can cook, but I want pasta please. Something super rich and full of goodness," I smile up at him. The thought of him cooking for me makes my heart flutter.

"On it," he says as he heading over into the kitchen.

I could get used to this. Cooking isn't something I enjoy at all, in fact, I suck at it. So he can take that one if he wants.

"Can you feed Niko too, please," I yell at his retreating back.

"I fed him two hours ago, Princess and his room is filled to the brim with snacks to tide him over till dinner time."

"Thank you!" I shout, impressed. Sharing this parenting load is turning out to be fun, everything I've always wanted.

"I can feed my own son you know, but you're welcome," he states and I just laugh, thankful for his presence once again.

30 minutes later, the most delicious smell wafts into the room. I look up sniffing the air, like a sniffer dog at the airport. The aroma is intoxicating, rich, mouth-watering.

"Ohhhhhhhh, sweet baby Jesus, what is that smell?" I ask, looking up to see Matteo standing in the doorway holding a bowl, looking so domestic just standing there.

"Tagliatelle al Giardino," Matteo states, like it was

baked beans on toast, like it's nothing special and he hasn't just make me something incredible.

"Gimme, gimme!" I say, holding my hands out. Matteo looks down at the floor and says, "I'm actually not sure how I'm meant to walk this over to you?"

Looking at the floor I realise it's littered with papers, there's a path through, but it's barely visible.

"Oh um, just walk over that file there. It's mainly receipts and stuff that might not be claimable anyway," I say, pointing to the left of the room.

I watch as Matteo tiptoe's through the paperwork like it's a maze of laser beams, and I'm reminded of something.

"Hey, remember when I asked if you would teach me Ninja skills? When are you going to teach me to be sneaky and stealthy like you over there, Mr Prima Ballerina?" I say, pointing to his tiptoeing, teasing him, enjoying this moment with him.

He just smiles at me, handing me my bowl, he kisses my head and twirls with his fucking arms in the air. The gesture is so unexpected, so playful and so completely not what I'd expect from the scary mafia boss.

"When did you wanna start learning, Princess?" he asks, tiptoeing back out of the mountains of paperwork I have piled up like the twelve apostles.

Honestly, the skills of this man astound me. He can be so tender, so playful, so completely different from what the world sees.

"Whenever you're ready, but not like next year, I mean now, when you're ready."

"As precise as ever," he says. "I can kick you outta bed an hour earlier to train, if you'd like. Otherwise, we can use the gym before bed," he says. "Maybe Niko could join us? Kid walks around like he has cement boots on," he grumbles.

"Gym?" I must have a look of confusion on my face, cause Matteo starts to laugh at me.

"Yes Princess, the gym. We have one. It's attached to the garage."

"Since when?" I reply, puzzled. I thought I'd opened every single door in this house by now, realising I've never actually been into the garage. This house really is enormous.

"Eat up, I'll come get you in a couple of hours," he says, continuing to laugh at me as he walks away.

Honestly, this house is so damn deceiving. I make a mental note to get Matteo to walk me through the entire place, so I don't leave any stone unturned. I hate mysteries, especially where I live.

Twirling my fork through the pasta Matteo's just brought me, I remember the first time he'd cooked it for me. The memory is so vivid, so clear. Almost, like it was yesterday instead of 12 years ago.

I was living in a small apartment next to Foley Park. Matteo had been knocking on my door every single night, for two weeks at that point. It was always super late when he turned up, but this time it was only 5 in the afternoon and he was laden down with shopping bags. He looked so out of place in my tiny apartment in his expensive suit and dangerous aura.

"You're earlier than usual?" I stated, confused by his early arrival.

"I wanted to cook for you tonight," Matteo said, like he

was telling me about the weather, like it was the most natural thing in the world.

"Cook for me?"

"Yes Princess, that's what boyfriends do. They cook dinner for their girlfriends," he laughed.

"Boyfriend now? Matteo this is going a bit quick don't you think?" I frowned. "I hardly know you."

"Princess, I told you two weeks ago, you are mine. So yes, I'm your boyfriend and you my girlfriend. I'll happily marry you tomorrow if that's what it takes for you to realise that you belong to me," he said walking down the hall to my kitchen. "Come and show me where you keep everything."

I stopped and took a deep breath. Fuck me this man was hot. I wasn't used to men this hot or put together. I was only eighteen and had only been with boys by this stage. Not men. Not like this. Nothing compared to Matteo, he seemed to ooze masculinity and sex. I didn't know what to do with it all. Let alone how to deal with it knocking on my doorstep every day. Brittney, my best friend, had told me to run a mile. But how do you run from a man who wants you, looks like a God, and tells you that you belong to him? You don't. You simply stand there and allow yourself to be swept along for the ride, like sand on the beach.

I knew what was happening wasn't normal. You didn't just allow strangers to enter your apartment, declare their ownership of you and reply with a simple thank you. But I did. I was a spider caught within Matteo's web and I wanted him to eat me. I'd wanted to be consumed by him.

That night, he'd made me Tagliatelle al Giardino. A

pasta dish with eggplant, tomato, zucchini and capsicum. It was the best thing I'd ever eaten, and Matteo had made it all from scratch; Excluding the pasta. But he'd claimed it was freshly handmade by a chef in a restaurant his family owned. Which I'd come to realise was Fratelli's. I mean, of course it was; Everything in his world was connected.

That was also the first night he'd stayed with me in the apartment. Every other night he'd just stopped in, he'd always climb into bed behind me and cuddle me till I'd fall asleep; Leaving me to wake up alone. But this night, it was the night he'd first kissed me. It was the night everything changed.

After he'd cooked for me, we sat down to eat. I'd decided it was time for some questions, I'd needed to understand what was happening between us.

"Matteo, why do you keep turning up on my doorstep?" I asked, my heart pounding in my chest.

"I thought I made that part pretty clear, Princess," he said, raising an eyebrow at me. "You're mine. It can't be any simpler than that."

"But why? And how? I mean, I met you in a tattoo shop, then bam, you turn up here every single day since?" I was confused and I was falling for him.

"Love at first sight," he said, raising one shoulder as he reached for his glass of wine with his other hand, like it was that simple, like love at first sight was real and explained everything.

"But I don't believe in love at first sight," I reply.

"That's okay, Princess, I do." He was so confident, so sure, so completely certain about it.

"You have a very twisted way of looking at things Matteo." I said, shaking my head.

"That might be true, but when you grow up in my world, you have to think and act differently compared to everyone else. You're younger than me and have not experienced half of what I have, so believe me when I tell you this." Matteo stood from his seat and walked over to stand next to my chair. His presence was overwhelming, his energy intoxicating. "The second my eyes met yours in that shop, my heart actually skipped a fucking beat. My stomach felt like I was going to vomit, and my hands were instantly clammy." He slowly pulled my seat away from the table, grabbing my hand and pulled me up to stand in front of him. "I've killed men before, and I've had a gun held to my head, yet not once have I ever felt scared. Until that moment. What if I'd died and never got a chance to talk to you? What if someone else got to you, before I could, and I'd never gotten the chance to kiss you?" he said as he lowered his lips to mine.

And he was right. I'd been scared of the same reasons he was. What if I'd never gotten a chance to taste this man? It might all end in flames, but it would've been worth it in the end.

His kiss was soft, so soft it was like his lips were ghosting over mine. I'd wanted more. I'd leaned in, deepening the kiss, pushing my tongue past his lips, and asked for entrance. I needed to see what he tasted like, needed to know if this was real.

"You're it for me, Eleanor," he smiled into our kiss. "You have me hook, line and sinker. There will never be *another. There will only ever be you," he'd said, before placing his hand on the back of my head and pulling me in.*

He was right. I had felt the connection, I just didn't want to believe it. But that kiss sealed my fate with his, like an invisible rope had intertwined and tied us together. I'd never ever wanted to lose it, but I was also so scared of whatever it was. That night Matteo held me until I'd fallen asleep, and when I'd woken, he was still right there, with his arms wrapped around me tightly, like he was afraid I would disappear, like he was afraid to let me go.

Matteo's voice jolts me from my memories, "You okay there, Princess?" He asks. I have no idea how much time has passed since he'd left me with the food. I've been lost in the past, lost in the beginning of us, lost in every bite of the pasta.

Looking up, I see a glint in his eye, like he knew cooking me that dish would remind me of our first kiss, like he planned it, wanting me to remember.

"I bet if I walked over there and kissed you, you would taste the same as you did 12 years ago," he smiles, his tone soft, tender and full of love.

"I think you would be right," I admit, blushing.

"Nice to see I still bring that colour to your cheeks," he smirks, "But it's almost time for the gym," he states as he walks away.

"Okay, let me get changed," I say, standing with the empty bowl in hand. I tip-toe through the paperwork and close the door behind me.

Chapter 21

Matteo Ricci

So, it turns out that teaching Eleanor and Niko to be stealthy is an impossible task. Niko has the heaviest footfalls known to man. I am going to have to get Angel and Spike to give him lessons every single day. No kid of mine is gonna sound like a mini elephant. Eleanor on the other hand is able to keep her feet quiet, but her breathing is like a drunk man snoring. How I've never noticed how loud she breathes, I'll never know. And teaching her to slow down and breathe softly isn't going to happen. Every time she tried, she has a mini panic attack. Safe to say she won't be any good at yoga or meditating. But I will continue to try to teach her, even though I would rather go for a round of root canals. Thinking about it, maybe some breath play in the bedroom will help her control her breathing? The thought makes my dick twitch.

I watch Eleanor move through the gym with such concentration on her face, she's trying so hard, pushing herself. She's doing it for me, and that kills me. She's so fucking beautiful when she's focused.

"Boss..." Spike says close to my ear.

I jump 6 feet into the air, quickly reaching for the gun in the back of my pants as my heart is races in my chest, my adrenaline spiking. Spike is a sneaky bastard. "Fucker," I spit out.

"Sorry, boss, you were too busy watching the two dipshits being elephants," Spike giggles.

"You're not fucking wrong there," I grimace. I was completely distracted by Eleanor, the way her body moves, the way she concentrates, the fact that she's here and she's mine.

"Want me and Angel to take over the kids' training?" Spike questions, pointing to where Niko is trying to stick to the shadows and all I can do is laugh. The kid is hopeless, he's loud, clumsy and kind of perfect.

"I was just thinking that," I reply with a sigh, turning to face Spike, "What's up?" I ask, already knowing something is wrong; Spike wouldn't interrupt me unless it was important.

"There has been some chatter about Tony. I was gonna head out and see what I could find out." Spike's voice is serious.

"Take the two dipshits manning the gate with you. It's changeover time, they can pull some overtime," I smile, knowing full well they have just done a 16-hour shift, but they'd pissed me off two days ago.

"What did they do wrong?" Spike snickers.

"Late for work two days ago," I state, raising my eyebrows. Punctuality is everything in this business, everything.

"Fucking dickheads," Spike says, shaking his head as he walks off towards the front door.

"Lemme know what you find, as you find it," I request, turning back around to watch the dipshits in front of me. I need more information.

"Sure thing, boss," Spike whispers into my ear, making me jump another 6 feet into the air. "Fucking, fuck! You're a cocksucker!" I growl at him, knowing he's doing it on purpose.

"Just keeping you on your toes, boss," Spike belly laughs and I watch to make sure he actually leave the room this time. The fucker.

I watch Eleanor and Niko finish up their training. They're both sweating, both exhausted, both absolutely perfect.

"Alright you two, that's enough for today. Let's go cook some dinner," I sigh, wondering if maybe I should go, have a shower and change my boxers. And now I'm thinking about Eleanor in the shower, about her wet skin and her under me. Gods this women can get me hard with just a single thought.

"What's for dinner, ol man?" Niko chimes.

"Nope, ol man doesn't work either," I sigh. "What's wrong with plain old dad?" I grumble, I like the sound of that. Just Dad. It means something.

"Really? I like ol man," Niko says, smiling at me.

"Why do I feel like the only reason you like it, is because I don't?" I ask, squinting my eyes at him. This little fucker thinks I don't know how he works, I was young and full of mischief once too. I secretly love it, though. But I'll never tell him that. I don't want to raise Niko like I was raised, but I'm not going to coddle him like Eleanor has either. The kid is too soft for this world, and I need to change that, but I also don't want to damage the kid either. I think delegating his teachings between myself, Angel and Spike will be best. Eleanor can keep the coddling for herself, she's good at it.

"What for dinner?" Niko asks, totally off topic. "I'm so hungry, I could eat an elephant," he says.

"Yeah, I'm sure we can arrange that with those feet of yours," I mumble.

"What?" Niko asks loudly.

"Nothing kid, come on let's get dinner started. I'm thinking chicken and mushroom risotto," I say as I throw an arm around Niko's shoulders. He feels so small under my arm, so young and so vulnerable.

"Eww, mushrooms!" Niko says with disgust.

"Hang on, you sure you're my kid? Hates Mushrooms?" I note, frowning over my shoulder at Eleanor. I'm teasing him, bonding with him, trying to be his father.

"Sorry Matteo, he hates them," she offers, raising a shoulder in half shrug.

"Well then, chicken and spinach risotto," I offer, looking at Niko with narrowed eyes. Kids these days, if I'd told my mamma I didn't like something, she would feed it to me every day of the week and then announce, "See, you do like it, you ate it! And that would be that." I'm secretly thinking of doing the same now, but I know Eleanor won't let me, Eleanor is too soft.

"Matteo, I see that glint in your eye," Eleanor whispers into my ear. She knows me, knows exactly what I'm thinking. "He hates mushrooms and celery. That's it, no need to feed it to him for a week."

I turn, seeing her walking off towards the dining room. I don't remember telling her that my mamma did that, but she knows, she's always known me. Even after 10 years, after all this time, she still knows me.

Moments later, she returns with two glasses of whiskey in hand as I'm just pulling the freezer door open to find the spinach. "Here," I say, handing her the ice tray.

"Thanks," she says as she takes it from me.

"I hope one of them is mine," I comment, placing the ingredients down on the bench, and reaching for the closest glass. I definitely need the whiskey.

"Yep," she replies, popping the 'p'. She hands me the empty ice tray and walks back out.

"I'm starting to feel like the bitch in this relationship," I grumble, jokingly, but it is sort of true.

"Well, one of us has to be," I hear thrown my way from what sounds like the stairs to our room.

"Dinner is in 30 minutes. Will I need to wake you up?" I yell after her.

"Nope, I'm showering," I hear back, and now I'm back to thinking of her naked in the shower… Fuck.

"Niko go shower too. That way dinner will be ready for both of you when you get out," I tell him, looking in his direction.

"On it, Da," he says, he called me Da.

"Da is Irish Niko…" I mumble.

"I know, felt strange to say it too." Niko says, pulling a face, before taking off downstairs to shower and get ready for dinner.

I don't mind this 'dad' gig. In fact, I love it. I love being his father, I love being Eleanor's partner.

I start preparing the risotto, placing rice into the pan with butter and onions. The smell is incredible. The process is meditative as my hands move through the motions automatically. I've made this a thousand times, but tonight feels different. Tonight, I'm cooking for my family.

~

As per usual both Eleanor and Niko have conveniently disappeared when it comes time to do the dishes. Releasing a breath, I realise that overnight I've pretty much become a mobster version of a housewife. What the fuck? And why don't I seem to care? This is some weird shit. Eleanor and her pussy have weakened the crap out of me, again. Just as I am internally berating myself on dishes and mobster bitches, my phone starts to vibrate in my pocket, pulling my attention back to the now.

"Spike…" I grunt into the phone.

"Boss, I got him," Spike's voice comes through the line, causing my entire body to go rigid.

"Office or warehouse?" I ask, already knowing the answer.

"Warehouse, boss."

"On my way," I say, leaving the dishes to clean themselves. This is it. this is the moment I find out exactly what Tony did to my woman.

I quickly race upstairs, changing into an all-black suit. It's a warm night and I don't feel like sweating, so I sling the jacket over my arm, ensuring I look the part.

Eleanor is in the library reading as I walked out of the room, fully dressed and ready to go. She looks up at me, like she's only just noticed I am even upstairs. Her eyes widening slightly as she takes in my appearance, she knows, she always knows.

"Good book?" I ask, trying to keep my voice casual in an attempt to hide what's about to happen.

Blushing from top to bottom she mumbles, "Um yes, it is, thank you." She's embarrassed. Ohh, I wonder what she is reading…

"Is my Princess reading a dirty book?" I tease, seeing the heat rising in her cheeks as she squirms in her seat.

"It's the only kind I read," she says, while clearing her throat and tugging on the collar of her t-shirt.

"Well, I hate to take you away from it, but I gotta deal with an issue. So, you've gotta go get dressed. Bring the book with you, I have a feeling you might need the distraction," I grimace. I can't leave her behind. As much as I want to, I can't, my brain simply won't allow me to be without her while the 3 men who hurt her still exist.

Raising her brows, she hands me the book. "Don't lose my page." She kisses me on the cheek and goes into our room to get dressed.

10 minutes later she's dressed in black slacks and a black v neck blouse, her hair is tied in a high ponytail, and with no makeup. She could wear a fucking potato sack and she would still be stunning.

I, however, am not ready to go. I decided to read the page she was reading, and let's just say if I did half of what the book describes, she would throat punch me. The thought makes me smile.

"Do women really like this sort of stuff? I mean she has 3 men, permanently, and they are all okay with it!" I say, frowning at her before turning the page. I'm genuinely confused and jealous of fictional men right now.

"Hey, I said don't lose my page," she says, snatching the book back. She flicks the pages to find where she was up to.

"If you didn't want me to read it, you would have used a bookmark," I say, with a smirk.

"Come on, I thought we had somewhere to be," she says as she walks up to me and palms my dick through my pants. "Nice to see someone else was enjoying the book," she laughs, walking down the stairs. I mean she isn't wrong, but now I'm wondering if she wants 3 men, if I'm not enough…

Rearranging myself, I do the only thing I know how, I follow her. Because I'll always follow her.

"Seriously, we need to talk about that book," I state, walking behind Eleanor towards the front door. When she gets to the door, she turns to face me.

"Matteo, why are you dressed and ready to leave the house at 7 pm?" That question sobers my thoughts.

"Right, okay, I'll tell you in the car," I say, rubbing the back of my neck.

"Is Angel here?" she asks looking around.

"Yes, he is downstairs with Niko doing tech stuff. He will put the kid to bed for us." I say, I'd already texted Angel, telling him to watch Niko, when I was reading her lady porn.

"Okay good, let's go then," Eleanor says, swinging her arms towards the door.

"Fuck okay yes, I'm getting distracted." Shit where is my mind at the moment?!

I lead us out to the car, getting her situated into the passenger seat before I jump into the driver's seat. I'm not sure how to start the conversation that needs to be had before we get to the warehouse. Taking a deep breath, I begin, "Okay Princess, we need to talk before we get there," I say, knowing full well this whole conversation isn't going to go well.

"Hit me with it, Matteo," she says, keeping her eyes on the road.

"I need you to follow each and every order I give you tonight. No questions, just do as you're told," I say, gripping the steering wheel tighter.

"Please," I add, cause I know how much she hates me ordering her around when it comes to things like this. The woman was born a fucking brat.

"Okay" is all she says. Just like that.

"Okay?" What a way to leave a man speechless, I'd expected a fight.

"Okay," she repeats.

"Right well, I'm not joking about this," I add, taking a deep breath through gritted teeth. "Spike has Tony," I mutter, barely audible. The words hang in the air between us, like a bomb waiting to explode.

"I gathered," she replies, looking out the front window of the car as we drive.

"Are you going to be okay watching us question him?" I ask. I didn't want to bring her, but I'm also never leaving her side again. Catch 22, I can't protect her if she's not with me. I can't keep her safe if she's not by my side.

"As long as you kill him when you're done, I don't mind," she states dryly, and it in that moment I realise how badly these men broke something in her. 10 years ago she wouldn't have said that, but now, now she has hardened, maybe even wants the revenge.

"Mobster life is rubbing off on you nicely, Princess," I smile.

"Let's hope not," she says.

"Let's," I agree.

But we both know it's too late.

She's already one of us.

Chapter 22

Eleanor Wang

Arriving at the warehouse, I feel my heart rate picking up, I don't want to be here, I don't want to see him, but I also know Matteo will never leave me alone again and I don't think Angel or Spike will ever be trusted with me either, until these men are gone.

As much as I hate it, I can understand why, I had thought the sentiment would extend to Niko but he seems to trust the others with him and granted the world doesn't know about him, but the thought still makes me nervous about what could happen if someone finds out about my son.

"Come on, Princess," Matteo says, opening my door for me. I hadn't even noticed he'd gotten out. Shit, I need to get my head in the game, I'm about to walk into a torture chamber and I need to be strong about it. I had known deep down in my soul that the second I had told Matteo about what had happened, he would go hunting. I knew he wouldn't stop till they were gone from this world, and I'm ok with it. I'm ok with him removing the things that scare me the most.

Matteo holds out his hand for me, like we're at a gala and I'm his plus one, only this time we're walking into a warehouse to torture a man into giving up the names of the others who raped me. I don't really want to know their names, I just want to know why, why me of all people, I mean clearly it was a play against Matteo, but he can't see a reason for it to have happened because they won the war and hurting me didn't affect the outcome, so what was the point of it all.

My steps falter a little as we walk, Matteo notices immediately and wraps his arm around my waist to help steady me before he places a kiss on my temple and tells me, "You're safe with me Princess," but I'm not sure I believe that right now, because we're walking into a room designed for torture.

"Can't I just stay in the car?" I ask, hoping for some kind of reprieve from what's about to happen.

"No, I don't trust anyone here enough with your safety, other than me. I'm sorry Princess, but you will be sitting in the room with me," he says, his tone firm but not too firm, he's scared and I understand why. I'm his, he needs to know I'm safe and he can't do that if I'm not in his line of sight.

The warehouse stinks like dead rats and chlorine, the smell instantly making my guts turn, I look at Matteo, asking him if the smell makes him want to vomit too.

"It used to, but I've gotten used to it now," he tells me, I can't help but to frown at him, because how is that even possible.

"Gotten used to it?" I ask him, genuinely confused about how anyone could get used to this smell.

"Dad bought this warehouse back in the 80s, I've been here a lot over the years, and unfortunately I'm used to it now," he explains and I shake my head, I don't think any number of years would get me used to this smell, I hold a hand up to my face in an attempt to shield it from the stench.

"Just breathe through your mouth," he suggests and I remove my hand to try it, yes it does make it a bit better, by a bit I mean like a very fucking small amount, but at least it's something. I want to walk in there with my head held high, smiling at one of the men who ruined my life, I want him to see me smiling and know that he didn't break me, because steel is forged in flame or so they say.

"Ready, Princess?" Matteo asks me, squeezing my side with his hand. I nod because I'm as ready as I'll ever be for this.

"As I'll ever be," I tell him.

"Remember what I said in the car?" he asks me with a stern voice, so different from the sweet voice he'd used earlier and I just nod because we both know, I'm either gonna listen or do the opposite, it depends on the factors at the time. After all, I'm not exactly known for my obedience.

Matteo turns the handle and we walk into what can only be described as a torture chamber, well more like a torture room really, the most concerning part of the room isn't the equipment hanging on the walls or the blow torch on the table. Nope, it's the fact that the room is sloped towards the middle, where a metal grate sits. Allowing gravity to do its job, so all the fluids can drain away; out of everything in here, that's what makes my knees go weak because it means this room has been used for the same purpose, many times before.

I feel Matteo's hand on my waist tighten as I start to sink towards the floor, my knees deciding they're 80 years old suddenly and no longer know how to work. Spike turns around, sees me struggling, quickly grabs me a chair and places it under my butt before I can end up on the ground.

"Thanks," I say to Spike, grateful for the support.

"She shouldn't be in here boss," Spike states, shooting a vicious look towards Matteo and I can see the concern in his eyes.

"She's okay, just give her a minute to compose herself," Matteo tells him. I appreciate that he's not dismissing my fear, but he's also not coddling me either.

Looking up I see a man hanging from the roof by chains, his toes barely touching the floor and his face is covered in blood, but I can still see who it is and my breath catches in my throat.

Tony.

One of the men who have haunted my nightmares for 10 years, whose name I'd never known, but had allowed to see me weak and fuck that, because I'm not going to let him see me like that again. No, I'm going to be strong, I'm going to face this fucker head on.

"Tony, nice to see you've joined us," Matteo laughs, walking towards him while rolling up the sleeves of his shirt. I can see a distinct bulge in his back pocket, a spew bag I assume and the thought of it helps to ground me; because that's right, it's lovely to know that a man like

Matteo, a big scary Mafia boss, has such a weak stomach that he can vomit on command. One would say it's humbling and kinda cute too, if I'm being honest about it. Focusing on his spew bag helps to ground me.

"I don't know what you want from me," Tony states, vitriol dripping from his words.

"Well, let's start with the names of the other two who'd accompanied you to Eleanor's apartment 10 years ago," Matteo says calmly. Gone is my Matteo, in his place is the Mafia leader and they are two really different people, one would say one is good, and one is bad; but I can't tell you, which is which because in this line of work, they're both necessary.

"I don't know what you're talking about," Tony replies and even I can hear the lie in his voice.

"Well let me refresh your memory, 10 years ago you forced your way into Eleanor's apartment, raped her along with two other men, then left her with a note to disappear," Matteo says calmly, while crossing his arms as he leans against the metal table, like he's discussing the weather and not about to torture someone.

"I'm going to let your first answer slide and tell you how this is going to go," Matteo states, grabbing the blow torch off the table and fiddling with the knob on the side, the sound of it is ominous, "I'm going to ask some questions and you're going to answer them, every wrong answer you give me will result in Spike cutting off a toe or finger and I'll burn the spot to stop the bleeding, got it?"

"But I don't know what you're talking about!" Tony yells, his voice desperate now.

"Please don't interrupt me, Tony, I haven't finished

talking," Matteo says, the flame igniting with a woosh as he lights the blow torch, "You will not be leaving here alive, tonight. I am going to kill you, but whether you leave in 50 pieces or in 2, is up to you," he shrugs, like he's not just signing this man's death warrant.

"So I'll ask you again, what are the other cunt's names?"

"No."

"No, what?" Matteo asks, raising his brow.

"I'm not going to talk, you can torture me, but I'll die with my secrets," Tony says, his defiance is his downfall.

With that Matteo lashes out, punching him in the gut and the sound is sickening, "Oh, you think so. I've never failed to get the information I've needed before," he says, grabbing Tonys foot and holding it still as Spike cuts off all the toes on his right foot with ease, as Matteo grabs the blow torch and burns the stumps to stop the bleeding, just as he said he would. I was okay with the visual, but what I didn't expect is the smell, because it smells like someone is cooking pork and that's now a meat I'll never eat again.

I close my eyes, trying to concentrate on breathing through my mouth, but the smell is coming through on my taste buds, making my mouth water and it's not the hungry kind. It's the I'm about to vomit kind. A finger runs down my face, before a soft voice murmurs in my ear and a plastic bag is placed in my hand, "It's okay, Princess, I brought extra bags tonight," Matteo whispers to me, before he straightens up and walks back over to Tony. I hadn't even heard him approach me to start with because he moves like a ghost.

I look down at the bag, wondering if I should use it to

hyperventilate or to vomit, because my body hasn't caught up with my mind just yet. I decide to just open the bag and wait for the vomit as I look back up to find Tony has now lost his toes from his other foot and the fingers on his right-hand. Watching this unfold is like watching the human centipede, where you're so fucking disgusted that you wanna vomit, but find yourself still looking at the screen, like it will just detonate and turn off on its own, that deer in headlights feeling. At that thought, a fresh wave of pork wafts my way and the vomit finally appears.

Don't let anyone fool you into thinking risotto is easy to vomit up, because it's not, little pieces of rice get stuck in every little pocket inside your mouth and nose, resulting in a hell of a lot of spitting to clean it out. There is nothing elegant about vomiting, there is also nothing elegant about sitting on a metal chair in a murder room because that is essentially what I am doing. Like a spectator at a tennis match, I watch Matteo asking questions, while Spike cuts off body parts and the amount of glee in Spike's eyes while he works, has me wondering if I should allow Niko around him at all, because clearly Spike hides his psychopathic tendencies well; I'd always known he was crazy, I just didn't realise he was completely insane, because you'd have to be insane to find the fun in this.

The men carry on like this for well over two hours. The smell of cooking flesh, shit and piss permeating the air, I haven't vomited again but I've held onto the bag like a lifeline, it's my anchor to sanity and I'm pretty sure this guy isn't going to last much longer. Matteo has the last two names he needs, but not the name for the guy who sent them and that's the information Tony won't part with, that's the one secret he's protecting.

For the first time in two hours, I decide to speak up. "Matteo?" I say softly, my voice is small and broken, causing Matteo's head to whip around, the shock on his face evident, like he'd forgotten I've been sitting here for two hours and he walks over to me immediately.

"Fuck, Princess, I'm sorry," he says, wiping his hands on a rag and I can see the blood under his fingernails, "You want to go home, Spike can finish up here," he adds, holding out his hand to me.

"Yes, but I wanna shoot him first," I point to Tony, I want to take my power back, I want to end this myself.

"You sure about that, we don't have who sent him yet?" he asks me as he grabs his gun from his waistband and hands it to me, giving me the choice, giving me the power.

"He isn't going to give it , Matteo," I reply, raising the gun in the air one-handed. I aim it at Tonys head from across the room, Spike doesn't move, just casually stands next to Tony like this is nothing, my hands are steady and my resolve is firm.

I fire off two shots, one to the dick and one to the centre of his forehead, killing him instantly. It really is like riding a bike, the recoil is familiar, the weight of the gun is familiar and I hand the gun back to Matteo.

"Can we go home now please?" I plead, looking up into his smouldering blue eyes. I really need some sleep, I need to process what just happened and to feel human again.

"Of course, Princess," Matteo states, leading me out to the car. He opens the door for me to jump in and I watch as he unbuttons his shirt, shrugging it off his shoulders, using it to wipe his face and arms that are spattered with blood.

It's strange how even in this moment, my eyes drag along his body. He is corded with muscle and a six-pack to match, yet I've not ever seen this man work out once since I've been back and with the amount of carbs we eat, I know he has to be doing something to maintain that physique because it's not natural.

"Keep looking at me like that Princess, and I'll end up fucking you on the bonnet of this car," Matteo says as he climbs into his seat, his voice is rough, his eyes are dark and I can feel the heat rising in my cheeks.

"Who says I don't want that?" I reply, my pussy clenching at the thought because it clearly didn't get the memo that Matteo is covered in blood, or that I've just shot and killed one of my abusers, but then again maybe that's why, one out of 3 down, one less to haunt my nightmares. adding to the fact Matteo is currently covered in the blood of a man who'd hurt me, Call me sick, but this world has changed me. I'd lived through months of war with Matteo 10 years ago, maybe I've just become immune to some parts of it, especially after Matteo used to turn up on my doorstep, covered in someone else's blood, it didn't put me off then but I also never knew whose blood it was. This is the first time Matteo has let me in so deeply, not hiding anything from me and as grateful as I am, I'm wondering if it's his way of making sure I can never climb back out of the hole he is digging for us. Not that I had planned on it anyway, I just didn't think most Mafia wives, or wives-to-be in my case, were privy to so much information, I mean that Enzo fellow had been shocked I was allowed in the room when they were talking. Which reminds me of something I need to discuss with Matteo.

"Matteo?" I say, my mind shifting to business.

"Yes, Princess," he replies, as he starts the car and takes off down the road. The streetlights lighting up his tattoos in intervals, making them look lusciously lick-able and I can't help but admire him, even covered in blood.

"I've been thinking about the proposal that Enzo came to you with," I tell him, watching his jaw tighten.

"What part of it?" he growls, an edge to his voice that tells me he's not happy about where this is going.

"The trafficking women part," I say, I feel him tense beside me.

"It's never going to happen, Princess, I'll never allow him to do that in my city, you don't have to worry," he says, looking at me as he reaches a blood-stained hand over to grab my thigh. His touch is possessive, his declaration absolute.

"I was thinking we should allow it... to an extent," I say, watching him shift in his seat, "If we can control the narrative, we can control the women who are sold. We can protect them, instead of letting Enzo do it his way, which would destroy them," I explain, because I need him to understand my reasoning.

"Hang on..." he says holding up his hand in a stop sign, "You want to traffic innocent, underage women through Sydney?!" he says, I can hear the horror in his voice that matches the look of shock on his face .

"No, I mean if we hold auctions for women who agree to be sold, with contracts to select buyers, then we can control what happens to them," I say, looking at Matteo, trying to make him understand my vision, "I mean there are plenty of women out there who want a rich daddy to look after them, there are also others who want to escape poverty to have a better life than they already have and if we have buyers sign contracts that these women can't be harmed, unless that's a kink of theirs, God only knows these days, then we can both profit and control the situation without causing an issue," I continue, shrugging like I haven't just proposed a new business venture to a mafia boss.

"Like a mail-order bride, but with contracts and a get-out-of-jail-free card to go with it?" Matteo says thoughtfully, I can see he's considering it, he's seeing the merit in what I'm saying.

"I mean we could essentially make it a business on the books, we could legitimise it and protect the women, while still making money," I say, shrugging because the more I think about it, the more sense it makes. We could control what happens to these women. If it's not us doing it, then someone else will, and those women will not come out the other side as well as I'm proposing.

"I'll think about it," he says, his voice is calmer now, "but it does look like a good solution for the issue with Enzo, could be win-win," he adds, I know he's going to do it because he always does what I suggest, if it makes sense.

With that I snuggle back into my seat, perving on his beautiful body as the streetlights continue to light up his tattoos, leaving shadows where the dips and grooves are.

"I don't think I've ever seen a man as beautiful as you, Matteo..." I admit, I mean it, he really is the most beautiful man I've ever seen.

"Are you checkin' me out from over there, Mrs Ricci?" he asks me with a smirk and a teasing edge to his voice.

"I sure am, but it's not Mrs Ricci yet, you might own this city but even you have to wait the 6-week grace period to sign a marriage certificate," I laugh, teasing him, playing with him.

"Only 3 more weeks Princess, although I'm thinking of just having Angel marry us today and sending the paperwork in now. It won't be stamped for three weeks, but it will be sitting in the court office, waiting," he says, he's already planned it, already decided and I'm not surprised by this, because Matteo always gets what he wants.

"Of course Angel is a celebrant!" I laugh, because nothing about the 3 of them surprises me anymore, "Let me guess, he did an online course when he got the flights booked from London?" I ask, he nods at me.

"He did, that guy is full of surprises," I say, shaking my head, because these men are insane but in the best way possible, "But a bit presumptuous don't you think, what if I'd said no?" I ask him, raising a brow, testing him.

"You and I both know, that would have never happened!" Matteo laughs at me, he's right, I would never say no to him. I don't think I could ever leave him again, not now, I'm not strong enough to resist this man.

"I could have though," I protest weakly. Why does this fucker know me, better than I know myself, how can he read me like an open book, when I've spent 10 years hiding from him.

"Nope," Matteo says, popping the 'p'. He's so confident in his answer that I can't even bother arguing with him, he's right and we both know it.

I lean back in my seat, watching him drive, watching as the streetlights continue to dance across his skin, watching the man I love take me home. One out of three that haunt my nightmares is dead, there's only two more to go and then maybe, just maybe, I can finally feel safe, after 10 years of being scared.

Chapter 23

Matteo Ricci

Eleanor, being Eleanor, fell asleep in the car on the way home; I swear she could sleep through an apocalypse. She seemed completely fine after watching me slice and dice a man, then roast him like he was a Creme Brule. after the initial horror and vomiting, she seemed to grow some sea legs, doing even better than I had for her first kill. I had not only vomited, but had a mini panic attack, although I was a hell of a lot younger. The truth of the matter is she's okay and I am not, because how does one allow their soulmate to watch them torture a man. I knew I'd have separation anxiety after Eleanor revealed her secret for leaving but taking her with me, I fucked up and I wasn't thinking of the consequences to my actions at the time, but now I am, but I'm also not sure I would do it any differently next time. Originally the thought of leaving her in the house without me made the vomit rise in the back of my throat, so no, I wouldn't and won't be leaving her behind, not now and not in the future. This is a guilt I am going to have to bear for the rest of my days.

Scooping her out of the car when we get home, I carry her up and into bed, laying her down on top of the doona. We both need to shower before we actually get into bed because our clothes need to be burned, and all DNA evidence needs to be dealt with. I shoot a text message to Angel, requesting to have the car cleaned, before I turn on the shower and wake Eleanor up, which is received with a promptly mumbled "Fuck off" in my direction until she wakes properly. I help her undress, then walk her into the shower, which is followed by more grumbling because she can be so prickly when she's woken up.

"Come here, Princess," I say, pulling her back to my front and wrapping my arms around her. I grab the closest shower puff and load it up with the new shower gel Eleanor's replaced mine with. I get to work, washing her from head to toe, I even make sure to wash her gorgeous hair 3 times, making sure it is clean because I need to know that every trace of tonight is gone from her body.

"Baby, I know you mean well, but if you shove any more shampoo into my hair it's going to start squeaking, let me add some conditioner to it please," she states, taking over. While Eleanor fixes the bird's nest I've created, I set to making sure I'm DNA-free, ensuring the water running off me is no longer pink. I know some had been washed away while I was washing Eleanor, but that doesn't stop me from looking down to make sure there is no traces left.

"You okay there, Matteo?" Eleanor asks, lifting my chin with her hand, so my eyes meet hers. I can see the concern in her eyes.

"I shouldn't have taken you with me tonight," I tell her,

I mean it, I'm wracked with guilt about what I made her witness.

"Yes, you should have," she says, smiling at me. I can see it's not one of happiness, it's one of sadness. She can see the rainbow at the end but she definitely doesn't enjoy the ride to get to it, "I needed the closure. I know that if I hadn't pulled the trigger myself, it would never have stopped the nightmares," she explains, and I understand what she's saying ,but it doesn't make me feel any better about it.

"I just…fuck Princess, I just can't leave you at home without me, I know it's irrational, but it's true," I admit, watching the water swirling around my feet. I feel Eleanor run her hands through my hair as she starts to scrub, I realise she's washing my hair just like I'd washed hers, it's such a tender moment that I almost can't handle it.

"Lean back, let me rinse it out," she says and I do as I'm told, standing there while she continues to wash it another two times, the care she's taking with me is almost undoing me.

"Nice and squeaky!" she states cheekily, calming the beast within. I'd known the moment I'd met her, from the moment our eyes met, and after our first kiss, they say love at first sight doesn't exist, but I'm walking proof that it does. I don't believe that both people feel it happen, I believe one does while the other has to catch up, relationships are built on one person chasing the other, and for me and Eleanor it's always been me chasing her. She's my catalyst, the person who made me change course so damn quickly, I've got whiplash. I didn't want to fall in love at the age of 20, I was having fun being a player, but one look from her and I was done, it's something that even to this day, I will never be able to explain to anyone. It was like the moment our souls collided, the world finally started to make sense.

"Whatever our souls are made of, hers and mine are the same," I whisper into her ear, the quote sums us up perfectly, it's the most accurate description of what we are to each other.

"You knew it before I did," she says, sadness lacing her voice because she didn't feel it right away, like I had.

"Yes, I did, and that's ok, one of us always has to play catch up Princess," I remind her, sealing my lips over hers. The groan that leaves her mouth has my dick standing to attention, even after everything tonight, after the violence and the blood, I still want her with every fibre of my being.

Laughing at me she says "Okay, okay let's get out, gotta leave some water for the whales," and she walks out of the shower, wrapping a towel around her body and I'm graced with sight of her bending over as she does that hair towel wrap thing that all women seem to do with ease and I can't help myself.

"Keep bending over like that Princess, and you'll get a dick shoved up your ass again," I tell her and my voice rough with need.

"Who says that's not what I want?" she replies, her eyes darkening with desire. I know exactly what she wants, because I want it too.

"Game on, Princess," I growl. I lunge towards her, wrapping my arms around her from behind and lifting her up into the air, so her feet are completely off the ground as her back crushes into my chest. I walk us into the bedroom laying her down face first onto the mattress.

"Don't move," I growl into her ear, causing her to shiver at my tone. I unwrap the towel from her body and the one from her head, allowing the water to roll off her onto the doona. I run my hands up the back of her thighs until I reach the bottom of her ass cheeks and I bring my hand down on the fleshy mass with a loud thwacking noise, slowly turning the cheeks pink before I run my palms back over them, soothing the sting. I listen as Eleanor whimpers and moans through every slap, it's the most beautiful sound I've ever heard.

"I love the colour pink on you, Princess," I tell her, because she looks absolutely stunning with her ass flushed pink from my hand.

"Mmm," is the only reply I get, telling me she's lost in the sensations I'm giving her.

"You wet yet?" I ask, reaching between her cheeks and running my hand down to find her cunt. I dip a finger in, finding her wet but not wet enough for what I need, so I grab her hips and pull them higher into the air, smacking her ass again. I check her pussy every so often and after another 10 hits I see she is dripping onto her thighs, just the way I like it, loving the sight of her so desperate for me.

"Fuck princess, I need to lick that up," I say as I lean down, running my tongue up to grab every drop. I begin to suck on her pussy lips, she tastes so sweet and musky, it's addictive, I could spend hours between her legs if she'd let me.

Shoving two fingers straight into her drenched pussy, I

feel her clenching down on the invasion, I start rubbing her clit with my left hand, while pumping the fingers on my right hand into her, I lick her cunt, working my way up to her back hole, giving it the same attention I'd given her clit. I run my tongue around the sensitive bud, making her writhe beneath me.

"I'm gonna cum," Eleanor gasps out as an orgasm hits her, her pussy squeezes down on my fingers as I continue to finger her through it, until she starts begging me to stop, I love that she's so responsive to me.

"Stop, stop… I can't take anymore!" she cries out. I pull my fingers free of her cunt and circle the bud above, as I slowly push my fingers in, being gentle with her because I know she's sensitive after that orgasm.

"Oh Matteo," Eleanor moans, her voice so needy, making my dick harden more, if that is even possible.

"Let me stretch you wide, Princess," I pump my fingers in slowly scissoring them inside to stretch her for, preparing her for what's coming next.

I pull my fingers free, leaning over to open the drawer of my bedside cabinet, I pull out a bottle of lube and a vibrator; I've been waiting to use this with her.

"I bought us a present," I announce, smiling. I watch her eyes widening with anticipation. I open the lube bottle, letting some drop down onto her bud while I grab the vibrator and slowly push it inside her cunt, letting the tickle bit rest on her clit. I climb back up behind her, grabbing my hard dick, I push it inside her ass, causing her to gasp at the sensation.

"Oh, fuck Matteo, that's it," Eleanor moans loudly, as she begins pushing back against me.

"Keep pushing back on to me, Princess, I want to watch your ass swallow me whole," I instruct her, watching as she pushes back until she is flush with my balls. I wait, allowing her to adjust before I click the button on the dildo, I leave it on the first setting, so it's lightly vibrating inside her and on her clit, I feel her jump a little with the sudden vibrations.

"Oh my God, Matteo," her voice is breathless as she starts wriggling, "I feel so full," she moans, I feel her clenching around me.

Bringing my free hand down on her ass, I feel her pussy clench around the vibrator at the contact, I can't help but smirk at her response.

"Oh, you like that, Princess," I snicker, doing it again, loving how she reacts to me.

"Fuck Matteo, I'm gonna cum so quick," she moans, the desperation in her voice clear.

I slowly start to move my hips, pulling out of her a little bit, then pushing back, keeping my hold on the dildo, so it moves in sync with me as she makes the most beautiful sounds.

"Oh shit, don't stop, Fuck, Matteo," she cries out. I start to move faster, knowing I'm not going to last much longer either. I can feel the vibrator rubbing against my dick through the wall of her ass, making my dick as hard as steel. The vibrations from the handle touching my balls cause them to draw up, and the sensations are amazing. I don't want this to end, but I know it's gonna be over quickly because it feels way too good.

I start thrusting faster, grabbing her hips with my free hand, I slam her back onto me with every thrust as I feel the tingle starting to take over my legs. Her ass clamps down on me, becoming impossibly tight as her orgasm hits and she screams out, dragging me right there with her.

"Oh Matteo, fuck!" Her pussy clamps down so tightly on the vibrator, I struggle to pull it out, while her ass milks my cock, pulling every drop of my cum out, making me see stars.

It's possibly the best orgasm I've ever had, the thought of being able to do that to her every day has my dick twitching, trying to come back to life, she's absolutely insatiable and I love it.

"I guess we need another shower," Eleanor laughs, as she tries to catch her breath while I'm attempting to do the same.

Pulling out of her, I help her up, smacking her ass again because I can't help myself, "Honestly Princess, your pink ass is really my favourite thing to see," I tell her, watching as the blush creeps along her cheekbones, she walks into the bathroom backwards and I follow her, because I'm not done with her yet, not by a long shot.

Chapter 24

Eleanor Wang

I thought staying out of the Ricci's business was what I wanted for myself, not witnessing Matteo work or being a part of that side of the business. That's what I thought 12 years ago when I'd met him, and when I'd first gotten back here with him this time. But now, after seeing him avenge me, after seeing how hard he works daily, I don't think I would have ever been happy just sitting on the sidelines, watching him build an empire from the shadows.

I also thought it would scare me to know just how insane he can really be, but the truth is, he isn't insane at all, he just has two faces; One for work, and one for home. But when it comes to me, no matter what face he has on, he is always impossibly soft with me and it's the most beautiful thing I've ever experienced, because I've never felt safer in my entire life.

Yes, he can kill someone without any remorse, but didn't I just do the same? I shot a guy and I've just slept better than I have in 10 years and the nightmares didn't come. For the first time, in a long time, I've woken up feeling like maybe, just maybe, I can finally breathe. Maybe I'm just as insane as he is. Maybe, this is what he'd seen in me 12 years ago, something I didn't realise is inside me, but he did, Maybe, I've been hiding something dark and broken that matches his own darkness.

"Princess?" Matteo speaks, clicking his fingers in front of my face to snap me out of my thoughts, I blink up at him, realising I've been lost in my own head again, lost in memories, possibilities and what-ifs.

"Shit sorry, what's up?" I ask looking up at Matteo. He's standing next to me and I can see the concern etched across his beautiful face.

"I called out to you three times, Eleanor. You sure you're okay?" Matteo frowns down at me. He's asked me this question every day for 4 days now. I think he is worried I resent him now, or am possibly scared of him since I've seen him work, when in fact it's the opposite. I respect him more than I've ever respected anyone and I feel safe with him in a way I've never thought I would feel safe again.

Maybe I should have stayed 10 years ago. I mean, there's not a lot I can change now, but maybe I would have been safe. But then I remember the men who attacked me were in his employ,, so no, I wouldn't have been safe. Matteo trusted more people back then. Now, it's only Angel and Spike and that's how I know he's changed, how I know he's evolved into someone better.

"I'm fine baby, just daydreaming," I say, smiling at him. He is impossibly handsome, standing in the afternoon light that streams through the office windows, his dark hair catching it just right. Doesn't help that a man in a suit is something any girl can drool over on a daily basis and I find myself doing exactly that.

Leaning down, Matteo places a small kiss on my lips, the touch is gentle, tender and so different from the man who tortured someone just a few days ago. "I hope it's a nice daydream," he smiles against my mouth and I can feel the care in his touch.

"Baby, any daydream that consists of you is nice," I reply, smiling back at him, because my daydreams are even better when he's in them, even my nightmares seem manageable when I know he's there.

"Well, thank you, Mrs Ricci," he laughs, a teasing edge lacing his voice that makes my heart skip.

"Still not your Mrs, yet; stop counting your chickens before they have hatched," I laugh back, teasing him about the marriage certificate that's waiting in the court office.

"Just over two weeks left, Princess, close enough!"

I place my hands in my armpits, make chicken wing motions at him, flapping them dramatically as he tries not to laugh at me.

"Don't make me turn your ass pink again!"

"As appealing as that sounds Matteo, I have a mountain of paperwork to do, thanks to you and your paperwork allergies," I reply, raising my brows in his direction, I'm only half joking because there really is a mountain of paperwork stacked on the desk that seems to grow, every single day.

"That shit gives me hives," he says, mock scratching his arms. He's being ridiculous and I love him for it.

"Thankfully you're rich enough to pay me double to do

it. I gonna need mental health pay too, for the amount of stress you're putting me through," I tell him, only half joking about that too because between managing his business and dealing with him, I'm exhausted in the best ways possible.

"Sorry, Princess, I've never been good at the whole paperwork side of it all; I prefer to be out on my feet, rather than in here on my ass," he says, shrugging at me, he's genuinely apologetic about it, even though we both know he's not really sorry. "Plus, you're a billionaire now, I think that's good enough compensation as mental health pay," he adds with a wink, mischief filling in his eyes.

"Fuck off, cunt," I say, throwing a pen at him, he catches it easily with one hand, like it's nothing, as he takes his seat by my side.

Angel got us matching chairs, so we now share the desk. I'd asked for my own, but Matteo being Matteo stated, "I'll just move over, we can knock elbows all day." As sweet as that sounded, it's fucking annoying, I like space and he is giving me none. I do get it, he lost me for 10 years and now can't deal, unless he can touch me at all times. Thankfully, the office has a bathroom in it, otherwise, I'm sure he would follow me down the hall and into one of the others one.

"I have a few things I need to set up for the four-seat meeting next week, and I need to find a new receptionist as well," Matteo says, while clicking away at his laptop. I look over at him, wondering what's going on in that beautiful head of his.

"Why a new receptionist? Is one of the girls leaving?" I

ask, genuinely curious about it because our receptionist team is solid.

"Nope," he says, popping the 'p', "I want to fire Becky," I hear the irritation in his voice, a barely contained anger simmering just beneath the surface.

"Why?" I ask, I have a feeling I know exactly where this is going, Becky has been making eyes at Matteo since the day I arrived.

"I don't like the way she acts towards me since she found out about you, and her advances have gotten worse," he sighs, the frustration clear on his face as his jaw clenches. "So, I need to replace her," he explains. I understand his reasoning completely, I've seen the way she looks at him and it makes my blood boil.

"I mean she pisses me off too, Matteo, but she is good at her job, and I'm confident enough in you that no matter what she does, nothing will happen. So, I'm not fussed if she stays or goes," I shrug because I really don't care about Becky and her pathetic attempts at flirting with my man.

"Oh, I know Princess, but she pisses me off. Most people who piss me off, get a bullet between their eyes. And she is heading that way, if she can't back off, hence why I need to fire her," he admits, his voice is deadly serious. I know he means it, Matteo doesn't make threats, he only makes promises.

"Okay, but maybe we can put it off for another couple of weeks? Maybe after the meeting? I have enough paperwork to keep me employed for the next 6 years, so I can't really help you just yet anyway. Plus, you have enough going on between work and the meeting. Let's just worry about it after?" I suggest, watching as he considers it, weighing the options in his mind.

"Yeah, I think that's actually a good idea," Matteo frowns. "But doesn't make seeing her face every day any easier," he admits, I see how much it's bothering him, how much her presence irritates him.

"And this is why I love you," I belly laugh at him. "Any other man would love the attention, yet you're acting like she has COVID!" He makes me swoon with how protective he is over me, how much he cares about my feelings.

"Princess, even after you left, I still didn't see any other women. You broke that part of me," he states, his voice vulnerable and honest in a way that makes my heart ache.

"Broke that part?" I ask him.

"Yep. You came in and smashed it. Every time I even looked at other women, all I'd see was how different they were to you," Matteo admits sheepishly. Fuck, he makes my knees weak and my mouth water. The sweet words make me wanna suck his dick, telling me that I'm the only one, that I've always been the only one.

"Dude, you can't say shit like that," I declare, pointing at him, "while I'm trying to dig you out of this paperwork hole," I say, pointing at the laptop screen. "I'm never going to get any work done if you keep making my undies wet and I'm constantly wanting to jump your bones," I sigh, only half joking because he really is distracting me, making it impossible to focus on anything other than him.

"I can always hire an admin lady," he winks at me, mischief in his eyes, I know he's trying to distract me from work.

"Then what would happen to my job?" I ask him, genuinely curious about what he's thinking.

"I can pay you to sit here and look pretty," he says, wiggling his eyebrows. He's being ridiculous, but I love it because this is the side of him that only I get to see.

"Fuck off, cunt, this is why I need my own desk. You're too distracting!" I say, throwing yet another pen at him, I know if he keeps this up, I'm going to run out of pens to throw at him soon.

He leans over and kisses my cheek, his touch is gentle, tender. "Get back to work, before I have to fire you," and with that, he stands, walking out of the room and I watch him go, already missing him the moment he's gone.

"Where are you going?" I call after him, already missing him, even though he only just left.

"To make sure the office is empty, and ready for the date I need," he calls back, I wonder what he's planning now, what surprise he has in store for me.

Is it weird that I want space from him cause he is smothering the hell outta me? Yet, when he leaves the room, I miss him. Is this Stockholm Syndrome or something, because I can't explain the feeling, I want him close but also need my own space. Somehow he manages to give me both, without me even asking.

I decide this is a better time than any to check my emails, I see I have two unread ones from Aela, aka Patrick. Well, most likely from both of them because I can see them now, fighting over the laptop to write the email, almost hearing them bicker about who gets to write it.

I open the first one, with the subject, "Miss you," and I read:

"Hey sexy lady," (I instantly I know it's Aela who's written this, I smile because I miss her so much it physically hurts.)
"I miss you!
How is it going?
Are you okay?
Can we come and visit you?
Please! I need to see with my own eyes that you are safe!
Patrick says hi, and that finding a PA as good as you, is impossible. He also hates you for leaving him.
But he also misses you and hopes you're okay. Love you,
Xoxo"

Awww, I miss her too. I've been gone for like 4 weeks now, but it feels like 6 months because so much has changed in the blink of an eye. All my belongings from London should be arriving via boat this week or next, I'm kind of hoping that only my belongings were packed and not the furniture, because I mean seriously where am I going to put it all. I already have a storage unit, Matteo said all my old stuff is in it. So fuck, now I'm gonna have two units of shit to go through, I'll just have to add it to my to-do list.

Maybe I can just get it all dropped at home in the empty room, that way I can go through it all, one box at a time. To have the ability to process everything in my own time. Shit, I'm off topic again, why am I so vague; maybe my magnesium levels are low, mental note to self, buy magnesium. But fuck, who am I kidding, I already know that's going to be the problem, adding another mental note to self, tell Angel to order magnesium because I need to be able to focus on what's in front of me.

Now, concentrating back on the laptop, I open the second email with the subject line, "Visiting," and it reads:

"Eleanor, We're going to come visit you.
We need to know that you are safe. Tell me a date that suits for us to fly in. X"

Now this one is Patrick, but them coming to visit, can't happen just yet, I need to figure out how to explain all of this to Matteo. I need to make sure he's comfortable with it.

I quickly email back:

"Subject: Can't wait
Aela,
I can't wait to see you guys! We're flat out with work right now though; I'm Matteo's PA now. Matteo is even worse with his paperwork than Patrick was. Can you imagine? I'll check a date with Matteo and let you know.
Love and miss you both,
Eleanor xoxo"

Shit. I want to see them so badly. I owe them my life. They'd kept me safe for 10 friggin years. I'll have to find a moment to bring this up with Matteo. Maybe after I've given him a blow job... he is always more open to suggestions then. Food for thought, knowing exactly how to get him to agree to anything I want. I'm not above using my body as a bargaining chip when it comes to the people I love.

Chapter 25

Matteo Ricci

"Eleanor, dinners ready!" I call up the stairs, the sound of my voice echoing throughout the house. It's my favourite time of the day, when I've gotten to come home and cook dinner for everyone. And by everyone, I mean Angel and Spike. They had always been permanent fixtures in my life, long before Eleanor and Niko came back, but now they are more prominent, they're essential to everything I do and I can't imagine my life without them here.

Some people might find it annoying, being around the same people every day, but not me. I'm obsessive, compulsive and if they weren't around me daily, I wouldn't be able to handle this life. I need the control, the structure, I need to know where everyone is at all times, what they're doing and if they're safe.

I stand in the kitchen, watching as the lasagna bubbles in the oven, the rich smell of tomato sauce and melted cheese permeates the air, making my mouth water. The salad is already made, it sits in a large wooden bowl on the counter, the fresh greens glistening with olive oil and lemon juice.

"Niko, can you set the table please?" I call from the kitchen, knowing full well that he's probably already done it, the kid is so eager to please.

"Already done, Pappy," he calls back, I can hear the smile in his voice.

"Nope, try again!" I respond, laughing at Niko's many attempts to find a name that should just be 'DAD.'

Dad. The word still feels foreign to me, not that I don't like it, it's actually quite the opposite. I really fucking like it, I just wish Eleanor would let me put another baby in her belly, one that I could raise with her from the beginning, one that has her eyes, my darkness and our love, all wrapped up in one perfect package.

Just thinking about it brings a smile to my face, imagining my arms wrapping around her belly from behind, it swollen with my child. Fuck, I'm getting hard just thinking of it, the image of her pregnant with my baby is the most beautiful thing I can imagine and I've been fantasising about it constantly.

I pull the lasagna out of the oven, the heat wafting over my face as I set it on the counter to cool slightly before serving. I can hear footsteps coming down the stairs.

"What's for dinner?" Eleanor asks from the doorway, her voice pulling me out of my daydream. I look up at her, noticing she's changed into something more comfortable, a soft sweater that hangs off one shoulder, showing the tattoos I've given her. "Need any help?"

"Princess, I don't need help cooking, only cleaning up after. At which point you and Niko always seem to magically disappear," I tell her, teasingly. I know exactly why she does it and I love her for it, she knows I need to do it, to take care of them in every way.

"Poof!" Eleanor singsongs, as she pops back out the door like the queen she is. I can't help but laugh because she's so fucking perfect I love her more than I'd ever thought possible when it comes to loving another person.

As long as it's only "poof" when it's dishes time, we will be just fine, I don't mind cooking, I actually love it, it's therapeutic for me. I also love that she manages to escape the cleanup, it shows me that she's comfortable here, that she's home.

Plating up the lasagna and salad I've made, I call out, "Come, grab your plates, Fuck Faces! I might cook it, but I don't bus the table too!" I can hear the shuffle of feet as they all come running, I can't help but smile, because this is what I've been missing, the chaos, this family.

"Coming!" I hear from 4 different people at once. It warms my heart knowing this is my family now, this chaotically beautiful mess of people, who would not only die for each other, but for me as well. At the end of the day I would burn the world down for any one of them.

Angel is the first to arrive at the table, his large frame filling the chair next to Spike as he immediately starts loading his plate with lasagna and salad, groaning in appreciation with his first bite.

"Fuck mate, this is incredible," Angel says with his mouth full. I watch as Eleanor wrinkles her nose at him in disgust, but she's smiling.

Niko slides into his chair next to Eleanor, looking at the food like it's the best thing he's ever seen, while

Eleanor helps him load up a plate, so he doesn't drip it all over the table, like he normally does.

Eleanor sits next to me and I immediately reach over and squeeze her thigh under the table, she gives me a look ,but she's still smiling behind it as she relaxes into my touch.

"So Niko," Angel says through a mouthful of lasagna, "how's school going?"

"It's good," Niko replies, shrugging as he takes a bite of his food. I watch him carefully, making sure he's eating enough, making sure he's happy. "My teacher is still trying to get my accent right."

"Your accent is Australian now," Eleanor laughs, reaching over to ruffles his hair, I watch as he leans into her touch. "You've been here for a month, you're picking it up faster than I did when I'd moved to England."

"Princess, you can take the Aussie outta the country, but you can't take the country outta the Aussie," I remind her as I lean over, kissing her temple. I inhale a waft of her shampoo, something floral and sweet that makes me want to bury my face in her hair.

"I know. I tried, but I sucked at it," she says primly. and we all burst out laughing because she's absolutely Australian accented.

"You sure did, Princess," I say, watching her try not to smile by taking another bite of her food.

Spike raises his glass of wine, he's been quiet for most of the meal, but now he's looking at all of us with something soft in his eyes. "To family," he says as we all raise ours, clinking them together. The moment is perfect, simple and everything I've ever wanted. I smile as I feel

Eleanor's hand finding mine under the table, squeezing it gently.

We eat, we talk and we laugh, the conversation flowing easily between us as we discuss everything, from Niko's school, to the new shipment that's come in at the warehouse, to Angel's terrible dating life. I find myself just watching Eleanor, watching the way her eyes light up when she laughs, the way she reaches over to wipe a bit of sauce from Niko's chin and the way she fits so perfectly into this life, into this family.

After dinner, Eleanor and Niko disappear as I start the dishes, just like they always do, leaving Angel and Spike to clear the table. I can hear them bustling around the house, Eleanor's singing off-key to some song on the radio while Niko's laughing at her, the sound of it making my chest ache, this is everything I've ever wanted, and I'd almost lost it.

I'm about to head upstairs to find Eleanor when Spike's phone rings, I watch his face change as he answers it, his entire demeanour shifting from relaxed to all business, in a matter of seconds.

"Yeah," he says into the phone, his tone strictly business now; clipped and professional. "Uh huh. How long ago?" He listens for a moment, before looking at me and nodding slowly. I can see the tension in his jaw. "We're on it. Send me the location," he states, hanging up and already moving, already pulling up whatever information is on his phone.

"What is it?" I ask him, feeling the shift in the air, the way everything changes when business calls. My body going rigid with the anticipation.

"Kim and Jeffreys found them hiding out in Redfern. They just grabbed them both and are heading to the warehouse now," Spike states and I can see the adrenaline pumping through him, the way his hands are already moving, already preparing. "Finally," he adds and I know exactly what he means, we've been waiting for this moment, waiting to get our hands on the men who hurt Eleanor.

Finally, we have them. Now we can find out who sent them 10 years ago, so we can find out who dared to touch what's mine.

"Princess!" I call up the stairs, my voice harder. I hear her moving around upstairs, probably in the library. "We gotta go out…"

"Really?" she yells back, the disappointment clear in her voice. "I was just about to have a bath."

"Sorry! And wear something black please," I call back at her, already moving toward the stairs, as I preparing myself mentally for what's about to happen. I get no response, causing me to wonder if my presence is starting to grate on her, if she's getting tired of me always needing her close, always needing to know where she is.

I hear footsteps on the stairs and Eleanor jumps, missing the last two steps, like she is a ninja. She lands perfectly in front of me as I catch her in my arms, before she can stumble, pulling her close to me.

"Hiya," she says with her hands in ninja chop-style, grinning at me like she hasn't a care in the world. I can't help but laugh at her, the woman can act like a 4-year-old one second, then a complete professional the next. I'll never understand how she does it, but I love her for it.

She's wearing black leggings and the same sweater as before, she looks so beautiful, I just want to wrap her up in my arms, all the time.

Still laughing at her antics, I urge, "Come on, Master Splinter, let's go," already pulling her toward the door, but she's resisting slightly, her eyes searching mine like she's trying to read what's about to happen.

"Splinter?!" She feigns a look of shock as I watch her trying to lighten the mood, trying to keep things playful, even though she can sense the shift in me. "It's Michelangelo! I mean can't you just imagine me spinning some nun chucks?" she mimics, spinning imaginary nun chucks. She's so fucking beautiful when she's like this, so free, so playful. I just want to protect that part of her forever.

"Actually, yes I can," I say, laughing at her as I wrap my arm around her waist, pulling her closer to me and burying my face in her hair for just a moment.

"We're lean, we're mean and we're green," she quotes, holding her hand over her heart, causing me to raise my eyebrows at her. I'm trying to stay present with her, even though my mind is already in the warehouse, already planning what I'm going to do to the men who hurt her.

"I didn't realise you were such a devoted fan," I comment, curious about this side of her that I've never seen before, the playful side that seems to come out more and more as she settles into her life with me.

"I'm not; it was Niko's favourite movie when he was little. I think I've sat through thousands of hours of the same movie. Safe to say, it's now ingrained in my psyche," she explains, love filling her eyes as she talks about Niko. It makes my heart ache, she's such a good mother and I'm so fucking grateful that she's here, that she came back to me.

"Well then, Michelangelo, may I have this honour?" I ask, holding out my arm for her to hook into, I watch her hesitate for just a moment, before she takes it. "We've got two bodies to extinguish," I add cheerfully, the excitement lighting up her gorgeous eyes, even as she tries to hide the fear that's lurking beneath the surface.

"Oh really? You found them?" Eleanor looks at me. I love that she's embracing this side of our life, that she's becoming part of my world, instead of running from it, that she's willing to walk into darkness with me.

"Your blood lust is taking over there, Princess," I laugh, trying to keep things light, even though I can feel the darkness rising inside me. "But yes, really."

"Okay, okay, let's go kill the past!" Eleanor exclaims, even though I can see she's lost a little colour in her cheeks, I know she's ready for this, I know she's strong enough for this because she's proven it to me, time and time again.

"It's gonna be okay, Princess, we'll go get the info on who sent them 10 years ago, then we can go. We can leave it all for Spike to handle. Unless you wanna show off your marksmanship skills again?" I offer shrugging, I watch her considering it, her eyes going dark with the same hunger I feel.

Wrapping my arm further around her lower back, I push her towards the front door, feeling her trembling slightly against me. I know deep down, she's strong enough for this, I know she can handle what's about to happen.

"Spike has the car out front waiting for us. Let's go, so we can get back to Niko," I tell her, needing her to know that this won't take as long, I'll get the information I need and then we'll come home, I'll hold her and make sure she knows that she's safe.

Taking in a deep breath Eleanor speaks up, "Okaaaay, you're right. Let's go," I watch her steeling herself for what's about to happen, her jaw tightens, her shoulders straighten as she prepares herself mentally for the violence that's about to unfold.

We walk out the front to the waiting car with Spike behind the wheel, and I can see the determination on his face, he knows what's coming, he knows what I'm capable of when someone hurts the people I love.

The night air is cool against my skin as we approach the car, hearing the distant sounds of the city, the traffic, the sirens, the life happening all around us as we prepare to step into darkness.

"Boss!" Spike greets as we slide into the back seat. Eleanor presses up against my side and I keep my arm around her, needing to feel her close to me.

"Spike, what's the low down?" I ask, while putting on my seatbelt. I feel Eleanor's hand find mine in the darkness of the car, before she squeezes it gently, grounding me, keeping me tethered to her and not the darkness.

"I just heard from them a couple of minutes ago, said they are at the warehouse now," Spike states as he pulls out of the front gate. The anticipation is building in my chest, the hunger for blood and answers.

"So, we're going to head over to the warehouse, hope-fully they'll have 'em tied up and waiting for us," Spike says, pulling out onto the road and I nod, that's exactly what I want, I want them restrained and ready for me to extract the information I need.

"Good! I wanna know who is behind this," I growl. Eleanor squeezes my hand tighter and I look over at her, she's staring out the window, her face pale but her expression is one of determination.

"We'll be there in 20, boss," Spike says, driving fast but controlled. I can feel the adrenaline coursing through my veins.

Leaning over to Eleanor, I grab her chin and pull her face towards mine, placing my lips softly onto hers, I pour everything I'm feeling into the kiss, all my love, my fear, my need to protect her. "It's okay, Princess. The big bad wolf will deal with it," I smile at her, wanting her to know that I'll protect her, that I'll always protect her, no one will ever hurt her again as long as I'm alive.

I watch her eyes growing round, a look of shock emerging on her face. I'm about to kiss her again, when I feel the impact. Everything happens in slow motion as something runs into the side of the car. I feel us become airborne, the world spinning around us as I throw my arms around her body and pull her close. The car flips, metal ripping and scraping,, glass shatters and then everything goes dark.

Chapter 26

Eleanor Wang

The car flips for what feels like forever, I feel like a ragdoll being thrown around in the back, my body slamming against the seats, the windows and I feel every impact, every movement, every bone-jarring collision as we tumble through the air. I'm screaming but I can't hear my own voice over the sound of metal tearing, glass shattering and the world spinning out of control.

Finally, we come to a stop, the silence is almost worse than the noise. All I can hear is ringing in my ears, a high-pitched whine that makes my head pound and throb, I can't think straight through the pain, through the fear and the overwhelming sense that something is terribly wrong.

We have landed the right way up, but the roof is caved in so low, I'm almost lying on the back seat. I can barely breathe because the space is so tight as I gasp for air, trying to figure out what just happened and where Matteo is.

"Eleanor?" I hear Spike calling my name from the

front, it sounds muffled, almost like we are underwater. I can't quite make out what he's saying at first, my ears still ringing and my head spinning.

"Eleanor?" I hear it again, each time it gets clearer and clearer. I try to respond, but my mouth feels like it's full of cotton and my throat is raw from screaming.

"Here…" I manage to groan back, my voice sounding strange and distant, even to my own ears. I try to move, but my body isn't responding the way I want it to.

"Boss?" Spike mutters next, with an urgency in his voice, the note of panic lacing his tone makes my heart rate spike even faster.

Reaching my hand out, I turn my head towards my right, where Matteo should be seated, I search for him in the darkness, reaching out within the crushed metal and the debris, my hand finding nothing but empty space and my stomach drops.

"What happened?" I whisper, not even sure if I'm asking Spike or myself.

"Boss!" Spike calls again, his voice becoming more frantic, more desperate.

"I can't see him!" I realise with a jolt, the panic rises in my throat like bile because he isn't in the back, he isn't where he should be. The realisation hits, I'm terrified that he's been thrown from the car or worse.

"Fuck!" Spike yells, I can hear him struggling, trying to move in the front seat. "We need to get out, can you move?"

"I don't think so, I'm pretty much laying on the seat back here," I reply, trying to stay calm, but my voice is shaking and I can feel tears starting to stream down my face because I can't find Matteo, I'm trapped and everything is wrong.

"Can you reach or see your door at all?" Spike groans, the desperation in his voice obvious.

"I can't even see you," I respond. The darkness is suffocating me and I'm starting to panic, my breathing becoming shallow and rapid as I realise just how trapped I am.

Then I hear it, footsteps running towards the car, fast, heavy and purposeful. Maybe it's help. Maybe, someone is coming to rescue us.

"Help! Help!" I shout, trying to move, trying to get their attention, trying to make myself visible to whoever is out there.

Then I hear metal on metal and I realise someone is cutting into the car. My heart leaps with hope because maybe they're cutting us out. Maybe, they're going to help us.

"Help!" I call again, reaching toward the sound, toward the light that's starting to pour in through the damaged metal.

"Eleanor stop!" Spike yells, his voice is sharp, urgent, and filled with a warning that makes my blood run cold. "There is no way the authorities got here that quick."

The blood freezes in my veins and I realise with a sickening clarity that these aren't rescuers, these are the people who hit us, these are the people who did this on purpose. My mind is racing, trying to figure out who they are and what they want from me.

"Who is it?" I say softly to no one, my voice is barely a whisper. I'm pressed back against the seat, trying to make myself as small as possible, trying to hide in the darkness.

"Argh!" I scream as a hand clamps around my ankle, The grip is brutal, painful, as light pours in through the door they have managed to open. The hand on my ankle pulls and pulls, the pain is excruciating, shooting up my leg like fire. By the feel of it, I think my leg is broken and they're pulling on it anyway, pulling me out of the car without any regard for my injuries.

"Fuck! Stop!" I scream, trying to kick at them, trying to fight back, trying to do anything to get away from this person, but I'm trapped and injured. I feel myself being dragged across the twisted metal and broken glass.

"Fuck, Eleanor!" Spike screams back, I hear him kicking as he tries to fight his way out of the front seat to get to me, I can hear the desperation in his voice, the rage, the need to protect me but he's trapped too. There's nothing he can do.

I feel the night air before it registers that they have managed to pull me out of the car. I'm gasping for breath as my eyes adjusting to the darkness. I can see shadows moving around me and I'm terrified, I don't know who these people are or what they want from me.

Arms wrap around my waist, hauling me up and carrying me towards a waiting car. I'm struggling, thrashing, trying to break free, but the pain in my leg is so intense that I can barely move. I'm lifted like I weigh nothing and carried away from the wreckage.

Who the fuck is it? What do they want from me? I'm screaming the questions inside my head, my thoughts racing a mile a minute as I'm trying to figure out what's happening and why this is happening.

Looking around I see a shadow lying on the ground about 20 metres away. My heart stops ,because I know, I just know that it's Matteo and he's not moving, he's not getting up. The world tilts on its axis.

Oh no, please no. Not Matteo. God no.

"No, no, no, no, no!" I scream, thrashing harder now, ignoring the pain in my leg, ignoring everything except the need to get back to him, to make sure he's okay.

"Matteo!" I scream over and over again, like if I scream loud enough he'll wake up, he'll get up, he'll come save me like he always does.

"Matteo, wake up!" I scream even louder, my voice is hoarse and raw as I beg him to wake up, begging the universe to let him be okay.

"Don't worry about that pretty boy over there," a dark voice says into my ear. The voice familiar in a way that makes my skin crawl and my blood run cold. "He is already dead."

My heart stops. It literally stops beating for a moment, I can't breathe, I can't think, I can't process what this person is telling me.

He can't be. Matteo can't be dead. He's too strong, too powerful, too much a part of me to just be gone.

Black dots start to dance in front of my eyes, I'm hyperventilating and I can't stop; I can't breathe. The world is spinning, I'm falling, I can't stop falling as the darkness is swallowing me whole, pulling me down into its depths. I welcome it, because I can't live in a world where Matteo is dead.

"ARE YOU SURE HE'S DEAD?" I HEAR SOMEONE SAYING, the voice familiar. I try to place it, but my brain feels like it's moving through molasses, everything is slow, heavy and wrong.

I try to sit up, but my body feels like lead, my eyelids refusing to move. I'm trapped in this space between consciousness and unconsciousness, I can't quite make it to either side.

"One hundred percent, I checked myself," another voice says, a note of finality to it that makes me want to scream.

Slowly, it all starts to come back to me. The memories crashing over me like waves and I'm drowning in them. Matteo lying on the road. The impact. The spinning. The darkness. The hands pulling me away from him.

Oh, Matteo no. Please no. Not him.

I refuse to believe it. I refuse to accept that he's gone, because if he's gone then I have nothing left, I have no reason to keep breathing, no reason to keep fighting.

Where the hell am I? The question floats through my mind, but I can't seem to focus on it long enough to figure out the answer.

I know I'm lying down, that much I can feel. There's something hard beneath me, something that feels like almost like a mattress, but it's too firm, too clinical, too much like a hospital bed.

My leg is throbbing so badly, there's no way it's not broken, every time I try to move it, the pain shoots through me like lightning and I have to bite my lip to keep from screaming.

"She's waking up," someone says next to me, the voice is closer now as I try to figure out who it is, but my brain is still foggy and confused.

Trying hard to lift my eyelids, I manage to make them flutter for a bit before they fully open. It's too damn bright in the room, everything looks white and there are lights on everywhere, the brightness stabbing into my eyes like needles. I can't help but groan.

I resort to trying to lift my arm, attempting to shield my eyes, but it gets stuck halfway up and I realise with a jolt that something is holding it down. I look down and see handcuffs, cold metal handcuffs, one side is attached to my wrist and the other is connected to the railing on the bed.

The bed is definitely a hospital bed, but the room doesn't look like a hospital. The realisation starts to sink in, I'm not in a hospital at all, I'm somewhere else, somewhere I don't recognise and I'm handcuffed to the bed.

The room is painted white, but the walls are covered in bookcases that are overflowing with books, hundreds of books, maybe even thousands of books, and that's it. There's nothing else, just books, white walls and the overwhelming sense that I'm in a prison.

Did I die and go to a heaven that just happens to be a library? What the hell is this place? The questions are swirling through my mind, but I can't seem to find any answers.

Turning to my left, I look at the man speaking, my breath catches in my lungs because I recognise him and I can't quite believe what I'm seeing.

No, it can't be.

"Patrick?" I whisper, my voice barely audible as I stare at him like he's a ghost. In a way he is, he's a ghost from my past, a person I'd thought I could trust, a person I'd thought was my friend.

"El," he says, smiling at me like we've just run into each other on the street, instead of me being handcuffed to a hospital bed in what appears to be a library prison.

"What the hell Patrick? What are you doing here?" I ask, trying to make sense of this, trying to understand what's happening, why Patrick is here and why I'm handcuffed.

"I've come to take you back home," he replies, his voice is calm and casual, like this is the most normal thing in the world.

"Home?" My head must be so scrambled, nothing he's saying is making sense. "I don't understand?"

"Home, El," he smiles at me, but there's something in his smile that makes my skin crawl, something possessive and dark that I've never seen before. "You belong to me."

"I think I must be suffering from some brain damage, Patrick; did you just say that I belong to you?" I frown up at his face, searching for some sign that he's joking, that this is some kind of sick prank, but his expression is serious and cold. I'm starting to realise I don't know this person at all.

"Yes, belong. You didn't think I did everything I've done for you, for no reason? Come on El, you're not that stupid are you?" He looks at me with humour in his eyes, but it's not a kind humour, it's cruel, twisted and makes my stomach turn.

Shaking my head, I look over at Patrick, I reply, "I don't understand. Why? I thought you were my friend?"

"I am your friend, El, but I also own you. I've owned you for a lot longer than you think," he says shrugging, like this is the most casual revelation in the world. My brain is struggling to process what he's actually telling me.

I think my brain is broken. It must be. None of this can be true. I love Patrick. I've trusted him. I owe him my life, yet he's telling me he owns me. I'm starting to realise with a sickening clarity that I've been played this entire time, everything he's done for me was part of some larger plan, I was just a pawn in his game.

"Where is Matteo?" I ask, scared of the answer. I'm terrified of what he's going to tell me because I already know, I already know that Matteo is dead and I'm going to have to live with that knowledge for the rest of my life.

"Dead," Patrick says with a shrug, like the world isn't falling apart around me, like he didn't just tell me that the love of my life is gone and I'll never going to see him again.

I feel like I can't breathe, I gasp for air, my chest tightening as I'm drowning in the realisation that Matteo is gone. I'm alone, I'm trapped and there's nothing I can do about any of it.

"And, and… Aela? Where is she?" I stammer, trying to comprehend my situation. Grasping at the hope that maybe Aela is here, maybe she can help me, maybe she can get me out of this nightmare.

"In London; she doesn't know about any of this," Patrick states with a note of satisfaction lacing his voice, like he's pleased that he's managed to keep it all a secret, that he's managed to orchestrate all of this without anyone knowing.

As I try to sit up, pain shoots up my leg and into my hip. I wince because the pain is worse than childbirth, worse than anything I've ever experienced and I realise that I'm not getting out of this bed anytime soon.

"Fuck," I wince, trying to move, but every movement sends waves of pain throughout my body.

"Stop moving, you silly lass; you've broken your leg and cracked a few ribs," Patrick informs me as he pushes me back down, his touch is rough and possessive, nothing like the gentle way Matteo would have touched me. "The doctor will be here in 5 minutes to give you some more painkillers. Just lay down and be patient; we can't fly till we get your bones set," he grumbles while checking his phone. I realise with horror that he's planning to take me somewhere, that this is just the beginning of my nightmare.

I look towards the other man in the room, whom I had completely forgotten was here. It's the man from Matteo's office the other week, the one who was with Enzo. My heart sinks, this is all connected to Matteo's world, this is connected to the mafia. I'm starting to understand that I've been caught in the crossfire of something much bigger than I ever could have realised.

Shocked, I say "Tino?" Trying to make sense of how he fits into it, how he's connected to Patrick.

"Was wondering if you remembered my handsome face," Tino beams at me like he's won the lotto and there's something unsettling about his smile, something that makes me want to recoil.

"Don't you work for Enzo?" I frown at him, trying to piece together the puzzle, but nothing is making sense.

"Yes," he smirks, I can see the satisfaction in his expression.

"Shut up, you two. Tino, go see what's taking the doctor so long; I need this leg dealt with so I can go home," Patrick orders. I realise that he's the one in charge here, he's orchestrated all of this. I'm at his mercy and there's nothing I can do to stop him.

"Yes, boss," Tino mutters as he walks out, leaving me alone with Patrick. My entire life has been a lie, the man I've trusted most in this world has been playing me this entire time, Matteo is dead, I'm trapped and there's no way out.

Chapter 27

Matteo Ricci

I wake to the sound of beeping. It's a steady, rhythmic sound, pulling me from the darkness as I struggle to understand where I am, and what's happening. My body feels like it's been hit by a truck, everything hurts.

"He's waking up," I hear a voice say, sounding relieved.

"Welcome back to the land of the living, boss," a male's voice says from the other side of me, I recognise it's Angel. I'm trying to figure out what the hell is going on, why I'm here and where here even is.

What the hell is going on? Why does my body feel so heavy and sluggish? Where is Eleanor? The questions swirl through my mind as I start to panic, I can't remember what happened and I can't find Eleanor in my thoughts.

"Princess…" I manage to force out past the desert that's taken refuge in my mouth, my voice is hoarse and weak, I barely recognise it as my own.

"Boss," I hear from my right, I know it's Spike's voice,

but he sounds urgent, desperate. "Boss, you need to wake up, mate."

Forcing my eyes to open, the first thing I notice is that we're in a makeshift hospital room inside the warehouse. If we're at the warehouse, then something has gone very wrong. I try to remember what happened.

Warehouse. Shit, fuck. The crash. Eleanor.

"Princess!" I try to yell out, but it comes out closer to a hoarse whisper. My throat is raw and painful. I look around the room, desperate to lock eyes with her, desperate to see her beautiful face, to know that she's okay.

"Where the fuck is Eleanor?!" I try to shout as my voice is getting stronger now. I'm Fuelled by panic, fear and the overwhelming need to find her, to make sure she's safe.

"She isn't here, boss, she was taken," I hear Spike declare, the words hitting me like a punch to the gut. I feel the black haze starting to creep over my vision as I struggle to breathe, struggling to process what he's telling me.

Eleanor was taken. She was taken from me. She was taken and I wasn't there to protect her.

My mind is swimming, I can feel myself slipping away as the black haze gets darker and I'm falling back into the darkness, but I don't want to go back there, because if I do, I might not come back.

"Boss, god dammit, don't you dare; I need you here to help me," Spike snarls into my face as he grabs my arm, snapping me back into the here and now, his grip is tight and painful, grounding me, keeping me tethered to reality.

"Who took her?" I ask, my voice desperate, pleading,

and filled with a rage that's building inside me, like a volcano about to erupt.

"I don't know, they turned up minutes after the crash, used the jaws of life on the car, grabbed her and left," Spike says, the guilt, the regret, the self-recrimination clear in his voice. "I was pinned by the steering wheel; I couldn't get out to help her. I'm sorry, boss," he explains, looking devastated as the tears build up in his eyes.

"Fuck, we gotta go get her," I declare, trying to sit up. I feel every ache and pain throughout my body as I begin moving. It's like my entire body is on fire causing me to gasp for a single breath, but I don't care, I need to find Eleanor, and I need to find her now.

"Sorry boss, you're not moving till the doctor has finished with the x-rays and tests," Spike looks at me pleadingly, the note of authority in his voice tells me he's not going to back down on this.

"I know you wanna go find her, but if you have internal bleeding, you will die before we get the chance to get her and that's just not helpful," he says. His words are making sense, but I don't want them to make sense, I need to be out there looking for her, I need to be doing something, instead of lying here in this bed like a useless bastard.

"Fuck!" I scream, as tears run down my face. I can feel the continuous stream of them flowing down my cheeks. I'm not even going to try to stop them, because I've failed her, I've failed to keep her safe and that's the one thing I'd promised her I would do.

"I didn't fucking keep her safe! I promised her I would keep her safe. I kept her with me at all times, so this wouldn't happen!" I blurt out as tears splash down my face. My voice breaking as I fall apart in front of Spike and I don't care, because my world has fallen apart.

"This is all my fault; she was safer in bloody London!" I scream, pulling at my hair. I try to get out of the bed, fighting against the restraints, but the pain and the overwhelming sense of failure has me struggling.

"Boss," Spike says, grabbing my shoulder, his grip is firm, grounding me. "I honestly don't think she was safe anywhere," he says, the tone of his voice making me pause as I look into his eyes, I see a hint of regret and I know he's holding something back.

"Alright, Spike, what are you not telling me?" I ask, my voice quieter now, more controlled, and I can see him struggling with whether he should tell me, or not.

Pulling up a chair, Spike sits down heavily, running a hand down his face, he looks exhausted, defeated and I know whatever he's about to tell me, is going to change everything.

"Angel found out some info after we'd left. All that digging he's been doing into the camera footage, and the people living in the apartment building that Eleanor lived in 10 years ago, pulled up a name we hadn't realised was important, until now." he says. He's choosing his words carefully, like he's trying to figure out how to tell me something that's going to destroy me.

"Whose?" I frown, leaning forward, despite the pain. I need to know, I need to understand what's happening.

"Patrick Murphy," Spike says, my blood instantly running cold.

"As in, the Patrick Murphy? The one from London.

The one who'd helped to hide her and keep Niko a secret?" my voice gets progressively louder as I speak. Starting to understand what this means and I don't fucking like where this is going. "How the fuck did that cunt's name come up?" I look over at Spike whose eyes are fixed on the ground, watching as he struggles with what he's about to tell me.

"Well, he owned the apartment building. In fact, he'd even owned the apartment building that Eleanor had first lived in; the one over in Glebe. I don't know what it all means, but he's been tied to her for as long as you have…" Spike states, the implications of it all starting to sink in as I start to realise this goes deeper than I could've ever thought. Patrick has been involved in Eleanor's life in ways I'd never known.

"What the fuck? This makes no sense," I say, trying to get my head around all this new info. I'm running through the timeline in my head, trying to figure out how it is even possible and what it means for Eleanor.

"Angel has been trying to get his head around it all too. He's been looking into his Australian bank statements and finances, but there's nothing on them other than rent from properties and money from the sales of buildings before and after the day she left Australia," Spike explains. I'm listening to every word, trying to piece together the puzzle.

"So, he left the same time she did, knowing exactly where she was going?" I ask, trying to piece it all together. I know the confusion is written all over my face, because this doesn't make sense. "Hang on. You don't think he was the one who had her raped?" I ask, the thought making me feel sick. If Patrick was involved in that, then I'm going to kill him slowly and painfully.

"I have no idea; he isn't affiliated with anyone or anything in Australia, or so Angel can see. He hasn't found any ties, anywhere," Spike explains. I can see him struggling over the lack of information.

"He isn't Irish Mafia, is he?" I ask, trying to figure out what his angle is, what his connection to Eleanor could possibly be.

"Not that Angel can find," Spike responds, sounding frustrated and defeated. We're missing something, we're missing a crucial piece of the puzzle.

I run my hand down my face, trying to process all of the information, trying to figure out what it all means. "This isn't happening. Who the fuck is Patrick Murphy?" I ask, my voice quiet and dangerous. I can feel the rage building inside me, like a bomb about to detonate.

"That's a question we're trying to work out," Spike huffs as the doctor walks back into the room, immediately distracting me with his presence.

"Doc, I need to get this sorted out now," I almost yell at him, watching him flinch at my tone, but I don't care. I need to get out of here, I need to find Eleanor.

"Okay, got it. I have your x-rays here. You have 3 cracked ribs, a fractured collarbone and cheekbone, you also have dislocated fingers but we have reset them already, and you also have a concussion. This is all consistent with being thrown from a moving vehicle. I want to put you through an MRI machine, now that you're awake, we can," he states, listing off my injuries like they're nothing, like I haven't just learnt that Eleanor has been taken and I'm lying here broken and useless.

"For fuck's sake," I snap, trying to sit up again, but the pain is too much and I fall back onto the bed, cursing under my breath because I need to be out there, I need to be finding Eleanor, but instead I'm stuck here, being poked and prodded by doctors.

IT TAKES THE DOCTOR WELL OVER TWO MORE HOURS TO declare that I do not have any internal bleeding and that I won't drop dead from my injuries if I walk out the door. I'm grateful for that at least because it means I can get out of here and start looking for Eleanor.

They've pulled my arm up under my damn chin to help with my collarbone and I've been given so many pain meds I can't feel my fingers or toes. Everything is numb and distant and I hate it, because I need to feel, I need to be sharp and focused if I'm going to find Eleanor.

The fucking arm-brace thing isn't gonna last much longer, because I need two hands and I'm going to need to be able to move freely, if I'm going to get Eleanor back.

Walking inside my front door, I head straight up the stairs to get changed. I'm moving slower than normal because every step sends waves of pain through my body, but I'm pushing through it, I need to be ready, I need to be prepared for whatever comes next.

After removing the fucking brace and allowing my arm to hang freely, I instantly feel the pull on my collarbone, the pain is sharp and intense, but I'm managing it. I'll just have to be careful and not use the arm unless I need to.

I pull on a pair of stretch jeans and a tight long sleeve black top, before heading back downstairs to Niko's room, knowing full well that everyone will be down in his little tech dungeon, where the answers are going to be found and where we're going to figure out where Eleanor is.

Walking down the last two stairs, I look into the open-plan lounge/gaming room to find they've turned it into a detective's office, the sight of it making my chest tighten because this is what we've been reduced to, searching for clues, trying to piece together the puzzle of where Eleanor is and who's taken her.

Whiteboards cover the walls, with names, connections and theories, while the pool table is covered with laptops and power cables that run all over the place. Workplace health and safety would have a field day in here, but I don't care. This is what it will take to find Eleanor.

"Dad," Niko almost yells from his spot on the floor as he jumps up and runs over to hug me. He wraps his arms around my waist, I can feel him trembling and realise he's been scared for me.

"I'm so glad you're okay," he says, his sweet voice is muffled by my top, where his face is currently squished. I feel his tears soaking through my shirt, my heart clenching at the action.

"I'm okay Niko," I say, cupping his face with my palm, trying to be strong for him; even though I'm falling apart inside. "But I need you to stop squeezing my ribs so hard," I laugh, trying to keep things light, even though everything is dark and heavy.

"Shit, sorry, Dad," Niko swears, the worry in his voice clear.

"Hey, no swearing," I say tapping the back of his head with my palm, trying to maintain some semblance of normalcy, even though nothing is normal anymore.

"Mum said I can swear as long as it's inside the house and not out in public," he grins at me, the mention of Eleanor makes my chest ache because she's not here, she should be here, I need to find her.

"Your mother...." I choke, hardly managing to get the rest out. "Has a funny way of parenting," I say, my voice is breaking as I think about Eleanor and how she's not here, how I don't know where she is, or if she's even safe, or if she's hurt.

I look at Niko, seeing the tears building in the corners of his eyes, watching as he tries to be brave for me; it's breaking my heart, this kid shouldn't have to be brave, he should be safe, happy and carefree.

I rub my hand over my heart, trying to compose myself. "But if she says it's okay, then it's okay," I say, trying to be the strong one here, trying to be the one who holds it together, even though I'm falling apart.

"Boss," Angel says, jumping up from his perch at the pool table, he looks worried. "Sit the fuck down, before you fall down!" he yells, concern filling his eyes.

"I can't sit, I need to find her," I state, already moving, already trying to figure out where to go and what to do next.

"Seriously cunt, put your fucking ass in a seat now, before I make you," Angel growls at me, the note of authority in his voice tells me he's serious. "I know we need to find her; that's what we are doing, but hurting yourself unnecessarily, is just plain stupid," he says. I know he's right, but I don't want to sit, I want to be out there looking for Eleanor.

Pulling out a random chair, I sit in it, watching Angel typing away on his laptop. I'm trying to be patient, but I'm struggling, every second that passes is a second that Eleanor is in danger, and I'm not there to protect her.

"What have you found so far?" I ask, my voice is urgent, desperate, filled with the need to know everything.

"Okay, so we have been combing for everything to do with Patrick. All his properties, possible flight details..." Angel huffs, not looking up from his laptop, I can see the exhaustion on his face, the way he's been working non-stop to find information.

"So far, I have found 3 properties in Sydney, two in Melbourne and one in Perth, that he still owns. He used to own 13 before he'd left 10 years ago, but since then he's been selling them all off..." Angel says. I'm listening to every word, trying to figure out which one Eleanor might be in.

"After having extensive renovations done by the same hired contractors," Niko chimes in. I look over at him, seeing the intelligence in his eyes, the way he's piecing things together.

Fuck this kid is smart, he doesn't get any of it from me. He's all Eleanor. Thinking of her sends a new wave of pain through me, I struggle to take a breath. I need to find her and I need to find her now.

Fuck Princess, where are you?

"The last 6 properties Patrick owns are yet to be renovated. They are what I would consider to be the best ones to renovate and sell," Niko says, dragging me from my thoughts, I'm grateful for the distraction because thinking about Eleanor, is making me want to scream.

Angel finally looks up from his laptop, determination set in his eyes. "So, if we take away Melbourne and Perth, we are left with 3 here in Sydney," he says, running his hand down his face. "That means we have 3 potential places where Eleanor could be," he states. I feel a spark of hope igniting inside me, we're getting closer, we're narrowing it down.

Fuck, now we're getting somewhere. "Where are they?" I ask, leaning forward despite the pain in my ribs, I need to know where these places are.

"One is a warehouse in Campsie, one is an old house in Botany, and the other is a strip of shops in Blacktown," Niko reads from his laptop. I commit the locations to memory, I know one of them is where Eleanor is, and I'm going to find her.

"The shops are derelict, haven't been used in 12 years, the warehouse is currently leased to a clothing company, and the house is rented to a 'Mrs Tinsdale', 63 years old. She was, in fact, the owner of the house before a foreclosure, Murphy bought it and leased it back to her for a hundred dollars a week," Niko continues. I'm listening to every detail, because details matter and details can lead us to Eleanor.

"The price hasn't changed once over the last 10 years..." Niko adds, confused. I watch as he struggles to understand why someone would rent a house for the same price for 10 years.

"Angel, look into Mrs. Tinsdale. Who is she when she's at home?" A new wave of energy surges through me, feel deep in my bones that this woman could be the link we are looking for, this woman might be connected to Patrick in some way we don't understand yet.

"Already on it," Angel states as he types furiously on his laptop.

"Says here, she's a widow, has been since she was 26; her husband died in a car accident," Angel reads. I'm listening, trying to figure out what this means and how it connects to Eleanor.

"Real accident or does it look like a hit?" I ask, starting to see a pattern emerging, a web of connections that Patrick has been weaving for years.

"Accident, a car ran a red light, and he was killed on impact," Angel answers. I nod because that's what makes sense, it fits with what we know.

"Work?" I ask, trying to figure out just how Mrs. Tinsdale fits into all of this.

"Hold on, just hacking the ATO," Niko says, my head snaps towards him, I take him in with a mixture of pride and concern.

"Hacking the what?!" I ask, looking at Niko, "You've got to be kidding me," I voice, torn between being impressed, and being horrified that my son is hacking government databases.

"Okay, I'm in… Right, so it seems she hasn't worked once in the last 10 years. She gets a pension for disability, but before that, she had been a paid nanny for a company called, 'Conners Building'" Niko reads. I listen, trying to figure out what it could mean. "Hang on, I'll see who the owner of the business was..." he adds as he types some more before concentrating.

"It says here she is on disability due to breaking her back at work," Angel reads, the picture starting to come together. "She fell down some stairs, got a payout for it, but has since needed the pension to survive," he adds. I nod, everything is starting to make sense.

"Um Dad......" Niko looks at me, his face as white as a ghost. the shock in his eyes clear. "The owner of the company was Conner - Conner Murphy," he says, the name hitting me like a punch to the gut as I realise what this means.

Patrick has been orchestrating this for years. He's been planning this, setting up his pieces on the board and Eleanor has always his target.

"For fuck's sake!" I say throwing the chair I'd been sitting on across the room, it smashes the TV mounted to the wall. I'm struggling to contain the rage that's built up inside me, I need to find Eleanor and I need to find her now.

"Watch your collarbone Boss," Angel huffs, the concern straining his voice, but I don't care about my collarbone, I care about Eleanor.

"Spike!" I call up the stairs, I hear him racing down. "Get the car ready, and strap up," I command, already moving towards the door because I know where Eleanor is and I'm going to get her back.

"Angel, we're going to pay a visit to Mrs Tinsdale," I state, the understanding registering on his face, he knows what I mean, he knows we're going to get answers and we're going to get Eleanor back.

"Niko, you're going into the storage room," I declare, watching the protest forming on his face, but I'm not going to let him come with us, I won't risk him.

"The storage room?" Niko looks at me confused with fear in his eyes.

"Yep, I'm not taking the chances of having you with us, but I'm also not taking the chance of leaving you unprotected," I point up towards the ceiling. The 'storage room' is essentially a massive safe; it houses money and guns; you can't get in or out without the pin. It also has security camera footage, that way you can see who is outside the door if you're inside; I need to know that Niko is going to be safe, while I go find Eleanor.

"Take your laptops with you," Angel states, already moving toward the stairs. "They work inside the room. You can keep an eye on us and help feed me information as I need it," he says, Niko nods in understanding, he knows that this is the best way to keep him safe.

"Okay…" says Niko as he gathers his things.

"Come on kid, I'll take you up," Angel indicates with his finger, pointing towards the stairs. I watch as they head upstairs, grateful that Angel is here, that he's taking care of Niko while I go find Eleanor.

"Niko," I say, looking over at him. I need him to know how much he means to me, I need him to understand that he's not just my son, he's my other reason for living. "I love you," I declare, my voice thick with emotion.

"Love you too, Dad," he says back without even a hint of hesitation. the words hit me like a punch to the gut. I thought there would be no way I could ever live without

Eleanor in my life, but this moment right here would be the only reason I would keep breathing.

He might not have been in my life long, but the love that I feel for him is insane, it's overwhelming and all-consuming. I realise that I have two people to fight for now, two people who depend on me, two people for whom I would burn the whole fucking world down for.

There is a piece of me and a piece of Eleanor in him. He is the most perfect thing I've ever created in my whole life, I'm going to make sure that I bring Eleanor back to him because he needs her, and I need her; we're not complete without her.

I wonder if my own parents ever cared about me as I do for Niko. I know the answer is no, they raised me to be a weapon, they raised me to be a Mafia king, not caring about my feelings or my happiness.

I grew up very differently from this kid. My parents didn't coddle me or show me any affection like Eleanor does with Niko. They raised me to be a Mafia king, whereas Eleanor is raising Niko to be a boy, to be kind, compassionate and loving. Looking at it now, I think I like Eleanor's style a whole lot more. I'm going to make sure that Niko grows up with that love and that care always, because he deserves it and Eleanor deserves to be the one here to give it to him.

I'm going to find Eleanor, I'm going to bring her home and I'm going to make whoever took her, pay for what they've done.

Chapter 28

Eleanor Wang

The doctor works methodically, his hands moving with a practiced precision as he manipulates the broken bone back into place. I can feel the grating sensation of the bone fragments as they slide against each other, back into place. It's the most horrifying feeling I've ever experienced. Every single movement he makes while setting the bone back and then wrapping the leg in the cast, sends waves oof pain throughout my body, making me want to scream. Instead, I bite my lip, trying to stay silent, I reach out, gripping the sides of the bed so hard, it feels like I may break my fingers, but I refuse to give Patrick the satisfaction of seeing me break.

"How's it looking?" Patrick asks the doctor, who is yet to tell me his name. He has ignoring my rounds of whispered questions since he first came into the room, I can hear the impatience in his voice and see the way he is tapping his foot against the floor.

"Nearly all done, just adding the last layers. It'll need one to two days to set properly, she can't be moved until then," he announces as he gives me a sly wink, my stomach flips not sure if he's on my side or if he's just being cruel. I search his face for some sign of sympathy, but find none.

"One to two days?!" Patrick yells. the frustration evident in his tone and the way he's losing patience with the situation. "For fucks sake."

"She will need different pain meds from those as well," he says concerned as he point to the Endone on the counter. "Those will make her stomach turn. I'll go and collect something that is a lot gentler on her stomach; we can't have her vomiting all over the new cast, that will set you back further," he explains. I'm grateful for his concern, even if it is just professional.

"Do whatever is needed," Patrick sighs, exhaustion saturating his voice, this is all becoming too much for him. "But I want to be back in London as soon as possible," he adds. the thought of London makes my heart ache because that's where Aela is, that's where my life was before all of this happened.

"I will leave now to go and grab them," the doctor says turning to Patrick. I watch him carefully, trying to memorise his face, just in case I need to identify him later. "Do I need a driver?"

"No, take my car, but be back within 40 minutes," Patrick advises, giving the doctor a cold stare. I watch as the fear flashes across the doctor's face because he knows what Patrick is capable of.

"Of course. I'll wash my hands and be on my way," the doctor says, moving quickly. He washes his hands in the sink, before disappearing out of the room, leaving me alone with Patrick and the sound of my own heartbeat pounding in my ears.

"How are you feeling?" Patrick turns his attention to me as he moves closer to the bed. I try to move away from him, but my leg is immobilised and I'm trapped.

"Like my whole life is a lie, and no one is telling me a thing!" I growl at Patrick, feeling the anger rising inside me. It's hot, fierce and all-consuming because I'm tired of being in the dark, I'm tired of not understanding what's happening to me.

"Hold on, if we are about to talk shop, I'll get us some tea and food," Patrick says, walking out of the room, leaving me alone with my thoughts, my fear and the over-whelming sense that my life is never going to be the same again.

He returns 10 minutes later with a hot bowl of soup and two cups of tea, moving like this is the most normal thing in the world, like he hasn't just kidnapped me, told me that Matteo is dead and informed me that apparently, I'm his property.

"Okay El, what do you want to know first?" Patrick asks while blowing on his tea, like we're out for lunch in a dainty tea shop, the normalcy of the gesture is so at odds with the situation; I feel like I'm going insane.

"Can you please explain to me how exactly I belong to you?" I start, asking the most pressing question, my voice shaking. I need to understand what's happening, I need to know how I got here. I have one day to work out what is happening and find a way out. Matteo isn't dead, I just know it in my bones. And even if he is, Angel or Spike will come. I have to hold on to that, I need to hold on to that, because if I don't have hope, then I have nothing.

"Do you remember your first apartment in Glebe? The one next to the park?" Patrick begins as he leans back in his chair, like he's about to tell me a story, like this is all some grand tale of romance, instead of the nightmare it actually is.

Frowning I look at him, trying to remember, trying to piece together the memories of my younger self. "Yes, of course I do; it was the first apartment I'd lived in after I moved out of home," I say, wondering where this is going, wondering what this has to do with anything.

"Well, I owned that building," he admits, smiling at me as he continues. My frown growing deeper as I start to understand that this goes back further than I'd originally thought. Patrick has been in my life in ways I'd never realised. "I bought it when I heard you moved into it," he says, the realisation starting to dawn on me. This man has been stalking me, has been orchestrating my life without my knowledge.

"But why?" I ask, my voice small and frightened as I searching his face for some explanation that makes sense.

"Do you remember a Mrs. Tinsdale?" he asks, the name sends a chill down my spine because Mrs. Tinsdale was my nanny, she was someone I'd trusted, someone I'd loved.

"Yes, she was my nanny for about two years when I was little," I answer, trying to figure out where this is going, trying to understand the connection.

"She was also mine, but she was mine for a lot longer than she was you," he says, smiling warmly, I recognise the satisfaction in his expression, the way he's enjoying telling me this story. "She showed me a photo of you and your family from the Sydney Telegraph, when your mum put that massive fundraiser for the children's hospital together. It was love at first sight for me. I knew you would be mine," he stated, like he wasn't the biggest stalker known to man. I feel sick, realising that this man has been obsessed with me since I was a child.

"I was 10 when my mum did that! You would have been, what, 18?" I say holding my hands out like a confused monkey. I'm trying to process what he's telling me, trying to understand how someone could become obsessed with a child they saw in a photograph.

"Yes, I was. It was also the same year my dad died. I'd inherited his business and the properties he bought to flip," he says, shrugging like it's all perfectly reasonable. "I also bought this place," he says, holding his hands up and spreading them wide, I see the pride in his expression. "This is Mrs. Tinsdale's house," he says. The realisation hitting me like a blow to the gut.

I think I need a break, my mind is getting jumbled up as I struggle to process all of the information. "Mrs. Tinsdale?" I ask, my voice weak and confused.

"Yes, yes, Mrs Tinsdale, keep up or are those pain meds making your mind cloudy? I swear you're a lot smarter than you're acting right now," Patrick sighs at me, a note of impatience in his voice that makes me want to scream at him.

"Sorry, my mind is taking a while to catch up…" I say, trying to organise my thoughts, to make sense of the web of lies and manipulation that Patrick has been weaving around me.

He smiles at me, it's a gentle smile, the kind of smile that would be comforting, if it wasn't coming from a man who's clearly insane. "It's okay sweetheart, eat your soup, you might need some food," he says, reaching for the bowl like he's about to feed me, like I'm a child.

Maybe I do need food, but my stomach doesn't seem to think so. It feels like it's had battery acid swirling around inside it as I struggle to keep down the bile that's rising in my throat.

Patrick reaches for soup and a spoon, taking to hand feeding me. I watch him with a mixture of fear and disgust, because this is so wrong, it is so twisted. I need to figure out how to escape, how to get away from this man.

"I can feed myself," I grumble, trying to push him away, but my body is weak, injured and I know I'm no match for him.

"Oh, I know you can, but I want to feed you," he says, leaning right over into my face. His breath is hot against my skin as I recoil from him. "I've been patient for 20 years, El. There have been so many things I've wanted to do, but wasn't able to. Having Aela helped me a lot after you had Niko, but it is always you I crave the most," he admits, the words are making my skin crawl. He's been using Aela, he's been manipulating her to get closer to me.

I push the bowl and spoon away from my face with as much force as I can muster. "I can't eat anymore. Please, just stop," I say, my voice is desperate, pleading, and filled with the need for him to leave me alone.

"You really need to eat more," he frowns at me, trying

to push the spoon back toward my mouth, but I turn my head away from him.

"I think I'm going to vomit," I announce, right as I feel the bile rising in my throat and I gag, my body convulsing as the nausea overwhelms me.

Patrick shoves an old white plastic ice cream container under my chin, right as I vomit up the few mouthfuls I'd managed to take. I'm heaving, my body wracking with the force of it. I'm crying, I know I'm trapped, I'm helpless and I don't know how I'm going to survive this.

"Where the fuck is that doctor?" Patrick growls, walking out of the room, leaving me alone with the container of my own vomit and an overwhelming sense of despair because I'm beginning to realise that no one is coming to save me, I'm completely and utterly alone in this nightmare and I have to figure out how to survive it on my own.

I lying back on the bed, staring at the ceiling as I try to hold onto the belief that Matteo is alive, that he's looking for me, that he's going to find me and take me home, but with each passing moment that belief is getting harder to hold onto and I'm starting to wonder if Patrick was telling the truth, if Matteo really is dead and I'm never going to see him again.

The thought is too much to bear, I close my eyes, trying to think of a way out of this, trying to figure out how to escape from a man who's been obsessed with me since I was a child, a man who clearly has no intention of letting me go.

Chapter 29

Matteo Ricci

Right now, it feels like that famous line from the stupid Titanic movie and I can almost hear it playing in my head as we crawl through the traffic. You know the one…. It's been 84 years, and I can still smell the fresh paint…. Yeah, that one and it's the most accurate description of how I feel right now because every second that passes, feels like an eternity, I'm dying inside knowing that Eleanor is out there somewhere, while I'm stuck in a car moving that's at a snail's pace through the city.

I need her back. Now. Not in an hour, not in 30 minutes, but right now. I can feel the desperation building inside me, I'm like a pressure cooker about to explode, struggling to keep it together; but I know if I lose it now then I'm no good to Eleanor.

Not knowing where she is, is tearing me apart, it's eating away at me from the inside out. I can feel my rage and fear mixing together in my chest while the thread that holds me together is getting thinner and thinner with each passing moment.

We have some leads, but they are nothing concrete. Every single second counts and I'm acutely aware that with each second that passes Eleanor could be in danger, she could be hurt, or suffering and I'm not there to protect her, just thinking about it is making me want to scream.

"There has to be a faster way through this traffic!" I growl at Spike who is driving us as fast as can the nighttime traffic of the city. I notice his knuckles are white as they wrap around the steering wheel because he's gripping it so hard. I know he's just as frustrated as I am. Even at 1 am, the traffic is bumper to bumper, it's like the entire city is conspiring against me, trying to keep me from getting to Eleanor.

"I'm going the fastest way, boss," Spike replies as he flips off another driver and cutting him off at the lights. I see the rage in his movements, the way he's channelling his own frustration into aggressively driving and I appreciate it, because it shows me that he cares, that he's just as invested in finding Eleanor, as I am.

Just then my phone rings, the sound cuts through the tension in the car like a knife. It's night security from the office, normally I would have Angel or Spike deal with the mess, but I don't want to leave anything to chance tonight, I need to be involved in every decision, I need to know everything that's happening.

"Ricci," I bark down the line, my voice sharp and dangerous. I feel the fear in the silence that follows.

"Boss, it's Nick here from night security," Nick says back in a rush with urgency in his voice, the way he's speaking quickly is like he's afraid I'm going to hang up on him. "I have a doctor here who desperately needs to talk to you. Says it's about Eleanor," he adds, the words hit me like a lightning bolt. I'm suddenly alert, suddenly focused on this one thing.

"Put him on the line," I command, already leaning forward in my seat knowing I need to hear what this doctor has to say, I need to know if he has information about Eleanor.

"Mr Ricci, Sir," I hear the trembling voice of a man, with fear lacing his voice, he's terrified of me and I'm grateful for that fear, it means he's going to take me seriously, and tell me the truth.

"Tell me where Eleanor is," I growl back in a low and dangerous tone. as the rage hits its peak inside me, I'm done with games, I'm done with waiting, I need to know where Eleanor is and I need to know now.

"If you can promise me the safety of my family, I will," the man practically gushes down the line, there's a desperation in his voice, the way he's begging me to protect his family and I understand, because I would do the same thing if I was in his position. "I know where she is. I just left her side 20 minutes ago. If I'm not back in 20 minutes, he'll know something has changed and Eleanor will be in danger," he says. The urgency in his voice is making my heart race, I know I'm running out of time, we're all running out of time.

"Give Nick the details of your family and I'll send a team to them the second I hang up," I promise, meaning it. I need this man to trust me, I need him to give me the information I need, in order to find Eleanor and I'm willing to do whatever it takes to make that happen.

"Thank you, Sir," I hear him give his name and address to Nick, I'm already signalling to Angel to get a team ready. I need to keep my promise, I need to protect this man's family and I need to do it now.

"Patrick Murphy has her holed up in his old nanny's place, down in Botany. She has a broken leg and broken ribs," he says, gasping for air as he explains in a rush. The words hit me like punches as I struggle to process what he's telling me. Eleanor is hurt, Eleanor is injured. She's been suffering and I'm not there to protect her.

"She has a broken leg and broken ribs," he repeats, the sympathy in his voice clear, the way he understands what this means to me. "I placed a cast on her leg that'll take longer than a day to set in the hopes that you can get there before he can move her. You will need to hurry. I won't be back in the allocated time, and I think the car that he gave me has a tracker," he says, panic seeping through his tone now, the way he's realising that he's made a mistake, that he's put himself in danger.

"Fuck!" I swear as I run my hand through my hair. This is getting more complicated by the second. I need to think, I need to figure out how to get Eleanor out of there without putting her in more danger.

"I wouldn't be surprised if he already knows where I am. You need to get there now," the man's voice wavers on the verge of full panic, he's terrified of what Patrick is going to do to him.

"What's the address?" I ask, just to cross reference it with where we are already heading and I'm already pulling up the map on my phone, needing to see where this house is, I need to figure out the fastest route to get there. I quickly place the phone on speaker, so Angel can hear the address and I see him leaning forward in his seat, ready to take down every detail.

"58 Serpentine Street in Botany. It's a little red brick house with a brick fence," he says as I commit the address to memory, I'm visualising the route in my head, already calculating how long it's going to take us to get there.

"Thank you," I offer, meaning it because this man has just given me the key to finding Eleanor, he's just given me the information I need to bring her home. "I owe you," I add, already thinking about how I can repay this debt because loyalty like this, deserves to be rewarded.

"Just so you know, she can't be moved. She has a nasty break in her leg. The moment you pick her up the leg will no longer be set in place, and she will be in immense pain," he states, the concern in his voice clear, he's worried about Eleanor's wellbeing and I appreciate that because it tells me that he's a good man, he's not just doing this for money or protection.

"Fuck, how do we get her out, then?" I ask, looking to the front where Angel and Spike are sitting, I watch them exchanging glances, knowing they're thinking the same thing I'm thinking, they're wondering how we're going to get Eleanor out of that house without causing her more pain.

"She can be wheeled out on the bed she is in," the doctor answers, relief filling his voice, as he comes up with a solution. "It's one of those hospital beds used in nursing homes," he explains. I'm grateful for this information, it means we have a plan, it means we can get Eleanor out without causing her more injury.

"Boss, I'll arrange a van to come to the house so we can wheel her out," Angel says, while tapping away on his phone, determination written all over his face, he's already putting the pieces together and making it happen.

"How long have you worked for Patrick?" I ask the doctor, trying to figure out who this man is, trying to understand his connection to Patrick and why he's helping us.

"I don't work for Patrick; I work for Enzo Morelli," he replies. The words hit me like a punch to the face as the car goes completely silent. This changes everything, this means that Enzo is involved in this, this means that there's something bigger going on here, bigger than I'd thought.

The silence in the car is deafening, the weight of what he just said settles over us like a heavy blanket as I start to process what this means, trying to figure out why Enzo would help us find Eleanor, trying to understand what his angle is because in this business, there's always an angle, there's always a reason.

Chapter 30

Eleanor Wang

Patrick comes back, bursting into the room, the sound of the door bouncing against the wall makes me jump. My heart rate spikes because I can see the panic on his face, the way he's moving with urgency and desperation, I know something has changed, something has gone wrong.

"We gotta go, El," he says, rushing at me with a small key in his hand. His movements are frantic, jerky, and filled with a kind of desperation that I've never seen in him before. I'm trying to figure out what's happened, what's making him so panicked.

"What? Where? What happened? The doctor said I can't move!" I say, trying to sit up but my body is weak and injured, I can barely move. I look at Patrick in confusion and fear because I don't understand what's happening.

"I don't care what the doctor said, the doctor is gone. We gotta go, love," he states, reaching for the cuff on my wrist that restrains me to the bed. His hands are shaking as he fumbles with the lock, I feel the cold metal of the cuffs release from my wrist.

"Patrick, we can't. The doctor said I cannot move!" I point to my leg, trying to make him understand that moving me is going to cause me serious injury, the cast isn't set yet and if I move, the bone could shift, causing permanent damage.

"I don't give a shit what the doctor said," Patrick replies while sliding one arm under my legs and one behind my back. I register the determination in his face, the way he's made up his mind and nothing is going to stop him from doing this.

"Fuck, Patrick!" I scream out in pain just from the small amount of contact he has made and he hasn't even picked me up yet. The pain is already so intense that I struggle to breathe as I grip his shoulders, trying to brace myself for what's coming.

"I'm sorry El, but this is going to hurt," he says as he heaves me up. The moment my body leaves the bed, the pain is so intense that I think I might die from it, the pain is so all-consuming, I can't think about anything else.

Holy fuck tards baking in the summer sun! That hurts! "Argh!" I scream as black dots scoot through my vision. I gasp for breath, trying to tell him to stop but the pain is too intense, I can barely form words.

"Patrick, stop!" I beg, clawing at his shoulders, trying to get him to put me down, trying to get him to stop moving because every step he takes sends waves of agony through my body and I know I'm on the verge of passing out.

"Seriously El, shut the fuck up," he growls in my ear as

he starts to walk out of the room with me. His voice is harsh, cold, it's nothing like the gentle Patrick I'd thought I knew. I quickly realising that I've never really known him at all.

I hear the faint sounds of a TV on down the hall and I can't help but wonder who's watching it, wondering if there's someone else in this house who might help me, but I'm too weak to call out, too injured to do anything but hang in Patrick's arms, suffering.

Just as I look in the direction of the sound, I hear the front door being kicked open and the distant sound of Matteo's voice screaming my name. My heart stops, because it's him, it's really him and he's come for me. He's alive.

"Eleanor!" I hear him scream, the sound of his voice is like a lifeline, a beacon of hope in the darkness as I struggle to respond, struggling to make my voice work.

"Eleanor!" His faint voice travels to me from the front of the house, it's getting closer and closer. I can feel the hope blooming inside me, because Matteo is here, he's going to save me and everything is going to be okay.

"Matteo!" I call back just as I feel my legs dropping to the floor. A hand wraps around my mouth and the sudden shift in weight sends a fresh wave of pain throughout my leg. I bite back a scream. I need Matteo to know where I am, I need him to find me.

"I said, shut the fuck up, El!" Patrick growls in my ear as his hand presses harder against my mouth. I'm struggling to breathe, I'm panicking because I can't call out to Matteo anymore, I can't let him know where I am.

Searing white pain shoots through my leg and I gag, as

vomit rises in my throat, my body convulses from the pain and the nausea. I'm struggling not to vomit, I know if I vomit with Patrick's hand over my mouth I could choke.

"Matteo!" I continue to scream, even though it's muffled by the hand covering my face. I try to make as much noise as I can, trying to give him an indication of where I am. I kick out with my good leg trying to make contact with Patrick's legs as I thrash against him, trying to break free, trying to do anything I can to get away from him.

I feel us moving backwards, back down the hall towards the rear of the house as I struggle against Patrick's grip, but he's stronger than me. I'm injured and weak, I'm no match for him and I continue to panic because I'm being taken further away from Matteo, from the one person who can save me.

"Eleanor!" I hear Matteo calling me, it's getting closer and closer as I'm trying to scream louder, trying to make more noise, trying to do anything to get his attention, but Patrick's hand is muffling my voice and I'm starting to lose hope.

I try hard to bite Patrick's hand, but I've got too much lip filler in to be able to reach it and I curse myself for my vanity, I curse myself for caring about my appearance, when I should have been focusing on survival. I struggle to find another way to fight back.

As we pass the rooms in the hall, a faint glow emits from one of them and I realise that must be where Mrs. Tinsdale is, and I'm wondering if she knows what's happening, I'm wondering if she's going to help me or if she's part of this nightmare too.

I feel Patrick stop moving as he lets go of my waist, reaching behind him to what I can only assume is a door. The weight of my body is on my legs now, it's excruciating. I feel the room beginning to darken around me, knowing I'm on the verge of passing out from the pain. I struggle to stay conscious, I need to be alert, I need to be ready for whatever comes next.

Just as the door swings open, Matteo's face comes into view, I can see him standing in the doorway and his face filled with rage, determination and relief. I've never been so happy to see anyone in my entire life.

"Eleanor!" I hear him scream, his voice is filled with desperation and love. I try to reach for him, but Patrick has his arm around my waist and I'm trapped.

"Let her go, now!" Matteo commands, his voice is cold and dangerous. I see the rage in his eyes, the way he's ready to tear Patrick apart with his bare hands.

"She isn't yours!" Patrick screams back at Matteo, a different form of desperation in his voice, he's losing control and I realise that he's not going to let me go without a fight.

I feel the cold hard metal of a gun being held to my head and I freeze because I know what this means, I know that Patrick is willing to kill me, rather than let me go. All I can think about is Matteo and Niko, and all the things I'm never going to get to do with them.

"Take another step and you will never see her again," Patrick states, his voice is steady and cold as I feel the barrel of the gun pressing harder against my temple. I hold my breath, terrified that he's going to pull the trigger.

I see Matteo's eyes widen in shock, watching as the

conflict takes over his face, the way he's torn between wanting to save me, and not wanting to risk my life. I'm trying to tell him with my eyes that it's okay, that he should do whatever he needs to do in order to survive.

My vision finally gives in to the pain and everything goes black. I hold onto the image of Matteo's face, holding onto the hope that somehow, someway, he's going to find a way to save me as I slip into the darkness, with his name on my lips.

Chapter 31

Matteo Ricci

Getting to Mrs. Tinsdale's house is a nightmare, acutely aware of the fact we will have at least 5 speeding tickets and 5 red-light camera tickets to deal with after this. Do I care about it? Not even the slightest, because Eleanor is in danger and nothing else matters, nothing else exists beyond the need to get to her and bring her home.

I jump out of the car, before Spike has even pulled into the driveway. My legs moving before my brain even has a chance to catch up, I'm running on pure adrenaline, desperation and the need to find Eleanor, to make sure she's safe.

Running up to the house I kick the front door in, calling out Eleanor's name as I go, the sound of my voice echoing through the empty house while I listen for a response, for any sign that she's here, any indication of where she might be. The house is so dark, except for a light emanating from the room a few doors down the hall, it's where I head there first, knowing that where the light is, it could be where Eleanor is.

I hear Spike and Angel coming in behind me, guns in hand. I'm grateful for their presence, I know I'm not thinking straight, I know I'm operating on emotion rather than logic, needing them to keep me grounded, needing them to keep me focused on the mission.

I walk straight into the room where the light is, only to find it empty, all bar a hospital-style bed with a set of handcuffs hanging off one of the railings, the sight of the handcuffs makes my blood boil, as I picture Eleanor lying in that bed, chained to it, suffering. The rage I'm filled with bubbling at tipping point by the mental image.

Running back out of the room, I keep calling out Eleanor's name, my voice is hoarse from the screaming as I move faster, pushing my body harder, knowing every second counts and I need to find her, now. She has to be here somewhere, this is the right house, that room only confirms, it but there isn't a car in the driveway, so I'm not sure if we are too late, the thought of that, makes me want to scream.

Running down the darkened hallway to the rear of the house, I spot her, my heart skipping, because there she is, being held up by Patrick, his hand covering her mouth while he's opening the back door. I recognise the pain on her face, see the way she's struggling against him and I move towards her without thinking about the consequences.

"Eleanor!" I gasp, her name like a prayer on my lips. "Let her go!" I command, my voice is cold and dangerous. I see the fear registering in Patrick's eyes, he knows what I'm capable of.

"She isn't yours!" Patrick screams back at me, pure

rage and insanity filling in his eyes. I quickly realise that this man, is completely unhinged, he's willing to do anything to keep Eleanor and I prepare myself for a fight.

I watch him raise a gun to her head, my entire world stopping as I watch the barrel of a gun be pressed against Eleanor's temple. I think about how fragile she is, how easily that bullet could end her life and I'm begin struggling to breathe.

"Take another step and you will never see her again," he states, his voice steady and cold. I know he means it. So I stop, trying to figure out what to do, trying to find a way to save her, without getting her killed.

The blood in my veins freezes, I'm standing here paralysed, caught between wanting to rush him and knowing that if I do, Eleanor will die and I can't let that happen, I can't lose her again.

"No!" I reply. Just as I'm about to move I see her body become limp in his arms, crumpling in on herself and I'm not sure what's happening. I'm not sure if she's been shot or if she's just passed out from the pain.

I feel a gun touch the spot between my shoulder blades, and a voice I've heard once before mutters behind my back. The reality of the situation hitting me like a punch to the face, because I know that voice, I know who that is.

"Take another step, and I'll shoot, Matteo," the voice says as I begin turning slowly. I need to see who's behind me, I need to know who's betrayed me.

"Tino," I say, trying to keep my voice steady, trying to keep my emotions in check, I need to think clearly, I need to figure out how to get out of this situation alive.

"Good guess," I hear him smirk from behind me, the satisfaction in his voice obvious, he's enjoying this moment of power over me.

"So, Enzo really is in on this..." I comment, trying to piece together what's happening, trying to understand how Enzo's gotten involved in this.

"A little bit of yes, and a little bit of no," Tino says in my ear, right as I feel the hot spray of blood splatter hitting the back of my head and shirt. I'm confused for a moment, not sure exactly what's happening, until it hits me, someone just shot Tino.

"That fucker talks too much," I hear Spike giggling beside me. I turn fully around to find a knife sticking out of Tino's neck, as blood continues to gush out all over the floor. I'm grateful for Spike's quick thinking, grateful that he's always got my back.

I swing back to Patrick, watching him as he leans down, trying to scoop Eleanor up off the floor and I move without thinking, lunging toward him with everything I have. I throw my shoulder into him, sending us both through the open doorway as we land on top of one another in the backyard; the impact is jarring and painful.

Pain slams into me, I know that my collarbone has to be shattered by now as I struggle to breathe, but I'm not stopping, I refuse to give up, because Eleanor is right there and I need to get to her, I need to make sure she's safe.

Instantly I feel a hard punch to the cheek, Realising quickly that Patrick isn't as weak as I'd thought, just clinically insane, I've underestimated him. I need to be more careful and more strategic about this fight.

"You can't have her, she's mine," Patrick declares, his

voice is filled with an obsession and madness that has me seeing red, because he's wrong, Eleanor is not his, she's mine and I'm going to make sure he understands that.

"Not a bloody chance," I respond, jumping on top of Patrick. I begin pummelling my fist into his face, over and over again, putting all of my rage and desperation into every punch, trying to beat the life out of the man who dared to take Eleanor from me.

As I'm punching him, I look down, seeing that Patrick still has the gun in his left hand, which he has now turned and is pointing up towards my chest, He fires off a shot that travels through the front of my chest and out of my shoulder. I feel a sudden white hot pain surging through my shoulder, the pain so intense that I think I might die from it.

I'm gasping for breath as I struggle to stay conscious because the pain is overwhelming. I know I'm losing blood as I start to feel woozy and weak.

"Boss!" I hear as I collapse forward on top of Patrick. I'm trying to stay awake, trying to keep fighting, but my body is shutting down on me.

I feel a boot push me off to the side as a rain of bullets falls into Patrick. All I hear is the pop, pop, pop, pop as Angel empties his clip into Patrick's chest, I'm grateful that Angel is here, grateful that he's finishing what I started.

"Fuck, boss!" I hear, seeing Angel rush over to me as he places a hand on my shoulder. Concern filling in his eyes, he's worried about me. I try to tell him that I'm okay, but I'm not sure if I am okay, I'm not sure if I'm going to survive this.

"We gotta get out of here, before someone calls the

cops!" Angel yells. He's right, we need to get out of here, we need to get Eleanor and me to safety.

Trying to sit, my head feels woozy, I'm struggling to focus, struggling to keep my eyes open because the pain is so intense. I'm losing blood and I'm not sure how much longer I can stay conscious.

"I don't think I can walk..." I admit, my voice weak and defeated. I hate myself for being weak, for not being able to protect Eleanor better.

"Fuck off, cunt. Stand the fuck up, let's go!" Angel demands as he starts pulling me up to my feet. He wraps an arm around my side and I'm grateful for his strength, grateful that he's here to help me because I'm not sure I could do it on my own.

Angel walks me back inside where I see Spike holding Eleanor in his arms as he walks down the hall to the front door. The sight of her in his arms makes my heart ache, I should be the one holding her, I should be the one carrying her to safety, but I'm too injured, too weak.

"The van should be out the front, go get Eleanor inside," Angel yells out at Spike's back. I'm trying to focus on the fact that Eleanor is safe, that we're getting her out of here, that we're going to make it.

"On it," I hear Spike reply as he moves quickly and efficiently, getting Eleanor to safety.

"Come on cunt, walk faster, we need to get some pressure on you before you bleed out on us," Angel grunts, trying to get me to walk faster. I'm trying to move my legs, trying to keep up with him, but my body is failing me and I'm struggling to stay upright.

Stepping out the front door, I see Spike loading

Eleanor into an ambulance, before he walks back to help Angel get me inside with her. I'm grateful that we have an ambulance, because I'm not sure how much longer I can stay conscious, I need medical attention soon or I'm going to bleed out.

I see her tiny frame lying on a bed in the back, that's when I actually realise we are piling into an ambulance, the confusion takes over for a moment because I'm not sure why there's an ambulance here, I'm not even sure where it's come from.

"Angel, why the fuck is there an ambulance here," I ask, frowning at him as I try to make sense of what's happening, trying to understand how we've gotten an ambulance so quickly.

"It's okay, they are under our employ. They will drop you guys off at the warehouse, the doctor's waiting," Angel states. I'm grateful for his foresight, grateful that he's already thinking ahead to what we need to do next.

"Since when have we had an ambulance on our payroll?" I ask Angel, trying to remember if I've authorised this, if I approved the expense.

"Since your son employed seven of them last week thinking it would be a good investment," Angel laughs at me. "Turns out the kid was right; might wanna give him a pay rise, boss!" he adds. I just shake my head, because it's so like Niko to do something like this without asking me first.

"Kid can have anything in this damn world that he wants," I exclaim, because Niko just saved our lives, Niko had made a decision that's enabled us to get Eleanor and myself to safety and I'm proud for that.

"Thanks, Dad, I've been eyeing off a new TV, seeing as I need a new one now," I hear Niko's voice, confused for a moment because I'm not sure where he is, not sure how he's talking to me.

"Where the fuck are you?" I growl, my voice is weak but filled with authority. "You're meant to be in the safe room," I snap, trying to figure out what he's doing, trying to make sure he's safe.

"Oh, don't worry I am. I've just hacked into the ambulances radio," he laughs at me and I can hear the pride in his voice, the way he's proud of his hacking skills, I just shake my head, because it's so like Niko.

"Fucking kids," I grumble, smiling even despite the pain. Niko is safe and Eleanor is safe and that's all that matters, that's all I care about right now.

I lay in the ambulance next to Eleanor, reaching over to take her hand, holding onto her like she's the only thing keeping me alive, because she is. She's the only thing that matters to me, she's the only reason I'm still fighting.

Chapter 32

Eleanor Wang

Waking up in two different places in a row, can suck a donkeys dick. I'm acutely aware that my body is becoming intimately familiar with strange beds and unfamiliar rooms. I'm starting to wonder if I'm ever going to sleep in my own bed again, and if I'm ever going to feel safe and comfortable again.

This time I wake up in an old room, in what can only be described as a makeshift hospital room. It has all the equipment, the monitors and machines that a real hospital would have, but the walls are not white and it's certainly not bright or clean. There's a staleness to the air that tells me we're somewhere that's not a hospital.

Looking to my left I see Matteo lying on a hospital bed similar to my own. His eyes are shut and my heart stops because he looks so pale. He's so still, so lifeless, I immediately panic because I can't lose him, I can't survive losing him again.

I struggle to get a breath and my chest is tightening as

the panic sets in, my mind running through all the worst thoughts, imagining all the ways this could go wrong.

"Matteo!" I call out to him, my voice shaking and desperate as I try to reach for him, but my body won't cooperate, my leg screaming in pain as I struggle to move.

"Matteo!" I yell, trying to practically scramble out of the bed as pain sears through my leg at the movement. I'm gasping, crying out because the pain is so intense, but I'm not thinking about my own injuries, I'm only thinking about getting to Matteo, about making sure he's alive.

Looking around I notice the door to the room is open, desperate, panicked, and not thinking clearly, I scream out,

"Help!" my voice is raw, filled with fear and desperation. I'm hoping someone can hear me, I'm hoping that someone comes to help me.

I instantly hear footsteps running towards the room as two faces step through, I try to focus on who they are, trying to recognise them through my panic.

Angel and Spike.

I don't think I've ever been happier to see them. I immediately reach for them, trying to communicate my fear and panic.

"Matteo," I point at his bed, my voice shaking as I try to tell them that something is wrong, Matteo isn't moving, I think he might be dead.

"It's okay, Eleanor, he is sedated. He got shot and the doc had to patch him up," Spike tells me as he wraps his arms around me giving me a hug. I feel the warmth of his embrace and the reassurance in his voice, I start to calm down, understanding that Matteo is okay, he's just sleeping.

"You scared the fucking shit out of me," Spike states, frowning at me. I can see the genuine fear in his eyes, the way he's worried about me. "Do that again, and I'll kill you myself," he states, but there's no heat in his words, only affection and concern.

"Fuck off," I hear Angel behind him as Spike steps out of the way. Angel is moving toward me with his arms open. "I'll fucking kill her," he states as he wraps his arms around me too, I'm surrounded by their warmth, their love and I feel safe for the first time since I'd woken up in that strange house.

I feel the tears pricking in my eyes as they begin to run down my cheeks. I'm crying, letting go all of the fear, trauma and pain I've been holding inside. I'm grateful that Angel and Spike are here, grateful that they're holding me and just allowing me to fall apart.

"What happened?" Angel asks, his voice is gentle and concerned. I try to piece together the memories, trying to remember what happened.

"I don't really know," I reply, my voice shaky and uncertain. "I woke up in that strange house and Patrick was there.... Oh shit, Patrick!" I say, looking around like he might pop up like Michael Myers seems to always do. I start to panic again, because I'm not sure if Patrick is dead, or if he's still a threat.

"Shhhh, it's okay. I emptied my clip into his chest," Angel informs me, I can hear the satisfaction in his voice as he gives me another hug and starts rubbing my back, I can tell he's pleased that he took care of Patrick. "He is gone," he assures me. I feel a wave of relief wash over me with the knowledge that Patrick is dead, because Patrick can't hurt me anymore, Patrick can't take me away from Matteo anymore.

"Fuck! What am I going to say to Aela?" I start crying again, thinking about my friend, I'm worried about how she's going to react when she finds out that her husband is dead, I feel guilty in a way, because even though Patrick was a monster, he was still her husband and I'm responsible for his death in a way.

"Seriously, that's what you worried about right now?" Spike looks at me in shock, the disbelief written all over his face, I know he's thinking I should be worried about myself instead of Aela.

Shrugging at him I say, "I suppose so; I don't know what to think at the moment," I say, being honest. my mind is a jumbled mess of emotions and thoughts. I'm struggling to process everything that's happened.

"I think you should stop hugging Angel, and hug me instead," I hear Matteo's voice grumble from his bed., I immediately turn towards him, peering out from Angels embrace, I see his eyes open. and I feel a rush of relief, so intense I might pass out again.

"Matteo..." I breathe out a sigh of relief., Getting a glimpse of Matteo, I can see the love in his eyes, the way he's looking at me like I'm the most precious thing in the world.

"Fuck off boss, this is my hug; get your own," Angel laughs at him, the affection in his voice clear, he's teasing Matteo, but also showing him that he cares.

"That's what I'm trying to do!" Matteo replies, his voice is weak but filled with determination. I watch him trying to move, trying to reach for me.

"Hang on, boss," I hear Spike say, before I hear the distant sound of brakes being let off the wheels on Matteo's bed. Spike pushes our beds next to each other, then I hear the sounds of the brakes engaging again, I'm thankful for Spike's quick thinking, he's making it possible for us to be close.

"Hey, Princess," Matteo says, holding out his hand to me. I reach for it immediately, holding onto it like it's the most precious thing in the world.

"Hey yourself," I reply, taking it in mine. I squeeze his hand gently, needing to feel him, needing to know that he's real, he's alive, he's here with me and I'm never letting him go again.

I look at him lying in the hospital bed, seeing the bandages across his chest and shoulder and I remember the moment when he was shot. A wave of guilt washes over me, because I'm the reason he was shot, he was hurt because of me and I struggle knowing that.

"You scared me," I say, my voice soft and filled with emotion as I look into his eyes. I can see his love there, I see the way he's looking at me, like I'm the reason he's alive, I'm the reason he's still fighting.

"I know, Princess," he says, squeezing my hand gently. "But I'm here now, and I'm not going anywhere," he assures me. I'm holding onto those words, holding onto the promise that he's not going to leave me, that we're going to get through this together.

Angel and Spike are watching us with smiles on their faces, the affection shining from their eyes, they're happy that we're together, they're happy that we've both made it through alive.

"We'll give you two some space," Angel says, gesturing to Spike before they both head towards the door. I'm thankful for their understanding, thankful that they know what we both need right now.

Chapter 33

Matteo Ricci

The sweet melody of Eleanor's voice pulls me from the dark weight of sleep that clouds my mind. It's the sweetest sound I've ever heard, I hold onto it like a lifeline, because if I can hear her, it means she's alive, it means she's here, and I haven't lost her.

Even though my eyelids refuse to open on command, I can clearly hear that the voices are content and okay. I lay here listening to her voice as she speaks with Angel and Spike, willing my eyelids to open, because I need to see her, I need to make sure she's really here and that it's not just a dream.

I feel pain throughout my chest and back, a dull but constant throb reminding me of the bullet that went through me. Clearly the doctor has filled me with some amazing painkillers because the pain is manageable. Being shot was a bitch, but seeing as I'm awake already means I must not have had a lot of damage either, and for that I'm grateful because I need to be here for Eleanor, I need to be here for my family.

Once my body has caught up with my mind, I am able to open my eyes into a decently lit room, I'm immediately wondering why they have so many lights on.

My eyes lock onto a woman, whose face is buried into Angel's chest as he rubs her back. And fuck, she is a sight to behold. I drink in the image of her alive, because I'd almost lost her, I almost didn't get to see her again. Just thinking about it makes my chest ache more than the gunshot wound.

Her long thick black hair is tangled up around her shoulders and I don't think I've ever seen her hair looking so dishevelled. She is always complaining that no matter what she does to her hair, it's always dead straight, she used to curse it. But now, that theory is out the window. I wonder if she will appreciate me telling her that her hair looks beautiful like this, that she looks beautiful like this, that even though she looks like she's been to hell and back, she's somehow still the most beautiful woman I've ever seen.

"Seriously, that's what you worried about right now?" Spike replies to Eleanor. I try to figure out what they're talking about, trying to piece together the conversation, but my mind is still foggy from the painkillers and from sleep.

"I think you should stop hugging Angel, and hug me instead," I manage to say to the room. My voice is hoarse and weak, but I'm putting all the authority I can muster into it, needing Eleanor to know that I'm awake, to know that I'm here.

"Matteo…" Eleanor breathes out a sigh of relief while attempting to detangle herself from Angel. She twists to look over at me, the tears building in her eyes as she looks at me like I'm the most precious thing in the world. It makes my heart ache, I love her so much and I'd almost lost her.

"Fuck off, boss, this is my hug, get your own," Angel laughs at me, I can hear the affection in his voice, the way he's teasing me, but also showing me that he cares; he's glad I'm awake.

"That's what I'm trying to do," I state, reaching out toward Eleanor, but my body is weak, I'm struggling to move; I hate myself for being so weak, for not being able to get to her on my own.

"Hang on, boss," Spike mutters, before pushing my bed closer to Eleanor's, making it so I can reach my hand out to touch hers. I'm appreciative for his quick thinking, grateful that he understands what I need, without me even having to ask.

My hand finds hers and I hold onto it like it's the most precious thing in the world, because to me it is, she is and I'm never letting her go again, I'll never allow anyone to take her away from me again.

"Hey, Princess," I greet her, my voice soft and filled with love, relief and all the emotions I've been holding back since I'd found out she was gone.

"Hey, yourself," Eleanor replies, squeezing my hand. I can feel the strength in her grip and it gives me hope, it tells me that she's going to be okay, that we're both, going to be okay.

"You feeling okay?" I ask, searching her face for any sign of pain or distress, needing to know that she's alright, that Patrick didn't hurt her too badly.

"I'll be fine; I wasn't the one who was shot," she says, pointing to the bandages on my chest and shoulder, the concern is shining from in her eyes, she's worried about me and it makes me love her even more, because even after everything she's been through, she's still thinking about me, still worried about my wellbeing.

"Well, seeing as I'm awake, I'm gonna assume I'll be just fine too," I say, winking terribly , trying to make her laugh, trying to lighten the mood. We've been through so much, and I want her to know that we're going to be okay, that everything is going to be okay. It's the thought that counts right?

"Um, did you just try to wink, boss?" Spike asks, looking at me as both his eyebrows creep into his hairline, the amusement lighting up his face, while he tries not to laugh.

"Yep!" I say, popping the 'p'. I grin, knowing full well that I probably looked ridiculous, but I don't care. Eleanor is smiling and that's all that matters.

"Ummm, well that wasn't a wink," Spike laughs at me, affection filling his voice, he may be teasing me, but in his own way he's also showing me that he's glad I'm awake and okay.

"Fuck off, cunt," I retort, but there's no heat in it, only affection and gratitude, because Spike helped save my life, Spike helped to save Eleanor's life and I'm going to make sure he knows how much I appreciate that.

"You two need to rest," Angel states, his voice serious

and I know he's right. I know that Eleanor and I both need to recover from what we've been through. "We have a lot to do," he adds. The weight in his words reminding me that there's still business to be handled, there's still the matter of Enzo and what he's involved in.

"Please, feel free to elaborate, Angel," I offer as I try to focus on what he's saying, trying to understand what still needs to be done.

"It can all wait, boss," Angel points at Eleanor. "You might wanna allow Eleanor some time to recover and let the new cast set on her leg," he says and I can see the wisdom in his words, he's right and I'm appreciative for his guidance.

Sighing, I know that Angel is very much correct. I ask, "Did the doctor put the correct cast on this time?" I'm asking because I want to make sure that Eleanor is going to heal properly, I want to make sure that she's going to be okay.

"What do you mean 'correct cast'?" Eleanor asks, confusion taking over her face, she doesn't understand what I'm talking about.

"The doc placed a plaster cast on you last time, knowing it'd take days to set, so he could create extra time for you," Angel explains, I watch as the realisation dawns on her face, understanding that the doctor had helped her all along. "He was then meant to go get different medica-tion for ya, which allowed him to go to the office in the city and alert us to your whereabouts," Angel continues and I'm thankful for the doctor's quick thinking, grateful that he was able to get us the information we needed.

"Really?" Eleanor asks, the shock in her voice evident,

realising that the doctor was on her side the whole time. "I was begging and pleading with him the whole time he set my leg, but he didn't respond to me once," she exclaims with a confused expression, I can see the hurt in her eyes, the way she thought he was ignoring her, when really he was protecting her.

"Patrick was holding the safety of his family over his head," Spike shrugs, I watch Eleanor's expression morph into understanding, the doctor was doing what he had to do, in order to protect his family.

"When he got to the office, he had night security call us, he demanded his families safety before he'd help you," Angel adds, I nod because I remember that conversation, I remember the fear in the doctor's voice when he asked for protection for his family.

"He works for Enzo," Angel says, pulling his phone out of his pocket. I'm listening carefully because this is the important part, this is the key to understanding what happened. "Well, he did work for Enzo," Angel corrects himself and I can hear the satisfaction in his voice, the way he's pleased that we've turned the doctor to our side.

"He now works for Matteo?" Eleanor smiles, I see the hope in her eyes, the way she's beginning to understands that we're building something, we're creating a new order.

"He now works for us, Princess," I say, making sure she remembers that she is the queen of the Ricci's now and that everything we do, we do together. I watch as the smile spreads across her face, accepting her place in my world.

"Yes, okay, for us," she smiles at me as I hold her hand through the bars on the bed. I'm grateful for this moment, grateful that we're here together and we're alive. "Angel, can you lower these god-forsaken rails, please?" she asks frustrated, she wants to be closer to me.

Angel walks over, he pulls the pin holding the rails up and lowers both sides down, understanding fully, he knows what Eleanor needs, without her even having to explain it.

Eleanor scoots herself closer to me, so she can semi-snuggle into my side and hold my hand properly, the feeling of her pressed against me is like a balm to my soul as I hold onto her, I breathe in the scent of her hair, glad that she's here, and that we've made it through.

"Thank you," she says to Angel, her voice is soft, filled with affection. "Now, fuck off so I can nap," she adds playfully.

Spike and Angel both laugh at her. "Anything you say, boss," they say in unison, which only makes them laugh harder as they leave the room. I'm thankful their loyalty, and their friendship, without them I wouldn't have Eleanor back.

"You sure you're okay, Princess?" I ask into her hair, which is currently tickling my chin.

"I'll be okay," she says, her voice soft and filled with exhaustion. "But I really do need to sleep. Whatever the doc gave me hasn't worn off and doing as little as I've just done feels like I've run a marathon," she explains, the tiredness taking over her voice, her body is shutting down from the trauma and the medication.

Chuckling a little into her hair I say, "Love you," and I mean it with every fibre of my being, I love her more than I love my own life, I love her more than I love anything in this world.

"Love you too," she murmurs, her voice drowsy as I

hold her closer. I listen to her breathing even out as she falls asleep, grateful for this moment, grateful that we're here together, we're alive and we are going to be okay.

Chapter 34

Matteo Ricci

Let it be known that shoulder wounds are pretty horrible, add in a fractured collarbone on top on the same side and you've got hell. I'm learning this the hard way as I try to find a comfortable position that doesn't send waves of pain through my entire body. It's becoming clear that sleep is going to be a luxury, I won't be having for a while.

You have to sleep sitting up, I swear this is how and what lazy-boy chairs were designed for. I find myself spending more time in the recliner, than I'd ever thought I would, it's a bitch to get in and out of. but they do deliver a level of comfort that one can't muster by being propped up in a bed. Trust me I've tried, but the pain is too intense and I can't find a position that works.

I don't like sleeping separately from Eleanor, I think that's the real problem, being away from her, even for a few hours, makes me anxious, paranoid and I find myself constantly wondering if she's okay, if she needs me, if she's in pain and I can't be there to help her.

I have had the chair placed next to the bed, so I can at least be in the same room, but the small amount of distance still sucks. I find myself reaching over in the middle of the night just to touch her hand, to make sure she's still here, to reassure myself that she hasn't disappeared again.

Thankfully, Angel or Spike are able to carry her upstairs to bed every night, to which I am thankful for, because I'm not strong enough to do it myself right now, and that's something I hate. I hate being weak and dependent on others, but Eleanor needs to be in a real bed and I'm not going to deny her that comfort, just because I am injured.

She has yet to master, stairs versus crutches, I'm not overly keen on allowing her to try either, I am terrified that she will fall, that she will re-injure her leg, that I will lose her again and I can't survive that, I can't handle losing her a third time.

We had only gotten a few hours of sleep in the makeshift hospital room at the warehouse, before Angel had us moved back home and I was definitely glad to be back in my own house.

We have 7 days till the four seats meeting, which means we have 7 days to work out how Enzo is involved in everything and who really hired the other two men. The 7 days are ticking away and I am acutely aware that time is running out, I need answers before I walk into that meeting.

At first Eleanor declares she wants to go and interrogate the two men herself, I have to admire her fierce determination, but being that it's only been 3 days since we've gotten home and quickly realising that the pain in her leg isn't going away, she relinquishes the role, handing it off to Spike and I could see the frustration on her face, she hates being sidelined, but she is smart enough to know her limitations.

Spike left 5 hours ago and we still haven't heard a word from the man. I'm starting to get anxious, but Angel assures us Spike is fine and he has a video link going, just to make sure it's all going okay and will give us any information that they find out, soon. I trust Angel, trust his judgment, but even I am still on edge.

Niko has taken to sleeping in our bed next to Eleanor every night, nearly losing her has done a number on him and he needs her close at all times. He only uses his dungeon downstairs to shower and change, choosing to follow his mother from room to room instead. I understand, because I feel the same way, I need her close, need to know she is safe.

It doesn't seem to bother Eleanor one bit, instead she's revelling in the attention and love he's showing her. I can see the way she's clinging to him, just as much as he's clinging to her. I sometimes feel like a spectator, watching my favourite show about the two people I love most in this world.

"Spike is heading home now," Angel announces from the dining table. I look up from where I am sitting in my recliner, as I try to find a comfortable position.

"I always forget that man has a house of his own," Eleanor frowns. I can see her mind working, she's planning something. "Matteo, I wanna buy the neighbour's houses. That way Angel and Spike live closer," she declares, I look over at her, worried she's lost her mind, but also loving her for thinking about our family, for wanting to keep them close.

Angel full-blown belly-laughs at her, the amusement lighting up his face, the way he finds her idea ridiculous.

"What is so damn funny?" she scolds, a note of indignation to her voice.

"You do not want me living next door, Eleanor," he continues to chuckle.

"Why not?" she says, crossing her arms and glaring at him. "It would make it easier to get to and from work, and I could keep an eye on you!" she declares and I can see the logic in her thinking.

"That right there is exactly why!" Angel says, grinning at her like he knows something she doesn't.

"I'm confused…" she continues to frown at him.

"You know how you love a form of voyeurism?" He smiles at her and I'm suddenly very interested in where this conversation is going.

"Yes…" she says dragging the word out as she tries to figure out what he means.

"Well, it's one of my favourite past times," Angel says, I bite back a laugh, because I know exactly where this is going now.

Eleanor's eyes go wide, her mouth dropping open at Angel's admission. "You do not," she says, her voice is filled with shock and disbelief.

"Oh, Eleanor, the last thing you want, is to be out hanging the washing in the morning and looking up at my balcony," he grins like a Cheshire cat and I can't help but laugh at the image he's painting.

"Ooh my God!" she declares, covering Niko's ears.

"You dirty, dirty, man," she says, bursting out laughing at him and I can see the flush on her cheeks, she's embarrassed but also amused.

"I think the view of the bay is all you need," Angel says, pointing out the window, and I watch as Eleanor looks out at the water, and the beautiful view we have from our home.

"I think you're right about that one," she says, looking over at me with a slight flush to her cheeks, and I can see the mischief in her eyes.

"I don't mind buying the neighbour's houses," I wink at her. Her eyes narrow at me,

"Oh, shut up," she says, throwing the pen she had been holding at me. "You're all a bunch of dirty men," she declares, but there's zero argument from anyone with that comment, we all know she's correct.

We all know that she loves us anyway, she's accepted us for who we are, dirty men and all.

A COUPLE OF HOURS LATER SPIKE TURNS UP, FRESHLY washed and dressed, I watch Eleanor's eyes narrowing as she takes in his appearance.

"What took you so long?" Eleanor questions from the seat she hasn't left since this morning, I can hear the concern in her voice, she's been worried about him.

"Had to go home and clean up," Spike shrugs, moving toward the couch.

"That's a long fucking shower!" Eleanor glares at him.

"Where do you live? Fucking Campbelltown?" She frowns at him.

"No, I have an apartment in Paddington," he frowns back at her. "What's with the interrogation?" he asks, struggling to hide the amusement from his face, I know he finds her concern endearing.

"She wants to buy the neighbour's houses and have us move in," Angel announces as he walks back into the room carrying popcorn like this is a daytime TV show, and I have to bite back a smile.

"She does know you're into voyeurism, right?" Spike looks at her mischievously.

"She does now," Angel comments as, the room fills with laughter.

"So, not keen to buy the neighbour's pads anymore?" Spike raises his eyebrows, grinning at her and I see Eleanor's face flush red.

"Yeah, Nah, I've changed my mind," she laughs back, trying to move past the embarrassment. "But seriously, what took you so long? I've been a bit worried," she frowns at him again, genuinely concerned.

"I usually like to blow off some steam after I've spent time doing what I was doing," Spike explains, using his fingers to do some air quotes and I understand what he's saying.

"Oh," Eleanor flushes bright red, "sorry," she mumbles at him and I notice the way she's embarrassed for asking.

Spike walks over to her and kisses the top of her head. "Thank you for caring but…" he whispers to her, the affection between them making it obvious, they've become family.

I love how sweet the Buffy clan is to her, they've taken her back into their Vampire den without blinking an eye. This right here is my family, blood or not blood, this is it and I am grateful for every single one of them.

"So, what did you find out?" I ask both Angel and Spike as Spike takes a seat next to Eleanor. I lean forward slightly, ignoring the pain in my shoulder because I need to hear what they've discovered.

"A lot actually, and I'm sure Angel has already done some digging as he got the information too," Spike looks at Angel and I can see the respect between them, the way they work together, so seamlessly.

"Yep!" Angel says, popping the 'p'. The satisfaction that crosses his face means he's pleased with what he's found.

"Okay, so...," Spike begins, as I settle back into my chair, preparing myself for what's coming.

"Umm, are we gonna talk with mini-me in the room?" Angel points at Niko. I look over at my son, at the way he's listening intently to every word.

"Even though I would love to say no," Eleanor admits, and I can see the conflict on her face, she wants to protect him, but she also knows he needs to understand. "I think it's time for Niko to understand the issues at hand; he is a Ricci after all." she sighs heavily, accepting his place in this world.

"You say that with such reverence!" I quip, shaking my head. I know she's trying to embrace her role as the queen of the Ricci's, while also trying to teach Niko about his legacy.

"Well, his father is the king of the underworld, is he

not?" she points at me, and I see the pride in her eyes, she's proud of who I am.

"And his mother is the queen," I retort, seeing a smile on her face, she's accepting the title.

"Are we gonna stay on topic today, children?" Spike asks, holding his hands up like a set of scales, while Angel just sits there eating his popcorn. I think maybe I should have gotten some popcorn too, because this is going to be a long conversation.

"Yes, sorry," Eleanor says and I can see her refocusing, putting on her business face.

"Okay well, for all intents and purposes, Fuckwit No.1 told me he was hired by a man named Tino to do the job," Spike begins. I listen intently, processing every word. "He had been on our payroll for years, but when Tino approached him, he made an offer he couldn't say no to," Spike continues. "He was paid 50k in cash up front for the job and he was assured that no one would find out and that the apartment security cameras would be removed the day before."

"So, I'm gonna take a guess and say this is the same Tino that was Enzo's right-hand man?" Eleanor states.

"Yes, one in the same," Spike replies and I can see the confirmation in his eyes, he's certain about this information.

"This makes sense, as the apartment building paperwork shows there was some security camera maintenance in the building the same week it all went down," Angel adds and I nod, because this is starting to make sense, it's all starting to come together.

"Right, well that's it for Fuckwit No.1," Spike declares as he prepares to move on to the next piece of information.

"As for Fuckwit No.2, this is where things get interesting," Spike eyes the room as he bites his bottom lip. I know this next part is important, this is where things get complicated.

"So, Fuckwit No.2 was the one who'd had the most amount of contact with Tino; he said Tino approached him on a building site where he was working and offered him the same deal as the rest," Spike takes a breath before continuing. "The only difference was, he was to do the scoping out of the building, arrange the day and time that worked best, and arrange everyone to execute their plan," Spike explains.

"They were meant to go in, rough you up, and get you to leave. That's it," Spike admits, anger flashing across his face, he's disgusted by what they did. "What they did was because he told them that was the plan; he'd changed it, to suit himself," Spike says. The information has the rage building inside me. This means the attack was worse than it should have been, this means someone deliberately made it worse.

"I ran his record; he had priors for rape and stalking," Angel adds. I feel sick, this man was a predator, this man was dangerous and he was let loose on Eleanor.

"So, was he on my payroll too?" I ask and I'm trying to figure out how this man got involved in all of this.

"No, he wasn't, but he was on the payroll of a company your family used for building," Angel looks me dead in the eye as I try to remember, trying to piece together the connections. "Remember when your dad had the club in the Cross refurbished into a strip club?" Angel asks.

"The gentleman's only one?" I ask, starting to remember the project, starting to recall the details.

"Yes," Spike says, seeing the confirmation in his eyes.

"That's the building site he was approached on," Angel states, I feel the pieces clicking into place, as I understand how this all connects.

"If I remember correctly, Enzo was against it; he wanted to turn it into a brothel?" I try hard to think back, and I can see the memory forming, remembering the conflict that arose from that decision. "But the council said no, and my dad was also against the idea," I state, remembering the arguments, and the tension that arose from the decision.

"I think that's when the rift between the two men started," Spike states, I can see the understanding in his eyes, the way he's pieced this all together.

"That was when the fighting began, and the issues between your dad and the four seats really started to show," Angel adds, I just nod, remembering it all, remembering the tension that was building during that time.

I'm trying to process all of this information, trying to understand how it all connects.

"Well, after they did what they did," Spike continues, side-eyeing Niko. He's clearly being careful about what he says in front of my son. "Tino met with him to confirm that it was done. When he told Tino what they had done, Tino was furious with him and threatened to kill him if he ever told anyone else," Spike explains. I understand that

Tino was trying to control the situation, trying to keep things from spiralling out of control.

"I suspect that if Patrick had found out, he wouldn't have been too happy; his obsession was already in full swing by then," Angel states and I realising that Patrick was already involved in this, his obsession with Eleanor had already been driving his actions.

"I still don't see how this ties Patrick and Enzo together. I mean they are clearly linked, but I just don't see how?" Eleanor frowns as she's trying hard to piece together the puzzle, trying to understand the connection.

"I agree. They are clearly working together, with Tino as the go-to guy between them, but why?" I ask, frustrated. I need to understand the motivation, I need to know why they're working together.

"Well, clearly Patrick is someone to Enzo," Niko chimes in for the first time.

"How? But…" Eleanor looks thoughtful and I watch as her mind works, trying to figure out the connection.

"Well, Enzo is old enough to be his dad," Niko states and I see where he's going with this. "I mean, the guy is the same age as your Dad would have been," Niko says. I nod because he's right, Enzo is old enough to be Patrick's father.

"True, my dad would have been 57 this year, but Enzo didn't have any kids that we know about; I don't think the guy ever even got married?" I state looking at Angel for confirmation as I try to remember if I've ever heard anything about Enzo having children.

"Nothing on record at all," Angel shakes his head, seeing the certainty in his eyes, he's done his research.

"I need something; I can't go into this meeting with Enzo and not kill him," I state, the rage building inside me. I know what's coming, I know that I'm going to have to face Enzo and I'm not sure I can control myself.

I already know I won't make it past the door without putting a bullet in his head and without any proof, the others will shoot me straight after. I'll be dead before I can explain myself and that's not acceptable, that's not how this is going to go down.

"How old is Patrick?" Niko asks.

"38 this year," Eleanor responds without any hesitation and I hate that she knew him so well, I hate that she'd considered him to be that close of a friend.

"So that makes him what... 19 when Patrick was born?" Spike shrugs as he works out the math in his head, trying to figure out the timeline.

"Only issue is, Patrick was born in Ireland," Eleanor states, with uncertainty in her voice. "Well, he'd told me he was born in Ireland, and his birth certificate was Irish, but I honestly don't know what's bloody true anymore," she adds. I can hear the frustration in her voice, the way she's realising that everything she thought she'd known about Patrick was a lie.

I am definitely going to bring this cunt back from the grave, just to kill him all over again and I am going to make it slow and painful this time and I'll enjoy every second of it.

Angel starts tapping away rapidly on his laptop, focusing intently, he's determined to find the answers we need. "Let me see what countries he has been to and when..." Angel says. The room goes silent, all bar the sound of Angel tapping away. I hold my breath, waiting for him to find something, anything that will help us understand what's happening.

"Don't our records show that Patrick's dad was Conner Murphy?" Spike interjects.

"Yes," Eleanor states, sadness saturating her voice. "His parents were Conner and Caitlin. They were both listed on his birth certificate. Patrick told me they died when he was 18 in a building accident. They left him with enough money to buy a few properties and start his investment business," she explains and I can't help but wonder if this is another lie, if Patrick's parents are even dead.

"Okay, so Enzo has never left Australia," Angel grumbles, frustrated. This information isn't help us.

"You're joking!" Spike exclaims, shocked.

"What about Patrick's parents?" Eleanor asks Angel, her mind working as she thinks about it from a different angle.

"What about them?" Angel asks, clearly confused.

"Have they been to Australia? And if yes, when and what dates?" she asks. "I mean, we know they have been, seeing as Patrick was here when he was younger, but did they move here before or after he was born?" she asks, I can see the brilliance in her thinking, she's connecting the dots that we missed.

"Good question, I'll check," Angel taps away as I lean back in my chair, feeling a sense of hope. I think Eleanor just found the missing piece of the puzzle.

Chapter 35

Matteo Ricci

6 days later, I find myself walking into my office knowing everything is about to change. Tonight is the night where I take back control of my empire and eliminate the threat that's been hanging over my head for far too long.

Eleanor has already set the room up for the meeting. In doing so, she's discovered a small mic tapped under the desk. Anger surges through me instantly, because someone has been listening to our conversations, someone has been spying on us.

Angel does some digging, finding that it leads back to Becky's phone. I'm not surprised. Becky has always been suspicious, always too interested in what happens in my office. Now I have proof that she's been working against me and I'm going to make sure she regrets it.

Both Eleanor and Angel do a full sweep of the room, but don't find anything else. I'm grateful for their thoroughness. This is why Becky had tried to follow me into the room for the other week. Now it all makes sense. Now I understand her motivation.

Angel combs back through all our surveillance footage. Becky has been planting a mic in the room before every four seats meeting and returning to collect it after. The anger builds inside of me knowing that this woman has been betraying me for years, feeding information to someone. And I need to know who.

We need to work out if she's an informant, if she works for Enzo, or is just plain insane. I'm leaning toward the latter. Anyone stupid enough to spy on me in my own office, clearly isn't thinking straight.

Eleanor has me fuck her over the table before we remove the mic completely. She wants to leave Becky with a parting gift. One I'm more than eager to oblige. The thought of Becky listening to us, hearing Eleanor and me together, knowing that Eleanor is mine—it's the perfect message to send.

The sex is strange and uncomfortable with Eleanor's leg cast and my healing shoulder, but hey, sex is sex. I'll take it as it comes. Besides, the discomfort is worth it because I get to mark my territory. I'm making sure Becky knows exactly what Eleanor means to me.

Eleanor even offers to have Angel stay, seeing as he likes to watch, and be watched so much. Angel just laughs and walks out of the room, closing the door behind him.

We send all the information we have obtained to Luca Gallo and Antoni Rossi. Both jump on board with my decision and back my response. I'm grateful for their support, grateful they understand that Enzo has become a liability and needs to be eliminated.

Enzo won't be walking back out of these doors tonight, I'm certain of that. This is the end of his reign and the beginning of a new era. The four seats will be three from this day forward. I'm prepared for the consequences of that decision.

Luca and Antoni arrive well before the allocated time slot. I notice the anticipation in both of their eyes, they're looking forward to what's about to happen.

"Matteo," Luca smiles as he grasps my hand and pulls me in for a back slap.

"Luca, good to see you again," I reply. I reach out my hand towards Antoni and do the same. I see the respect in his eyes, he's acknowledging me as an equal.

"Matteo," Antoni says. His voice warm and filled with understanding.

We walk into the boardroom and take our seats, while we wait for the guest of honour. I settle into my chair, preparing myself mentally for what's about to happen. I need to be in control of this situation.

"Is Eleanor here?" Luca asks while looking around the room, like she might be hiding in the shadows. I can see the curiosity on his face, he's interested in meeting the woman who started all of this.

"Yes, but she isn't hiding under the tables," I laugh. The amusement snaking its way across his face. "She is holed up in my office, waiting for me," I say. I'm grateful that Eleanor is safe, she's not here to witness what's about to happen. I want to protect her from the violence that's coming.

"Do we get to meet the woman who started and has

now ended all this?" Antoni smiles at me, obvious respect in his eyes.

"Yes," I say leaning back in my seat. I feel a sense of pride knowing Eleanor is mine. She's proven herself to be worthy of being the queen of the Ricci's. "But, maybe after we have finished with the meeting, mate," I say.

Luca smiles at me, and I see the understanding in his eyes. "Of course," he says. I'm grateful for his respect for the order of things.

Leaning forwards I grab a glass and the decanter of whiskey. Pouring carefully, I make sure each glass is filled to the right level. "Drink?" I ask, offering it to the other men. I settle into the familiar ritual of preparing for a meeting.

"Yes, please, neat," Luca states.

"Rocks please," Antoni smiles.

"Still a pussy I see," Luca laughs at him with affection in his voice, they've known each other for years.

"I just enjoy having taste buds, mate," Antoni chuckles back.

"Nice to see nothing has changed," I laugh along with them. I'm grateful for a moment of levity before the storm comes.

"Only our ages," Antoni smiles.

I hear a crackle through the mic in my ear as Angel's voice comes through clear and steady. "He is heading up in the lift now," Angel states. The adrenaline starting to build inside me. This is it. This is the moment where everything changes.

"He is on his way up," I let them know. The shift in the

room obvious, as the energy changes and we prepare for Enzo's arrival.

"Let the games begin," Luca smiles like the Cheshire cat, with a predatory look to match in his eyes, he's been looking forward to this moment.

The fucker is insane. Luca has always been like this, always been willing to do whatever it takes to maintain his power. It's moments like these that remind me I'm swimming with sharks. I need to be careful, because one wrong move could be my last.

I sit back in my chair, getting comfortable as I hear the ding of the lift bell from down the hallway. The sound is loud and ominous, barely detectable during the day with all the background noise. But now, in the quiet of the moment it's like a death knell, like the universe is announcing that death is coming.

The room goes silent as we sip on our drinks, listening to the footsteps as they get closer to the room. Waiting for this fucker to arrive, is like waiting for the scary part of a movie—you're either gonna jump 10 feet into the air or be disappointed. I'm hoping for the latter, because I want to be in control of this situation.

Enzo walks into the room like he owns the place and he doesn't have a care in the world. I can see the confidence on his face, the way he thinks he's untouchable. I'm going to enjoy proving him wrong.

"Evening," he announces as he pours himself some whiskey. I see the casual way he's moving, he has no idea what's about to happen.

"Evening," we all reply in unison. I hear the weight in

our voices, we're all in agreement about what needs to happen here.

"Why all the long faces? You all look like the Pope died," Enzo says with raised brows. Theres confusion on his face, he's trying to figure out what's going on.

"I wouldn't say the Pope," I quip, leaning forward in my chair. I've been preparing myself for his reaction. "But Patrick did," I add, watching his face carefully, waiting to see how he reacts to this news.

Enzo chokes on his whiskey and looks up at me. I can see the shock in his eyes, the way he wasn't expecting this news. I'm satisfied with his reaction, because it means he didn't know.

I see Luca raise a gun and point it at Enzo. I can see the threat in the gesture, the way Luca is making sure Enzo understands, he's not going anywhere.

"Patrick…" Enzo manages to cough out. I can hear the confusion in his voice, the way he's trying to process what I just told him.

"Yes, your son Patrick is dead," I smile at him. My smile is cold and filled with satisfaction, after all, Patrick deserved to die.

His face goes white as he bolts out of his chair into a standing position. I watch the panic in his eyes, as he realises that something is very wrong here.

"What the fuck is this," he snarls at us, the anger and fear mixing together in his voice.

"Haven't you been wondering where your right-hand man is?" I ask, as I lean back in my chair, making sure he understands that we know everything.

"Tino?" he looks confused. His mind is working over-time, he's trying to figure out what's happened.

"Yes, Tino," I say, watching as the realisation starts to dawn on him.

Tino isn't where he said he would be. I see the moment of understanding on his face, the moment when he realises that Tino is dead.

The text messages Angel's sent from his phone to Enzo's stated he was going to head to London with Patrick to help keep him safe. His return flight would have been tomorrow. I'm satisfied with the way Angel has set it all up, he made it believable, so Enzo wouldn't suspect anything.

"He is away in London," Enzo tries for false hope, desperation cracking his voice, he's grasping at straws.

"Nope, he is currently swimming with the sharks in the harbour," I smirk at him.

"So, you have killed my son and my right-hand man?" Enzo asks. His voice small and weak. I see the way he's falling apart internally, he's realising that he's lost everything.

"You're the only one left," I say, pointing at him, making sure he's understanding what that means; he's about to die.

He sits back down in his seat. The moment it all hits home for him is visible. He knows he's a dead man walk-ing. He knows that we now know his biggest secrets. I see the defeat in his eyes, the way he's given up the fight before it's even begun.

"How did you find out?" Enzo sighs, placing his head

in his hands. The resignation in his voice clear, he's accepted his fate.

"Patrick staged a kidnapping of Eleanor and left me for dead," I state, leaning back in my chair like I don't have a care in the world. I watch his reaction carefully, making sure he understands the full extent of what we've discovered. "We managed to track him down by the properties he owns, or did own. We realised he's had a connection to Eleanor for longer than I have," I continue, the understanding dawning on his face.

"He'd been in love with her since he was 18," Enzo states, a bitterness lacing his voice, he's thinking about Patrick's obsession.

"She was only 10. Didn't that set off some alarm bells?" I ask. My voice filled with nothing but contempt, because this man knew his son was obsessed with a child and he did nothing about it.

Enzo just shrugs, like it isn't an issue. The man makes my stomach turn, because he's a monster, he's someone who enables predators and I'm disgusted by him. I'm glad that I'm about to end his life.

"Well after we worked it all out and went to retrieve her, guess who we found holed up with him in Mrs. Tinsdale's house?" I pause to take a sip of my drink. I'm savouring this moment, savouring the way Enzo is about to realise that we know everything. "None other than Tino. So, as you can now see, we realised that this is actually all linked to you," I say, pointing my glass in his direction. I watch as his face pales, realising that his carefully constructed web of lies is unravelling.

"So, it seems," Enzo states, his voice weak and defeated.

"So, naturally, Angel did some digging for me. He saw that Caitlin, Patrick's mother, was a cleaner in your family home, when you were 18," I say, watching his reaction carefully, waiting for him to confirm what we've discovered.

At Caitlin's name he raises his eyes to me and I can see the pain there, the way this woman means something to him. "Caitlin was more than just a cleaner," he states. His voice filled with emotion. "She was a lot more than that, to me." he says.

"Clearly, she didn't feel the same," I raise my eyebrows at him as I lean back in my chair, enjoying the way this is playing out. "She works for you for 6 months, then returns back home to Ireland. She meets Conner, gets married, and has Patrick 7 months later," I say, laying out all the evidence, making sure he knows that we know everything.

"Good to see you did your homework, well," Enzo mumbles, a bitterness in his voice. "But you're missing the most important part," he says.

"What's that?" I ask, waiting for him to reveal the final piece of the puzzle.

"She returned to Sydney when Patrick was 8. She was begging me for money, telling me about Patrick, begging me to get her out of the marriage she was in," Enzo says.

"That's why you funded Conner's building business?" I ask, piecing together the rest of the connections, understanding how all of it is linked.

"Yes, but the slut didn't leave him," he snarls, and I can hear the anger and bitterness in his voice. "She stayed, claimed she had to for Patrick. She said she would leave him when he was 18," he then smiles cruelly at me. "She wasn't careful with our conversations though. Patrick found out everything. He killed both his father and his mother, covering it up as a building accident," Enzo says. I feel sick because this man is admitting to knowing that his son murdered his parents, and he did nothing about it.

"Like father, like son," I state, my voice cold and filled with contempt.

Enzo's beams, smiling from ear to ear, the pride lighting up his eyes. He's proud of what Patrick did. "Apple doesn't fall far from the tree," he says.

"That's why you helped him get rid of Eleanor 10 years ago?" I ask. I'm waiting for him to confirm what I already know.

"Yes, my son wanted his girl. I know what it feels like not to have mine. So, I helped him," Enzo says. His voice filled with a twisted sense of understanding. "Granted, it wasn't the original plan we had, but it all worked out," he shrugs at me. The rage threatens to take over, knowing this man helped take Eleanor away from me.

"Then why did you come to me and give me Eleanor's location?" I ask, trying to understand his motivation, trying to figure out why he would do that.

"Patrick refused to move back to Australia. I was over fighting with him about it. He needed to learn that I'm in charge. He followed that bitch around like a fucking lap dog. It made me sick to see my boy ruled by a fucking cunt," Enzo yells at me, furiously, he's angry at Patrick for being controlled by Eleanor. "I had to get her back to Australia, so I could get him back here too," he says. I'm understanding now that Enzo was trying to manipulate the situation, trying to get Patrick back under his control.

"Well, that backfired for you, mate," I say, leaning back in my chair, savouring this moment, knowing exactly what's coming next.

"So, it seems," Enzo sinks into his chair, defeated, looking like a man who has lost everything.

"So what now?" he asks, his voice small and weak. I stand up and reach for my gun.

"Now you die," I shrug, as I raise the gun to his chest. I fire off two rounds, watching as he falls forward, watching as the life drains from his body.

I fire off another shot into his head, just for shits and giggles.

"I hope you have clean-up on standby," Luca smiles, the approval clear on his face, he's pleased with what I did.

"Yes, I do," I reply as I lean forward and refill my whiskey. I take a moment to process what just happened, to take in the fact that Enzo is dead, that this chapter of my life is finally closed.

"More?" I ask the others.

After refilling everyone's drinks I stand and move toward the door. "This way gentlemen," I say, as I walk out of the room and down the hall towards my office. I pass the cleaning crew I have on standby and give them a single nod of acknowledgement.

I knock twice on the door and wait for it to open, holding my breath because I know Eleanor is in there.

It opens with a gun pointed at my face, and I can't help but smile because I fucking love this woman.

"Princess," I smile as the gun is removed and the safety

is clicked back into place. I can see the relief on her face, she's been waiting for me.

"Matteo…" her voice is like a balm to my soul, as I reach for her, pulling her close to me.

"He is dead," I tell her and kiss her head. I feel her relax against me, the weight of everything lifting off her shoulders. "Please, go sit at my desk so I can introduce you to the other members of the seats," I say, watching as her sexy ass hobbles over and sits in her seat, placing her hands on the wooden top.

"Luca and Antoni, this is Eleanor," I say, sweeping my good arm wide like I would if I was showing off the Mona Lisa. To me, that's what she is—one of the world's most precious things.

"Hello Eleanor," Antoni states and sits in the chair across the desk. There's a respect in his eyes, he's acknowledging her as the queen of the Ricci's.

Luca just shakes his head, the amusement written all over his face. "A tiny thing like you, causes all this?" he laughs, the disbelief lacing his voice. "Well, I'll be damned," he says. I have to smile, because he's right. Eleanor is small, but she's mighty. She's caused more chaos and change than anyone I've ever met.

With that we all start laughing because we all know, he ain't wrong. I let out a breath, feeling the tension in the room dissipate.

The rest of the night runs smoothly. We run over all the agendas and logistics that need to be straightened out. I'm grateful that everything is going according to plan, thankful that we're finally moving forward.

"Okay, is there anything left to discuss, or can I fuck off home?" I ask the room.

"Only one," Luca states. I look at him with curiosity, wondering what else there is to discuss.

We all look to him, seeing the seriousness on his face.

"I would like to start the initiation process for my son to take over my seat," Luca says. I lean forward, interested in what he has to say.

"Gabe will be taking my seat in the next 12 months," Luca smiles, proudly. "He's gonna ruffle a lot of feathers boys, so watch out," he adds.

"God help us all," I say, shaking my head. I have a feeling that Gabe is going to be a force to be reckoned with.

I'm not sure if the underworld is ready for what's coming next.

Epilogue - Eleanor Wang

8 years later

I find myself sitting in the afternoon sun, watching the world go by. They say, time flies when you're having fun, and they didn't lie. I don't think I've ever been happier in my life.

Today, Niko turns 18. Holy nuns in a whorehouse! I am not prepared for this moment. The man Niko is today, isn't the one I'd envisioned all those years ago. But it isn't one I would change either. Niko Ricci is a man now. Well, that's what they say when you turn the ripe old age of 18.

And that little fucker isn't even spending the day with us. Nope, he has hired a boat and is currently floating out on the harbour with his friends. Parents are still super uncool to hang around with, apparently.

"Here, Princess," Matteo hands me a margarita. The condensation drips down the glass and I can feel the coolness of it in my hand.

"Thank you," I say, taking a long sip. The lime and tequila hitting my tongue perfectly.

We're currently sitting in the afternoon sun, looking out over the bay. The water sparkles in the light and I can see the boats dotting the horizon. It's peaceful here with Matteo. It's home.

"You still mad he wouldn't allow you to go to his party?" Matteo smiles at me, seeing the amusement in his eyes, he knows exactly how I'm feeling.

"Yes, I mean seriously, I'm fun!" I say pointing at my chest. I'm genuinely offended that Niko doesn't want me at his party. I'm the cool parent. I know I am.

"Yes, you are fun, Princess," he smiles at me, "but parents at your 18th birthday party isn't the cool thing."

"But what if there are drugs?" I ask, genuinely concerned about Niko's safety, even if he is 18 now.

"I can guarantee there is," he replies. I turn to glare at Matteo, I can't believe he just said that so casually.

"Tell me you didn't supply the boat with drugs, Matteo?" I grumble, already imagining all the ways this could go wrong.

"I was 18 once too, you know," Matteo states. "If I hadn't supplied them, then they would have come from god knows where. This way I've controlled what and how much has entered the boat," Matteo states, like he's done something awesome. I can see the logic in his argument, but I still don't like it.

I just shake my head at him, knowing full well I'm not going to win this argument.

"I don't like my son doing drugs, Matteo," I say firmly, needing him to understand how serious I am about this.

"Princess, you might not believe this, but he actually doesn't. I think being on this side of the fence gave him a different view of them," Matteo states, and I can hear the truth in his voice, he's been watching Niko grow up. "Plus Angel is on the boat with him. If anything gets out of hand, he will reel it all back in," he adds. I'm grateful that Angel is there, and thankful that Matteo is being so responsible about this.

"Still can't believe he allowed Angel to go and not me!" I say, throwing my hands up in frustration.

"That boat is a floating nerd's dream right now," Matteo laughs at me. I can hear the affection in his voice. "I mean seriously, the kid's friends are all in his tech class at Uni."

Which is true. Niko got into Uni two years early, due to his tech studies and homeschooling. There isn't a lot the kid can't hack. He'd made a bunch of friends when he started Uni, and thankfully they are just as nerdy as he is. I'm proud of him for that.

"I have something that will take your mind off it all, if you want..." Matteo smirks at me. I can see the mischief in his eyes, the way he's planning something.

"What's that old man?" I tease, knowing exactly how to get under his skin.

"40 isn't old," Matteo raises his brows at me and stands out of his chair with ease, "See, I can still stand without an easy chair." I watch the way he's showing off, he's proving his point.

"Is that how we now gauge age now?" I laugh at him.

He walks over to stand in front of me, holding out his hand for me to take. Sliding my hand into his, I allow him to pull me up and out of my seat. His grip is warm, strong, and makes me feel safe in his presence.

"And I can still do this!" he says as he throws an arm under my legs and lifts me bridal style. I feel weightless in his arms, even after all these years.

Squealing a little, I throw my arms around Matteo's neck. "Shit Matteo, warn me next time!" I say as I slap his chest, "I nearly popped a poopoo valve!" I laugh, as his chest shakes with his own laughter beneath my hands.

Matteo leans his face down and licks the tip of my nose, then starts walking us inside and up the stairs. The cool air in the house wraps around us as we move through the rooms. I can smell the familiar scent of home, the scent of Matteo.

"This isn't another one of those, 'I have a present for you upstairs things' and it just ends up being your dick with a red bow tied around it?" I look up at Matteo, genuinely curious about what he has planned.

"But you love that gift!" Matteo fakes a shocked face, the playfulness seeping from his expression.

"Ah, let's just agree to disagree," I say, trying to hide my smile.

"Well, this gift isn't a bow on my dick," Matteo laughs cryptically. I can hear the amusement in his voice, he's enjoying keeping me in suspense.

I narrow my eyes at him. Matteo's gifts are always one of two things. Jewellery; like lots and lots of it; over the years I have been given enough to sink the Titanic all over again. Or it is simply his dick. So, now I'm definitely intrigued.

Walking over the threshold of our room, I see a

rectangular box sitting in the middle of the bed. My curiosity spikes immediately. What could be in there?

Matteo places my feet back down on the carpet, "Well go on, open it," he urges, right before I see him rub his lower back.

"Can't hide your old age from me, mate," I laugh, teasing him about the way he's rubbing his back.

"Open the box, Princess," Matteo just smirks at me, the anticipation filling his eyes.

I hurry over, climbing onto the bed and open the lid of the box. Inside is a skin-coloured dildo. I look up at Matteo, confused. "Um, don't we already own enough?" I smile at him. We have quite the collection at this point.

"Yes, we do, but none of them are mine," he points to himself, and I can see the pride on his face, he's pleased with this gift.

"What do you mean 'you'?" Confused, I look at the penis once again. How can a dildo be him?

"Well, if you crawl over here and have a good look, you will understand," Matteo states in a hushed voice. His voice is low and filled with desire, and I feel my body responding immediately.

Slowly the implication starts to become clearer, and my curiosity gets the better of me. He's had his dick moulded into a dildo. The thought sends a shiver down my spine.

Leaning forward on my hands and knees, I crawl across the bed, so my face is level with Matteo's crotch. I feel the heat radiating off his body, smelling the familiar scent of him. My heart is races with anticipation.

Leaning back on my heels, I undo his belt and trousers,

finding him already starting to get hard, and I pull his dick out, popping him free of his boxers.

Swiping my thumb over the tip, I lean forward and suck him into my mouth, working him with my hand till his dick is rock hard and leaking precum. I can taste him on my tongue, and I'm savouring every second of this moment. The weight of him in my mouth feels perfect, feels right.

I then lean back and grab the dildo, holding it next to his. It's exactly the same. He's actually had his dick moulded into a dildo.

"This way, I can take both your holes at the same time, and know it's only me inside you," Matteo says; his lust-filled eyes looking down at me, seeing the intensity in his gaze, he's thought about this, planned this.

"Prove it," I challenge, wanting to feel him inside me in every way possible.

"Turn around and shove your face into the doona," Matteo states as he grabs the dildo out of my hand. His voice is commanding, and I feel my body respond immediately to his tone.

Turning around, I raise my ass in the air and place my face on the doona. I can feel the cool fabric against my cheek, as I wait patiently for what comes next. The anticipation is almost unbearable.

"Good girl," he growls, before leaning forward and licking me from clit to ass, till I'm squirming on the spot. The sensation is incredible, I can feel my body coming alive under his touch. His tongue is skilled and knowing, already pushing me close to the edge.

I feel the cold blunt end of the dildo as Matteo slowly

works it into my core, inch by delicious inch. I'm gasping for breath, my body responding to every movement. The sensation of being filled is incredible, and I'm already begging for more.

"That's it, Princess, I wanna see you swallow my dick in that pretty pink pussy," Matteo says. His voice filled with desire, and I can feel the way he's enjoying this.

"Fuck Matteo, that feels so good," I mumble over the doona cover. I can barely form words, my mind is so focused on the sensations coursing through my body.

Matteo fucks me slowly like that for ages, pulling me to the edge over and over again, but always stopping when I start to reach the peak. It's torture and pleasure all at once, as I beg him for a release.

"Please, Matteo," I whine, needing him to let me come, needing the release that's building inside me.

Standing up behind me, I feel Matteo pull the dildo out, leaving me empty and wanting. I gasp for breath, my body aching for more.

Leaning over to the nightstand, he grabs a bottle of lube and lets a few drops fall onto my ass, before he massages it into my bud with his fingers, slowly stretching me.

He then places the dildo on my bud and slowly pushes it inside. The sensation is intense, but I breathe through it, allowing my body to adjust.

"Ooh my God, Fuck, Matteo!" I cry out. The sensation is overwhelming, and I'm on the edge of coming already.

"That's it, Princess, push back on to it," Matteo encourages.

I push back towards Matteo, relaxing my muscles as I

go, focusing on my breathing, on the sensations coursing through my body. Every nerve ending is alive and firing.

Matteo's hand winds itself down between my legs as he rubs my clit, and pushes the dildo in and out of my ass at a very slow pace. The dual sensation is incredible, and I'm teetering on the edge of an orgasm.

"Please Matteo" I whine, needing him to let me come, needing the release.

"Not yet, Princess," Matteo says as he pushes the dildo all the way to the end and holds it still. I'm trembling with need, my body begging for release.

His hand leaves my clit, and I notice he is lining his dick up with my pussy. I hold my breath, waiting for him to enter me.

"Fuck," I state as he pushes himself inside. The sensation of being filled in both places at once is overwhelming, and has me gasping for breath.

I feel so full. It's amazing. The sensation is beyond anything I've ever experienced before.

Matteo starts to move in and out with his dick, while moving the one in my ass in tandem. The feeling is incredible, all my nerve endings are firing at once, as I get lost in the sensation, lost in the moment.

My orgasm rips through me so unexpectedly. My pussy tightening like a vice, as my ass clenches so tight, the dildo can't be pushed back in. I' cry out his name as my body convulses with pleasure.

"That's it, Princess, grip me tight," Matteo growls, reaching down to stroke my clit. Once it passes, Matteo starts to move again, this time he hits harder and faster, no longer moving the dildo in my ass; instead, he's holding it in with his hand as he pumps my pussy with his dick.

He is working me back up to another orgasm. The sensation is intense, and I'm already close to the edge again.

"Not yet, Princess," he growls as he rubs my clit a bit faster. I'm trying to hold back, trying to wait for his command.

"I'm not gonna last," I say, feeling the orgasm building inside me, threatening to break free.

"Now," he says as he pinches my clit with his fingertips. That's all it takes.

My orgasm sends me sailing, almost sending me blind with pleasure. I'm crying out, my body convulsing with the intensity of it. Every muscle in my body clenches, and I'm lost in the sensation.

"Fuck, Princess, you milk my dick so well." I feel Matteo stiffen behind me as he fills me with his cum. I feel the warmth of him inside me, as I savour every second of this moment.

Once I'm full, he leans his body over the top of mine and kisses my spine. The tenderness of the gesture is beautiful, and I feel a rush of love for this man.

"Told you it wasn't a bow on my dick," he laughs as he pulls out of my pussy and slips the dildo out of my ass. Slapping my ass, that is still up in the air, he says, "Come on, Princess let me run you a bath. That way you can fall asleep and snore the house down."

I'm laughing and exhausted, my body completely satisfied. I'm thankful for this man, grateful for the life we've built together. As he helps me up and leads me to the bath-room, I think about how far we've come from that first moment in the tattoo shop. The day this man had taken one look at me, and turned my whole world upside down.

The End

About Cassandra Doon

Cassandra hates writing about herself in the third person, but here we are. With over 33 novels penned and no signs of stopping, she writes across multiple genres. Unable to be pinned down by just one, you'll find Fantasy, Dark Romance, Young Adult, and even a Detective series in the mix.

Having grown up in a small country town and later lived in the city, Cassandra found a perfect spot she likes to call an 'in-between place'—complete with rolling hills and just a stone's throw from the Gold Coast in Queensland Australia.

While she may have had social media in the past, Cassandra has since declared it's not for her. Her website is now the best place to find out what's happening in her world and to see what upcoming books are on the horizon.

Also by Cassandra Doon

The 4 Seats Series:

Matteo

Felix

Gabriel

Catcher

Ruhn & Frost

The 4 Seats Extended World:

Aces

Obsessed Shadows

Adrian Romano

The Moretti Brothers

Standalone:

The Kings of Willows Peak

Damaged Goods

Tuesday May

The Devils Cut

The Detectives Mate

Dark Dahlias Rite

A Field of Tulips and Bones

Follow Poppy

To Her

Blood moon

Unit 9

Broken Creek Ranch

The Dead Zone

Eclipsion (Coming Soon)

~

Oakland Harbour Series:

Missing

Found

Home

~

The Boys Series

The Boys Of Hastings House Part 1

The Boys Of Hastings House Part 2

The Boys of Nightsbane University Part 1

The Boys of Nightsbane University Part 2

The Boys of Winchester U (Coming Soon)

~

Second Chances Series:

The Waterfall

Wicked Bonds

Writhe (Coming Soon)

The Restaurant (Coming Soon)

~

Umbravivus Series:

The Lost Kingdom of Umbravivus (Coming Soon)

The Crowned King of Umbravivus (Coming Soon)

The Queen of Umbravivus (Coming Soon)

~

Butcher and the Witch Series:

Poison is always in the Prettiest Bottle

Candles make Great Alibis

Socials with a Slice of Pie

~

Hemlock Hollow

Pumpkin Spice Apothecary 

Also By C.L. Doon

The Rain Dang Detective Series:

Still Waters

Moving Waters

Standalone:

Second Chances at The Riverbend Café

Lavender (Coming Soon)